INSTRUCTIONS
FOR MURDER . . .

Sarah Hopkins had let Paul Marnay suspect she was following him. But she hadn't decided how she would kill him. The letter hadn't been clear about that and had only insisted that the death must look like an accident. The instructions had been a little desperate, basing their appeal on irrationalities and vague threats. Sarah wouldn't have paid any attention to the letter if it hadn't been for its opening sentence: *There is someone you wish were dead.* The simple truth of that statement was irresistible. And so Sarah Hopkins agreed to play Chainmaster's ingenious game. . . .

Books by Ken Greenhall

The Companion
Deathchain

Published by POCKET BOOKS

DEATH CHAIN

KEN GREENHALL

POCKET BOOKS

New York   London   Toronto   Sydney   Tokyo   Singapore

An *Original* Publication of POCKET BOOKS

POCKET BOOKS, a division of Simon & Schuster Inc.
1230 Avenue of the Americas, New York, NY 10020

ISBN: 0-671-69407-3

First Pocket Books printing December 1991

10 9 8 7 6 5 4 3 2 1

POCKET and colophon are registered trademarks of
Simon & Schuster Inc.

Cover art by Jeffrey Adams

Printed in the U.S.A.

Chapter 1

He was pleased to find that she was slovenly and eccentric, that she led the kind of life he didn't feel remorseful about ending. She reminded him of his mother.

He had followed the instructions that were in the letter. He had been observant and patient, and he was being rewarded with the perfect conditions. It was Sunday morning, and a cold, early-spring rain was falling. Sensible people would hold to their winter habits by staying indoors. But Dwight knew that Edna Denning was not a sensible person. She didn't behave sensibly or dress sensibly. He had seen dozens of women like her during his months at the hospital. They had, unknowingly, helped him recover from his nervous breakdown. He would stare at them and tell himself: I am not like them. I will be strong again.

And now Dwight felt strong as he walked toward Falls Park. His strength, he thought, was a gift of time. He understood that time brings to each person in turn strength, decline, and death. He knew time more intimately than most people did. He saw it pictured and measured in the movements of the clocks he repaired. To know and control time is to know and control life—your own life and others'. Time protects those who understand it.

Dwight felt invulnerable—warm and dry—as the

rain sluiced down the folds of his army-surplus poncho, which, like every article of clothing he owned, had been made for issue by the armed services. Dwight had once thought of enlisting in the army but changed his mind when a recruitment sergeant laughed at him for asking if he would have to undress in front of other men. It seemed outrageous to Dwight that he should be laughed at when he was announcing that he was willing to die for his country. Perhaps the sergeant had not understood, Dwight thought, that I was not merely willing to die but that I had absolutely no fear of death. A man with my traits could be valuable.

And now someone—the person who had sent him the letter—had recognized that valuable trait. Dwight could take Mrs. Denning's life or anyone else's life without a qualm. What had prevented him from taking lives previously was not the fear of causing and witnessing death but the fear of being caught and sent to prison. Now that possibility had been removed.

It wasn't that Dwight sought the death of other people as an end in itself; his goal was to bring others the gift of time, not the extinction of time. But before he could use his gift, two people would have to sacrifice a few of their futile later years. And their sacrifice would eventually bring a new order to many lives.

The old woman had wrapped herself in a ludicrous cocoon of transparent plastic. She was apparently wearing several of the large bags that dry cleaners use to cover suits and coats. One of the bags had slipped down around her ankles, impeding her movement, and she was partially hobbled. She punched a hole in the plastic through which she dropped pieces of dried bread. Three pigeons emerged from their shelter in the eaves of a nearby building to investigate the offering.

Dwight Bailey was disgusted by the display of human degradation and animal greed. Maneuvering behind dense hedges, Dwight moved closer to Mrs. Denning. He was sure that because of the fogged plastic that covered most of her face, she would not see him until she was in his grasp. He moved forward, stopping occasionally to look around. He could see no one, and the area of clear visibility seemed to be decreasing in fog. He and Mrs. Denning were alone together. His plan had been to wait until the woman approached the edge of the park to view the falls, as she usually did, but he realized now that the weather might keep her from doing that. She was standing about fifty feet from the waist-high wall that ran along the edge of the park—a wall that concealed a precipitous drop to a rocky riverbed. Only the strongest person was likely to survive a fall to the river, and only an accomplished swimmer could stay afloat in the water's strong springtime currents.

Dwight took a final look around the park, but a wind-driven sheet of rain swept across his face, blinding him for a moment. He panicked. He rubbed his eyes and blinked heavily, and when his vision cleared, he rushed up behind Mrs. Denning, grabbing her shoulders and turning her toward him. Then he crouched and pushed his shoulder into her midsection, doubling her forward and lifting her as he straightened up. A pigeon rose in confused flight, brushing its wings against Dwight's head.

As he suspected, the woman was remarkably easy to carry. She was only bones and dirty skin. But she didn't seem as feeble as he had expected. There was a strength in her body that he hadn't seen; there was a look in her eyes, during the instant they exchanged glances, that showed a terror and passion that old women didn't experience. The woman's crotch was against his shoulder. He was vaguely aroused, but he didn't hesitate. As he ran toward the wall with her, a piece of the plastic she was draped in blew across Dwight's face. He saw the words, *Dangerous: Keep Away from Children.* He gulped for air as the plastic fastened across his mouth and nostrils. He hesitated. How had he come to be in this situation? Perhaps he should drop this pitiful, disgusting burden and leave.

Then he realized the woman was screaming—an event he hadn't anticipated. He couldn't put his hand over her mouth because the top of her body was bent over his back, and her face was out of his reach. What was she screaming? Obscenities. Words that his mother used—words that no woman should use. Yes, this woman is like my mother, Dwight thought. Without my devotion, my mother would have been this way: living in the streets, being devoted to filthy, useless birds, her head filled with nothing but vile words. Neither woman should be spared.

The screaming seemed louder. Dwight moved ahead frantically, and then he stumbled and his knees scraped against stone. It was the wall. He threw Mrs. Denning's body forward, and for an instant her scream became more insistent, more terrifying. Then there were only the sounds of the rain and wind. He looked down into the barely visible swirling water. Mrs. Denning's body seemed limp and unstruggling. But it had snagged against a rock. There now appeared to be a slow, general twisting of the woman's torso. She must still be alive. Her arm continued to move feebly. I have to be sure, Dwight thought, and he began to climb over the wall. But as he did so, the woman's body was suddenly swept free of the rocks. In one convulsive movement, a movement of finality and conclusion, the body vanished into the foaming water.

Now that the job was done, Dwight's panic subsided quickly. He turned slowly and looked across the vague, misty horizon of the park. He was alone. He was safe, unaccusable. As he started to move away, his foot caught in a torn sheet of transparent plastic bearing the words, *Keep Away from Children.* Were these words an omen? Dwight attended closely to the omens of his life.

As he hurried out of the park, he became aware of moisture on his body. Delicate beads of wetness were running down his back, collecting between his buttocks. Had his clothing failed to protect him? Had he torn his poncho in his exertions? No. He had confidence in his clothing. He was simply perspiring. It was emotion. It was fear, and perhaps guilt. Whatever those emotions might be, they were quickly subsiding and changing. The emotions that were replacing them were not familiar ones to him: joy and optimism.

But the new emotions reverted quickly to terror when Dwight found himself confronted by a small form that stepped out from behind a tree. A boy.

Keep Away from Children.

The boy looked to be about ten. A dangerous age, an observant, inquisitive age. What had he seen?

"Hi," Dwight said.

"Hi."

They stared at each other for a moment. Dwight didn't sense any fear in the boy's gaze, no particular curiosity. The best thing to do was to leave and minimize the chance of making a lasting impression.

Dwight moved quickly past the boy and began to jog. He didn't approve of the practice of public exercise—of the people who exposed their thighs and wore silly shoes with synthetic names displayed on them. But now he was grateful for the jogging fad. No one looked twice at someone running in the streets—someone fleeing the scene of a secret act. But I'm not running away from something, Dwight thought. I'm running toward something—toward a new life.

When he got home, he went to his bedroom and removed his clothes. It was nap time. He could hear the wet, grating snores of his mother, who was lying on the other side of the wall.

It was the time he formerly would have spent recalling the most attractive woman he had seen that week and imagining how she would look undressed. He would have imagined her kneeling above him and speaking certain words.

But now the words he thought of were those he had memorized from the letter:

Dear Mr. Bailey:

There is someone you wish were dead.

I know that is true, and I also know that you are perceptive enough to believe in the power of chain messages.

This chain is called the deathchain, and it will bring you the happiness that has escaped you.

If you follow the instructions in this letter, the person you most dislike and resent will be killed in a way that will cast no suspicion on you.

But as you know, the scriptures say an eye shall be taken for an eye. Therefore, I ask you to demonstrate your deservedness by taking the life of a certain person—an insignificant person.

WHAT YOU MUST DO

Take the life of Mrs. Edna Denning, who lives at 351 Center Street. Mrs. Denning is sixty years old and lives alone. As you will discover, she is a woman of fixed habits. Each afternoon at three o'clock, she scatters crumbs for the pigeons in Falls Park, and she stands for a few moments at the edge of the falls to admire the view. You are to push her into the water, being certain that no one sees you do it. Choose an unpleasant, overcast or rainy day. As long as you are unobserved, it will be assumed that Mrs. Denning's death was an accident, and there will be no way of connecting you with the event.

After completing your assignment, send me the name of the person whose life you want ended. Tell me about that person's habits and how to arrange for that person to have a fatal accident.

WHAT I WILL DO

I will send your designated victim's name to the next person in the chain, a person who—like you, Dwight—is careful and resourceful and who respects the power behind this chain. The person who has blighted your life will be removed, and you will know happiness.

I'm sure I need not point out to you the importance of secrecy. Telling anyone of the chain is as dangerous as choosing not to obey your instructions.

I welcome you to our exclusive club, Dwight. I'm certain you feel as fortunate to have our help as we feel to have yours.

> Respectfully,
> Chainmaster
> Box 1264
> General Post Office
> New York, NY 10001

It's all in my brain now, Dwight Bailey said to himself. Maybe one or two words are wrong, but it's inside. There was a feeling in his head that he had never experienced before; a feeling of energy, as if his brain were expanding and could explode within his skull. He placed his hands, fingers interwoven, on top of his head and pressed down. It was better to have his head filled with the words of the letter than with the words of imagined women. Certain words from the letter pleased him particularly: *perceptive, careful and resourceful.* No one had applied those terms to him before—certainly not his mother. In two or three minutes she would turn over and the snoring would end with a choking sound. After thirty-seven years of living with that sound, Dwight continued to hope that the choking would be real and fatal.

But now he didn't have to rely on hope. He could take action. He *had* taken action.

Now he must patiently await his reward. But Dwight Bailey was patient as well as obedient. Chainmaster had known that. Chainmaster had known so much about Dwight. It was good to be noticed. It was good to have a future—good to be able to use his gift constructively and without interference. I've been careful and resourceful. He clasped his hands over the top of his head and began to think of what he would say in his letter to his new friend, his benefactor.

"Dear Chainmaster . . ."

Chapter 2

If his family had allowed it, Paul Marnay might have spent his life painting a series of peculiarly static still lifes, collecting antique mirrors, and reading mystery novels.

But the family's business (they thought of it as a profession) was the production and worldwide distribution of French cognac, and every member of the family was expected to help sell the product in some way. The Marnay family had two types of members: the "snails" and the "sea gulls." The snails kept themselves dourly within the massive stone shell of their estate a few kilometers from the town of Cognac and distilled some of the most distinctive and expensive of the region's brandies. The sea gulls, who were sociable and urbane, acted as the family's merchants and had established themselves in the major cities of the world.

Paul was one of the few Marnays who didn't fit either category, but he was tolerated because he helped keep the Marnay product visible among a few wealthy and influential families in New York State. He lived in the town of Dale Falls and spent each August in nearby Saratoga during the racing, ballet, and theater season, using whatever charm he could summon up to promote his family's reputation at the expense of his own. His efforts were successful enough, however, to gain him his family's limited esteem and a generous salary.

Because Paul was by nature reticent and moderate, his social duties put a substantial strain on his nervous system—a strain that he, appropriately, relieved with frequent nips of the family's product. For emergencies, he carried with him an elegant glass-lined silver pocket flask. But he could easily control his trips to the flask, and he resented the fact that so many people were beginning to think of alcohol as an enemy. For example, in the admittedly bad practice of drunk driving, no one ever seemed to suggest that people cut down on driving instead of drinking.

Judicious consumption of cognac had improved Paul's life in several ways. Principally, it was clear that if he hadn't been raised in a bibulous family, Paul would probably never have become an accomplished portrait painter. His natural impulse was to look at people from a distance with admiration and fascination without making the harsh judgments that a good portraitist has to make. A drink or two gave him the paradoxical vision that simultaneously sharpened the image and softened its edges.

Also, Paul knew that if he had been a teetotaler, people would have respected him more but liked him less. And though being liked didn't seem like the highest of goals in itself, both of his income-producing activities depended to some extent on his being liked. Only independently wealthy people didn't have to worry about being obnoxious.

Avoiding a freestanding Victorian wardrobe mirror —one of twenty-seven antique mirrors in his studio —Paul went to an easel and removed a linen dustcover labeled "Pigeon Lady." Beneath the cloth was a head-and-shoulders oil portrait of Edna Denning, whom Paul had met in Falls Park and had persuaded to sit for him. The woman's features combined strength and weakness—compassion and contempt—in a remarkable way. Her wide, flat-planed forehead and well-spaced, alert eyes were admirable and handsome, but her prominent nose, which had obviously been broken at some time, led to a pinched, down-turned mouth and a weak, retreating chin. Paul had thought the painting was completed at the last sitting, but after putting it out of his sight for a week, he had decided to ask the woman in for one more sitting. He was sure she wouldn't mind—not because she had any interest in the portrait (she had never asked to see it) but because she was greatly interested in the fifty dollars an hour he paid her to sit for him.

Paul had felt guilty about sending his son, Luke, out into the rain on the boy's visiting day to fetch the old woman, but there was no other way to reach her. She had no telephone, and except during the coldest weeks of winter, she went to her house only to sleep. The park was where she lived, and the pigeons were what she lived for.

Paul didn't have as simple an explanation of what he himself lived for. That wasn't the sort of question he often asked himself. In fact, he seldom asked himself questions of any kind—primarily because he thought self-analysis would probably just add to the vague dissatisfaction he felt with his life. He didn't think of himself as being any weaker or less virtuous than most people he knew, but he believed there was a discovery he hadn't yet made, a discovery not about himself but about his world. He felt as if there were a room he hadn't been able to enter. The door to the room was guarded, and he was waiting for someone to whisper the password in his ear. It was a situation that called for patience, not for thought.

In the meantime, he put aside some hours each week for painting as a personal act that seemed somehow to be fulfilling a serious obligation. He thought of it as paying his life-dues, and the only obligation that rivaled it was his effort to give his son, Luke, whatever assistance or pleasure the boy and his mother would allow him to give. At the moment, that wasn't much: Saturday outings each week. So Paul's hours at the easel were usually the most important of the day.

One of the many things Paul enjoyed about painting was that it involved him in hours of intense concentration but didn't require him to have even the most rudimentary of thoughts. He was interested in experience but not in abstractions of meaning. The term *abstract painter* had never made sense to him. There was nothing abstract about paint, canvas, or paper; they were tangible things. What was abstract was any attempt to think or talk about paintings.

So Paul never talked about painting. He *did* talk about drinking, but that was an obligation growing out of his family's involvement with the production and distribution of cognac. Paul made a comfortable living painting the portraits of paying customers, but it was income from the family business that made it possible for him to spend a great deal of his time working on uncommissioned portraits like the one that he was looking at now.

And it allowed him to collect antique mirrors without concerning himself with the cost. If anyone asked him—as people often and enviously did—whether his life wasn't a bit self-indulgent, he said yes. His life consisted of a self-indulgent devotion to the concept of likeness.

Paul stared at his painting of the pigeon lady, wondering why he was dissatisfied with it and assuming that if he stared long enough the answer would come to him. He was still staring about fifteen minutes later when his son burst into the studio, wet and elated. Another aspect of likeness, Paul thought. Luke had lived most of his life under the direct control of his mother, Sherril, but he was unlike her in almost every way. Sherril, although she had not divorced Paul, had begun using her premarriage surname again as soon as they separated: Stone. The name was appropriate to her stolid temperament and heavy, firm body. Her head was like a sculpture, a blending of Mayan exoticism and Roman classicism, large features that—as Paul should have realized before his marriage—were meant to appeal to someone who enjoyed suffering more than he did. Sherril had none of her son's and husband's volatility and need to envelop other people—what she called the parasitic weed tendency. She had established a successful career as a real estate agent, using her stern, massive presence to intimidate people into pledging hundreds of thousands of dollars for homes that were usually inappropriate or unsound. People purchased not her houses but her air of authority; they loved her strength and were eager to be exploited by her, as Paul and Luke had been at various times. We love her, Paul thought, the way a plant's roots love the unnourishing but anchoring rock.

Luke took off his shoes—plain canvas sneakers—and wrung them out, forming a puddle of water on the elaborately parqueted floor. His father smiled at him, thinking: He's making a mess to thank me for allowing messes.

"She wasn't there," Luke said. "The pigeon lady, I mean."

"You look upset. I'd think you'd be pleased."

"There was some other creep there. I thought he was going to kill me."

"He had a weapon?"

"No. It was just the way he looked."

Paul realized that what he had seen as elation in his son was actually fear.

Luke said, "Why are there so many creepolas around?"

"It's part of growing up, Luke. If you work at it, you too can become a creepola."

Luke smiled. His life will be difficult, Paul thought. Luke was interested in architecture—in the engineering aspects rather than the esthetic elements. Show him an oak beam, and he wouldn't wonder where it could be placed to reveal its beauty but where it should be placed to make maximum use of its strength. Luke is like me, Paul thought: He's interested in the wrong kind of stress. Paul dreamed almost every night of buildings in which he was the only inhabitant—vast, deteriorating buildings. But when he was awake, he sought out people and involved himself, against his will, in their stresses. People gave him their affection because they sensed how much effort his interest required.

"The pigeon lady had been there," Luke said. "There was soggy bread on the ground."

"It doesn't matter. Maybe the painting is finished after all. What do you think?"

Luke walked hesitantly to the canvas. He never seemed comfortable when he looked at his father's paintings. "It looks like her . . . crazy and dirty." He turned away. "Why would you want to paint somebody like that?" he asked.

Luke's question seemed sincere, so his father answered truthfully: "I don't know. Maybe I'm the crazy one. Your mother thinks I am."

Luke, who didn't discuss either of his parents with the other, didn't comment. He went to a workbench in a corner of the studio, where he was constructing something Paul thought was more pointless than the pigeon-lady portrait: a fragile platform made of thin strips of balsa wood glued together in an interlocking series of rectangles and triangles, like the framework of a miniature building about a foot square and two feet high. Although the platform hardly looked sturdy enough to support its own weight, Luke maintained it would support his father's 150 pounds when it was completed. It was a science-fair stunt demonstrating some basic principles of structural engineering.

Paul wondered whether the portraits he painted were stunts as well—unlikely constructions that could produce oohs and aahs in those who hadn't learned the principles; that could occasionally be beautiful. It was beauty that Paul had never mastered, and he suspected that Luke never would either. So be it. Paul sometimes wondered if beauty wasn't just a distraction in any case, a point of dispute for frivolous people.

Paul turned to look again at the pigeon-lady portrait. No beauty there—in the woman or on the canvas. Maybe with another sitting or two the painting would take on some beauty. No. Paul looked at his watch, calculating, as he did too often, how many hours and minutes until five o'clock, the time when he allowed himself to have his first *official* cognac of the day—publicly and from a tulip glass.

Luke's robust alto voice interrupted: "Here I stand."

Paul turned to find his son standing triumphantly and heavily atop the fragile, unbending balsa wood construction. Luke's arms were folded across his narrow chest. He's a skinny kid, Paul thought, and he'll be a skinny man, an ectomorph, like his father. Likeness.

Paul asked, "How much do you weigh?"

"I don't know."

"Don't you weigh yourself?"

"No."

"Why not?"

"That's nothing that interests me."

Paul was pleased that Luke was the kind of person who decided for himself what he should be interested in. He said, "You probably weigh about seventy-five pounds—half of what I weigh." Before Paul could ask if the platform would hold one hundred fifty pounds, Luke began to lose his balance, and there was a soft cracking and squeaking noise within the framework of the platform. It twisted slowly for a second or two and then collapsed.

Luke didn't seem surprised or upset. He knelt and examined the wreckage. "Torque," he said, and smiled.

"I've felt some of that myself on occasion," Paul said.

Luke stopped smiling. *He* was feeling it," he said.

"Who?"

"The creep in the park."

Paul remembered those words the next day when, at the breakfast table, he read the brief newspaper item under the one-column headline: Woman Drowns. She had been sixty years old, her name was Edna Denning, and her death was considered accidental.

Chapter 3

"Mama," Dwight Bailey said, "I'm going to take a little vacation."

His mother squinted at him, deepening the heavy creases across her forehead. "Say that again, will you?"

"A little vacation. A few days in Florida, maybe."

Dwight was afraid she might shout her reply, but it was more like a gentle growl: "Are you fuckin' crazy? You are, aren't you?"

What bothered Dwight most about his mother was her profanity. It was one thing to be ill-tempered, but it was another to talk like a factory worker. Dwight had learned to repair watches so that he wouldn't have to work in a factory, so that he could work at home under conditions he created. His language, which he used sparingly, was like his workroom: meticulously clean and orderly. The only disorderly element in his world was his mother's presence. If it hadn't been for his mother and the popularity of battery-operated, nonmechanical watches, Dwight's life would have met all of his requirements.

"What do you need a vacation for?" his mother continued. "You don't do anything but spend my pension and fuck around with your stupid watches. Do you think I'll let you go to Florida on my money? Not a chance."

"I've got my own money, Mother. I've been getting some antique clocks to repair. I'm getting a reputation."

"You've always *had* a reputation . . . for being prissy and loony."

Dwight ignored the accusation. He heard it almost daily. "I'm going to take the trip, Mother, regardless of what you say. And it won't be entirely pleasure. I might buy some old clocks to fix up and sell."

But he thought: It *would* be all pleasure. Being away from his mother; visiting junk stores, or "collectibles" stores as they tended to be called now. An old clock was useless to people who could not restore time to the intricate jumble of metal. Dwight thought of himself as a magician . . . an alchemist who could change useless objects into valuable ones.

The biggest pleasure of his trip, however, would be the telephone call he would receive: the sympathetic voice describing his mother's accident and asking him to return to make arrangements for her funeral and burial.

Dwight had received a letter from Chainmaster commending him for the efficiency with which he had carried out his assignment and asking him for the name of the chain's next victim together with a description of the person's habits. Chainmaster said it was best if Dwight could arrange to be out of town during the time the next link would be added to the deathchain. Dwight had replied:

Dear Chainmaster:

I did what you said.

Now I get to name a person. I name my mother, Mrs. Angela Bailey. She lives with me at 512 Albany Street and doesn't go out much. But she goes every Friday to the Victory Regional Hospital to the twelfth floor (where the mental cases are). She will talk to anyone who asks her about astrology, and there's a window that can open at the end of the corridor by the elevator. I've thought sometimes of pushing her out of that window. The doctor pays her to come in and answer questions into a microphone. She's part of a study that goes on and on that we don't understand. Otherwise, the back door to our house is always unlocked. I'm going to be out of town from April 1 to 13.

Sincerely,
Dwight Bailey

His mother's voice brought him back to the present: "What are you going to do without your mommy, Dwight? How are you going to go more than a day without curling your lip at me? You can still hate me long distance, I know, but it won't be the same, will it?"

She was right. Dwight was devoted to his distaste for her. He would have to learn to live without his hate. But he could do it. The deathchain had given him the courage; it had distracted him. He looked at his mother, and the queasiness he usually felt was hardly noticeable. He was thinking, delightedly, that somewhere nearby was another person who had received instructions from Chainmaster, someone who would be watching and following his mother. Bye-bye, Mama. Soon, in the spring darkness, a face would appear at the window. Getting to know you. The better to kill you with, my dear. There, Dwight thought. You said it: kill. Why was it so difficult to say? People killed people all the time; they always had. Wars, massacres, uprisings, feuds, conspiracies, domestic disputes. Thou shalt not. Like adultery: Thou shalt not but thou does (doest?). Sex. Maybe that's next for me, Dwight thought. I've killed, now I'll fornicate. On my vacation. After the phone call comes about mother. Before I return to make the funeral arrangements, I'll spend a few minutes celebrating in my room with one of the women who sit at the bar in a hotel—an Oriental woman, perhaps. Chainmaster will break my chains.

Two days later, Dwight's mother said to him, "Some woman followed me today."

Dwight was pleased by the announcement. He had received a note from Chainmaster the day before telling him that his wish would be carried out but warning him not to try to learn how, when, or by whom.

He said to his mother, "What reason would anyone have to follow you?"

"People don't need reasons. Half the people walking around this town are loony. *You,* of all people, know that. Itching to interfere with someone for no reason . . . no fucking reason at all."

Just as there's no reason to say that word, Dwight thought. Maybe if you didn't constantly say that word, the person wouldn't be following you. You wouldn't be on the list.

The list. Dwight wasn't usually inquisitive, but the thought of the list intrigued him. In a way, the people in the chain were his relatives—his family. "What did she look like, the woman who followed you?"

"One of those women who wants to be a man—to be a *rich* man. Yuppy, yucky, whatever they're called. Suit, tie, briefcase. Smart-ass expression. Fucks for exercise, not for fun."

I could get to know her, Dwight thought. Follow her. But Chainmaster had said to make no attempt to learn how, when, or by whom. Chainmaster was right. It would be dangerous to know someone else who was in the chain. Maybe Dwight had already met someone who was in the chain, but as long as he didn't *know* that the person was in the chain, no harm could be done. Dwight had restored antique clocks for young women like the one his mother described—lawyers and executives. He had disliked them; the dislike was mutual. They could kill easily, he thought. They should be avoided. Let their cold-bloodedness work for me, not against me.

The next day, Dwight boarded a plane for Miami. His heart was beating so erratically that he thought it might set off an alarm when he went through the security checkpoint. What emotion was he feeling? He had always had difficulty distinguishing joy from guilt.

Chapter 4

Paul Marnay would watch television news programs only if asked to do so by someone he was fond of. There was no one he was more fond of than Luke, his son—and Luke wanted company while waiting to see the coverage of a major earthquake that had struck Mexico City. Luke, of course, wanted to see the structural damage that had been done to the city's buildings.

Paul wasn't interested in disasters or in most things that TV journalists were interested in. The truth didn't seem well served when it was funneled through a video camera. People are much too respectful of cameras, Paul thought. They pretend that the camera is the bringer of truth, but they know it neglects something important. The most exciting images Paul had seen on the news were sketches an artist had done in a courtroom from which cameras were excluded. There was a drama in the sketches, a concentration on essentials, a selectiveness that couldn't be achieved with a camera. Also, as Paul knew from dealing with his subject-clients, the camera image doesn't seem unique to people in the way that a sketch or painting does.

Luke was watching the earthquake sequence now. A tape was in the VCR, and the boy would play it back later in stop motion. He claimed to be looking at it from the standpoint of a would-be structural engineer and architect, but Paul suspected there was more to it than that. The sense of disaster was also an attraction.

Paul was made uneasy by events involving large numbers of people, whether the events were tragic or not. He liked to deal with people on an individual basis, and with people who, if they happened to do something that would interest a reporter or editor, would take pains to avoid having it discovered. Few people seemed to value privacy and decorum.

Though Paul preferred being with one person at a time, he found it necessary to have a large number of individuals to choose from. His marriage had ended during one of his uncontrollable urges to extend his "acquaintanceships." His wife, Sherril, had discovered him in a bar on a rainy afternoon in obvious thrall with a woman whose portrait he had been commissioned to paint. Sherril might have been more understanding if the woman had been beautiful and sensual and had been going to bed with Paul. But the woman was plain and too virtuous to share anything more than a drink with Paul. That's all he required, Sherril realized. He would, as she had suspected when she married him, love every woman he painted. Although Paul's infidelities were frequent, they were innocent and predictable enough to be tolerable to Sherril. But they were just one of the more obvious parts of a larger and more complex problem. Even Luke wasn't surprised when his mother suddenly took him to live with her in a separate household across town.

Luke now spent one day a week with his father and seemed to believe, as his parents did, that the arrangement was satisfactory. During the boy's visits, Paul usually did what his son wanted to do. And today seemed to be exclusively devoted to television (fortunately, a rare occurrence). The earthquake coverage had ended, and a local tragedy was being examined. A medical team was shown lifting a woman's corpse onto a trolley. She had jumped or fallen from a window. Paul wondered why that had to be shown. A voice was explaining that the police were trying to locate the woman's son, Dwight Bailey. Then his picture was shown. It was an institutional photograph made with emotional indifference and technical competence. It was bad.

"That's him," Luke said.

"Who?"

"The creep I saw in the park when I went to get the pigeon lady the day she got killed."

Paul and Luke hadn't mentioned the pigeon lady's death to each other. Her portrait, still covered, stood on an easel in a corner of the studio. Paul had twice started to destroy it, but had hesitated each time. It was a good portrait, spontaneous and well executed. It revealed the woman's emotional quirks. Nevertheless, who besides Paul would want it?

Luke continued to watch the news in a lethargic way, giving it just the minimum amount of attention —the degree that the program's producers expected their viewers to make available. Although his son had apparently forgotten once more about the creepola whose mother had fallen from the window, Paul could think of nothing else.

Two women had died in falls. Dwight was near the scene in the first instance and possibly also in the second instance. Paul supposed that he and his son were the only people who had that information. Were the two violent deaths simply a coincidence? Should the police be told on the chance that a crime or crimes had been committed? Probably. But Paul was interested in justice only in an abstract way. Justice should be done, but he didn't want to do it. And besides, his ability to make a living—to obtain commissions—depended to a large extent on his social image. If he was to get involved in a criminal investigation, even peripherally, it could mean that a few of his more snobbish acquaintances might decide he was not one of them and that they didn't need a portrait after all. It wasn't that Paul was totally servile. He was, for example, usually willing to risk sexual adventures among his clients, and a few commissions had been canceled by irate husbands whose wives had agreed to adjourn their sittings to the bedroom. But a certain amount of rakishness was expected of an artist. Getting involved in criminal misadventures among members of the lower socioeconomic groups was another thing altogether. It would not be discreet. Paul was not proud of his overdeveloped sense of discretion, but he usually deferred to it.

Leaving his son in front of the TV, Paul got up and went to his studio. He unshrouded the portrait of the pigeon lady. There was a strength and aggressiveness in her expression that could only exist in a person who was at war with her environment, someone who was not concerned with discretion. She was stronger and possibly more honorable than I am, Paul thought. She wasn't the sort of person who would voluntarily surrender her life or be careless with it.

So? Painting someone's picture didn't make you responsible for that person, did it? Maybe it did. Portraiture was an intimate act. It forced you to look at a person more closely than most lovers or close relatives. By insisting on painting this woman—Edna Denning—Paul had become responsible for her. He went to the telephone and called the local police department.

It turned out to be an unsatisfactory call for several reasons. It wasn't until the call went through that Paul realized he wasn't sure what he wanted to say. Did he have a question? Did he want to make an accusation? He mentioned the names of Edna Denning and Dwight Bailey to the person who answered the call and was eventually connected with someone who said, "Ray here." Paul wasn't sure whether Ray was a first name or a last name, and he couldn't tell from the voice whether the officer was a man or a woman. Telephones made Paul aggressive, particularly when he was talking to someone he had never seen. People's voices were more deceptive than their faces, he thought. Except for a few instances with children, he had never seen a person (including two transsexuals) whose sex wasn't obvious from their appearance. But voices could be ambiguous.

Officer Ray was a woman, Paul decided. He made his decision not on the evidence of the officer's voice but on the assumption that a police department would be more likely to hire a woman than to hire a man who sounded like a woman. But that still left Paul with the problem of what to say to the officer. He came up with, "I saw Dwight Bailey's picture on television."

The police officer said, "We've found out where he was, if that's what you wanted to tell us . . . in Florida . . . he's on his way back."

"Oh," Paul said. If the creep had been in Florida, Paul's theory became embarrassingly thin.

"Are you a friend of his?" the officer asked.

Paul hung up. He removed the portrait of Edna Denning from its easel and put it into a cupboard labeled "Misc." He reached for his flask, but hesitated when he remembered that Luke was in the other room. Paul went to the doorway and for the next fifteen minutes watched his son watching television. I'm a cobbler attending to my last, he said to himself, and then wondered what a last might be.

Paul had never tried to paint Luke but had once thought, frivolously, of doing a portrait that would be a composite of himself and his son. Paul would set up a mirror so that it reflected his own image, and then Luke would pose sitting next to the mirror. It would be a portrait of the artist's genetic dominance. But in a sense, Luke was himself a portrait—a living portrait —of his father. And in any case, Paul knew that he and Luke were the worst subject for a portrait. They had the kind of features that were not well represented in repose. Their faces were too mobile to be recognizable when not in motion. Maybe this was an instance where a camera—a movie camera or video camera— was superior to a brush. Luke's face, even now when he was relaxed, was never completely immobile. His reactions to what he saw were transferred to the muscles of his face and body. One or both of his remarkably heavy eyebrows moved at all times, and his wide mouth was seldom closed, accommodating itself constantly to smiles, pursings, and an obtruding tongue. Luke wasn't handsome, but he was exciting to watch. To look at him was to have an adventure.

Paul didn't like adventure; he liked convivial repose. He was glad Officer Ray had not needed his suspicions.

Chapter 5

Connie Nickens had spent most of her twenty-five years in a state of excitement. What made her life difficult was that she didn't distinguish among the various kinds of excitement she experienced. And after adolescence arrived and added exhausting new depths to her repertoire of emotions, Connie had been forced to ask several therapists and social agencies to help her contain her excitement. They had helped moderate her behavior by converting her fondness for drugs and promiscuity into the more socially acceptable channels of avarice and ambition. She became successively a bartender, hostess, and manager in an ever-posher series of lounges and restaurants. She learned to support her instinctive charm and conventional beauty with an understanding of bribery, creative bookkeeping, and betrayal. She was becoming solvent and respectable when one of her few confidants—Freddy Stella—turned out to be not a lover, as she had thought, but an extortionist. Freddy was an obstacle that Connie thought she might not be able to remove. Then she received an unusual letter.

Connie assumed the letter was an answer to her prayers. She had been taught to pray by a recruiter for Alcoholics Anonymous, and although she had continued to drink, she added informal daily prayer to her activities. She had no difficulty seeing Chainmaster as God, and she easily accepted the assignment outlined in the letter—the ending of Angela Bailey's life—especially after she spent a few hours following Mrs. Bailey and getting to know a little about the old woman's dreary activities. Connie thought an existence as unexciting and resigned as Mrs. Bailey's could be considered a nonlife. Killing her would be killing in its most minimal sense—a technicality.

This would be the final act of Connie's misspent youth—an act of purification. As she prepared for her encounter with Mrs. Bailey, Connie began to feel like a bride-to-be. And when, a few days later, she found herself alone with Mrs. Bailey in the corridor of the hospital, next to the open window, Connie experienced no hesitation, felt no sense of wrongdoing—she pushed the old woman neatly and effortlessly out into unobstructed space.

Connie's sense of justification increased when she turned from the window and had the good luck to hear a bell signaling the arrival of an elevator—an empty elevator that took her quickly and unobserved to the lobby and away from the scene.

She stopped at the mailbox outside the entrance to the hospital and mailed a letter. It was addressed to Chainmaster, and it named Freddy Stella as her choice of the chain's next victim.

Paul Marnay, feeling the first tinglings of arousal, watched in delight as Connie Nickens, the restaurant's hostess, moved the table and allowed Hillary Brock, his date, to slide into a banquette. The two women smiled insincerely at each other, trying only feebly to hide their mutual dislike. As Paul moved into the banquette next to Hillary, he reflected that the only things the women had in common were good teeth and ash blond hair. In Connie's case, the hair and many of the teeth were artificial, whereas Hillary's were as nature had supplied them. But Connie had paid top price for her cosmetic work, Paul thought. She probably had the work done out of town, maybe going as far as New York City for the dentistry. The teeth were just the right shape for her broad, Slavic features and were artfully unsymmetrical. The hair color was believable in itself but seemed wrong for the hair's brushlike texture.

Paul had known Connie for several years and had helped her find her two most recent jobs. He had taught her about wines and would have accepted occasional invitations to share her bed if she hadn't insisted on keeping a couple of unfortunate connections—apparently romantic—with men that Paul found terrifying and that the police, he had been told, found worthy of surveillance.

Because of her sinister private life, Connie's artifice seemed more real than Hillary's delicate naturalness. Hillary radiated refinement and sincerity. She was a social worker in the local hospital, with a psychotherapy practice on the side. Connie, until recently, had been one of the less fortunate, but, partly on the basis of Paul's recommendation, she had joined the staff of the Postroad, one of the town's better, if more conservative, restaurants. Paul had persuaded the skeptical owner that Connie's combination of shrewdness, sexiness, and intimidating toughness were the right qualities for a maîtresse d'. The owner said that Connie was doing well, but he also contended (how seriously, Paul wasn't sure) that the restaurant had begun attracting members of the masochist branch of the sadomasochist set. Mild-mannered men had begun showing up without reservations, which would subject them to a scolding by Connie and a long wait for a bad table. The proprietor claimed he didn't mind because the men seemed to enjoy such treatment; and since they tended to be listed in the region's social register, they raised the tone of the place.

Hillary Brock was also listed prominently in the register. There was some feeling that the Brock family was too wealthy to be among the truly elite, but so much of their money was channeled toward the three *C*s—charity, culture, and clubbiness, that they were reduced, after donations and parties, almost to the upper-middle income regions, which fortified their social status.

Hillary was a minor blossom in the family orchard —the 1980s equivalent of a spinster. She was allowed to do good works and to sleep around at a certain level of respectability—the one that Paul represented— but it was assumed she would not marry. Paul liked her because she was beautiful and passionate and because she didn't try to capitalize on either fact. He was less enthusiastic about her tendency to control people and about her interest in psychotherapy. It seemed particularly unfortunate to Paul that a social worker would do psychotherapy, which implied that people who were poor or uneducated or in trouble with the law got that way by being mentally ill. But Paul didn't express his opinion to Hillary.

The conversation at that particular lunch, however, was a little more interesting to Paul than usual. As Connie seated him and Hillary side by side in a banquette, recited the obligatory, "Enjoy your meal," and was about to walk away, Hillary said to her, with what Paul thought was a prying tone, "I don't mean to pry, Connie, but were you having a problem at the hospital Saturday? You seemed unsettled. I might be able to help if there's a problem there."

Connie's self-confidence seemed to waver, and she turned pale for a moment. Paul thought it might be her version of a blush. But she recovered immediately, touching Hillary's shoulder and saying, "No problem, thanks, Miss Brock. Just visiting a friend. Serious illness in a friend can be unsettling."

As Connie moved quickly away, Hillary turned to Paul and said, "I thought hostesses—or whatever she is—were supposed to keep their hands to themselves. And it wasn't during visiting hours when I saw her."

"Saturday," Paul said. "Wasn't that when the woman—Mrs. Bailey—went out the window?"

"Mmm. I had to work with some of the staff who tried to revive her. They're used to death but not that kind."

"What kind is that?"

"Public suicide."

"Don't ask me to explain why," Paul said, "but I thought for a while that her son had pushed her out."

Hillary looked at Paul with an expression he couldn't read, but it was in the area of shock-fear-disbelief. She obviously wasn't going to respond.

"I was wrong," Paul continued.

A waiter intervened to take their drink orders. Hillary ordered a vodka gimlet instead of her usual half bottle of champagne—a further sign of distress. Paul ordered the only drink he ever ordered before a meal—one of the competition's cognacs. Doing research, he called it. He would order his own brand after the meal. I need solace, Paul thought. While waiting for the solace to arrive, he moved his hand along the table to Hillary's, which turned out to be cold and tense rather than, as he had expected, warm, moist, and supple.

Paul decided that too much of his time recently had been taken up with thoughts of violent death. He took Hillary's elaborately folded napkin, unfurled it, and placed it on her lap. Then he placed his hand under the napkin between Hillary's thighs, which were their usual warm selves. Hillary always wore either a long skirt or some kind of trousers, and when she wore stockings at all, they were usually knee-highs. She had told Paul that she didn't like to feel pressure on her thighs except under certain private circumstances.

The current circumstances weren't exactly private, and Hillary turned to Paul with her eyebrows raised in questioning surprise. He said, "I need comforting."

"We all need that. But there's a time and a place, my sweet."

"I've been thinking about death," Paul said. "It's all around us."

"I work in a hospital—remember? One of my basic jobs is to help survivors deal with loss."

We *both* think of death too often, Paul thought. He asked, "How do the experts say a person is supposed to deal with loss?"

"First, you go crazy a little bit—you let yourself grieve. The danger is when you don't mourn or grieve. That way lies pathology."

"But someone like you can't grieve at every death you get involved in. You wouldn't have time for anything else."

"I have my acts of mourning. Haven't you noticed?" Hillary squeezed her thighs together, catching Paul's fingers in a remarkably tight grip.

"That seems more like passion than mourning," he said.

"It *is* passion, but not sexual passion."

"Just a form of pathology?" Paul said.

"That, but not *just* that."

The waiter brought their drinks. Paul retrieved his hand, and he wondered if it was true that Hillary was a little crazy. Probably. But he believed that if you looked closely enough at *any* person, you would find some craziness. And someone who helps other people cope must have to share their stress to some extent. He had heard that psychiatrists have a startlingly high suicide rate. He clinked glasses with Hillary. She looked feverish. He remembered that she had once talked about the big turnover among hospital social workers—the large number who gave up and went into something more restful, such as air traffic controlling. She called the syndrome burnout.

Hillary finished her drink in two swallows and waved the empty glass at the waiter. Quenching the flames, Paul thought. Soon those flames were out, and after sharing food and gossip, Paul and Hillary adjourned to her apartment and started some other emotional fires. *"Vive la pathologie,"* Paul said to himself at one particularly conflagrational moment.

Chapter 6

Like many bright but undereducated people, Connie Nickens had the advantage of tending to define things in her own way, on the basis of her own experience. And according to her definition, a bad person wasn't one who had sometimes done bad things but one who kept doing the same bad thing over and over again. Freddy Stella was a bad person.

Freddy kept asking Connie for money in return for his silence about some funds she appropriated from a former employer. Freddy had made a profession of capitalizing on other people's mistakes, and Connie was sure it hadn't occurred to him that his profession itself might be a big, although temporarily successful, mistake.

Freddy was a large, unfastidious man whose well-developed muscles were concealed by a layer of fat. Because of the combination of his physique and his taste for gossip, Freddy called himself, proudly, a mud wrestler. Although it now seemed incredible to her, there had been a time when Connie found that combination of qualities attractive. Her fondness for Freddy taught her that she had a tendency to confuse strength with worth and that people should occasionally try to overcome their tendencies; it also developed in her a desire to see Freddy discreetly and quickly removed from the world.

Another of Freddy's qualities was a need to drive automobiles faster than they could safely be driven—a fact that Connie stressed in the letter she sent to Chainmaster and that resulted in the selection of Lamb Johnson, an auto mechanic, as the next person in the deathchain.

No one who knew Freddy Stella was surprised when his car went out of control on a rainy night, smashing headlong into the concrete-and-steel support of an overpass. The highway patrol officers who were sent to the scene of the crash thought at first that the driver had been thrown free. Then they realized that Freddy Stella's body had simply become an indistinguishable part of the car's twisted, compressed remains.

One of the few people to be disturbed by Freddy Stella's death was Paul Marnay. The limits of coincidence had been exceeded. Something was going on. The pigeon lady fell into the river when Dwight Bailey was nearby. Dwight's mother fell out of a window when Connie Nickens was nearby. Now Connie's friend Freddy has a fatal accident. Something was definitely going on. A chain of violent deaths. But what was the pattern? The first two murders could have been committed by a psychopath who randomly attacked seedy old women. Why would the murderer also kill Freddy, though?

Paul wondered why he should get himself involved, even if he was able to see a pattern in the killings. For though he was interested in fictional mysteries, he had never seen them as being strongly connected to reality —not because there weren't any real mysteries. On the contrary. Paul thought there were too many mysteries in everyday life. But in real life, the mysteries seldom got solved; that's why there were so many of them.

For Paul, there always seemed to be some implied meaning, something that was a little beyond him in the way things looked or the way events related to one another. He liked the paintings of Magritte in which everyday, conventionally depicted elements were combined in a sinister way: the house in the darkened lane with deep shadows and a lighted street lamp, all under a sunny daytime sky. I'm too ready to see shadows, Paul thought. But he did want to talk to someone about his concern. Not the police. Who else? Who was sympathetic company and would be willing to believe in the existence of homicidal maniacs? Paul picked up the phone and called Hillary Brock.

"Hillary?"

"Paul—business, I assume." As a defense against inappropriate entanglements, Paul had a rule against seeing the same woman socially more often than once every two weeks.

"Sort of business."

"But not entirely? Beware. I'm liable to get the idea you're after more than just my body."

"I am."

"More than just my mind and body?"

"Yes."

"More than just my money and mind and body?"

"What else is there?" Paul asked. He was serious.

"My soul, of course."

"Of course. That, too." It had never occurred to Paul that a social worker would think in terms of the soul. He thought social workers were supposed to be secular. He said, "I didn't know your intervention (one of her favorite words in talking about her work) was divine."

"I'm divine in every sense, *mon cher.*"

Paul was feeling uneasy. He wasn't religious himself, but joking about religion upset him. Among his forebears were both Catholics and Jews who had been persecuted for their beliefs. The jokes always seemed like the leading edge of intolerance to him. One of the reasons he wouldn't join a church was that the very existence of a church—even one that preached tolerance—implied that all other churches were somehow inferior. And eventually someone always wants to eliminate the freedoms, if not the lives, of the inferiors.

"Hey," said Hillary, reminding Paul that he had fallen silent.

"I'm still here," he said. "Can we have dinner tonight?"

"We can have anything you want tonight."

"Just food and talk," Paul said.

"What kind of food?"

"Soul food?"

"And what kind of talk?"

"Body talk," Paul said.

Hillary produced a pleased "Mmmm."

"Dead-body talk, actually."

It was Hillary's turn to be silent. After a moment, she said, "Not funny."

"It wasn't meant to be."

"Dead bodies are a little out of my line . . .

personally and professionally. I deal with bodies that still have personalities attached."

"Personalities are another thing I want to talk about—homicidal personalities."

"Not my favorite dinner-table topic."

"We could make it pillow talk." Paul had an image, more tactile than visual of Hillary's long, smooth body; her pale, sparse, nonconcealing pubic hair.

"That's better," Hillary said, but it didn't sound to Paul as if she meant it. It's remarkable, he thought, how just three spoken syllables could reveal apprehensiveness. He arranged to pick her up at seven that night, even though he was beginning to think the meeting would be a mistake.

Although Paul had mentioned soul food to Hillary, he wasn't really sure what soul food was or where you could get it. And because he was looking for professional advice tonight, he let Hillary lead him to a place that was attached to the side of a run-down frame house and that seemed not to be a restaurant but an extension of someone's family kitchen. Paul couldn't decide—even after eating the meal—what nationality the family might be. His best guess would be that they were part Thai and part North African. Paul liked the way the chef looked better than the way she cooked, and he had to restrain himself from asking her—a pudgy, cynical-expressioned, fiftyish woman—to pose for him.

Paul also restrained his conversation, and it wasn't until he and Hillary adjourned to a hotel bar for the requisite after-dinner drink that the unpleasant subject was introduced. His restraint wasn't just an effort to let Hillary enjoy her dinner; it was also the result of a growing uncertainty. As he tried to decide how to explain his suspicions, he began to think they might be idiotic. He finally decided to wait and see if Hillary would bring the matter up. While he waited, he watched. Hillary's face was not expressive—not as expressive as her voice, he thought. She seemed to make a conscious effort to keep her features from reflecting any feelings or attitudes—perhaps as a result of her training in interviewing people. It could also have been the result of vanity, wanting nothing to disturb the smooth symmetry that her face had in repose.

"I thought you wanted to talk," Hillary said.

"I decided to stare a bit first."

"Some people consider that impolite," Hillary said, "but I've never understood why."

That's obvious, Paul thought. A woman who goes braless while wearing a silk blouse—as Hillary was doing—isn't going to mind a few intense gazes. "Staring is an act of aggression," he said. "There's no defense. If I see you, I possess you. That's why we have—or had—hoods and veils."

"Then you're an extremely aggressive person."

"I suppose I am, in a nonaggressive way. I'm certainly not lethal."

"Fortunately, few of us are."

"But some are. That's what I want you to tell me about. What kind of people kill other people?"

As Paul had expected, Hillary's look of pleasure and receptiveness instantly vanished. However, her expression changed not to a professional objectivity, as he had anticipated, but to something more complex; something that seemed to include irritation. Her answer was professional and calm, though: "In most cases, killers are ordinary people who are in an extreme state of anger, fear, or jealousy and who happen to get their hands on a deadly weapon before the emotion subsides."

"I'm not talking about most cases," Paul said. "I'm

talking about people who kill without emotion, carefully, undetected."

"That sort of thing happens in books, *mon cher*—which means that it doesn't really happen."

"It doesn't happen often. But sometimes. Crazies like Son of Sam or the Hillside Strangler."

Hillary looked at Paul disapprovingly. "That's a little different. I thought you meant someone with a formal motive like jealousy. You mean a psychotic—the paranoia-prone single child whose parents abuse him. Never marries; never makes a satisfactory sexual arrangement. The quiet young man next door whose idea of a date is a weekend strangulation. Is that what interests you, Bunky?"

"I don't know what my interest is," Paul said, and he told Hillary about the three deaths. As he spoke, he began to feel ridiculous. Hillary's face set into a rigid, troubled frown, and she stared down at her drink. She's worried about me, Paul thought. Paul let his story trail off inconclusively.

Hillary took his hand. "Our little world is too much with you, Paul. People have accidents, and in a smallish city like this, people's lives coincide in one way or another. And you're too much aware of other people anyway."

"I suppose. Do I need therapy?"

"It might help if you spent a weekend in New York City . . . new faces . . . a museum or two, some galleries . . . with an amorous friend, perhaps."

Paul had often wondered why Hillary didn't live in New York City. She drove down almost every week, claiming she had work to do or a conference to attend. At first Paul thought she must have a lover in the city, but that came to seem unlikely as he got to know her better. To make her visits to New York, Hillary worked a difficult split schedule at the hospital. With her private practice and a fairly active social life, she looked overwrought most of the time. However, she was a person whose attractiveness increased as she approached exhaustion. Tension made her look as if she were fighting off a wave of sexual desire. But there was also something else in Hillary's emotional intensity—something that had made the thought of spending more than a night with her seem unappealing to him. There was a forbidding aspect to Hillary, and considering how knowledgeable she was about the human mind, Paul assumed she was living according to some kind of distinctive, admirable principles. But on the other hand, it sometimes occurred to him that doctors get sick, too. Maybe she and he were both sick, Paul thought.

"Okay," he said. "Are you available to nibble *La Grande Pomme* next weekend?"

"I'll nibble whatever you'd like."

"Where shall we stay?"

"At the Hilton. I've already got a room reserved. I'm taking part in an orthopsychiatry workshop there."

"What's orthopsychiatry?"

"I'm not sure."

"I won't have to attend the workshop?"

"You just have to attend to me."

"An irresistible assignment," Paul said. "Shall I arrange with the hotel for double occupancy?"

"I always make that arrangement."

"Just in case a friend needs emergency treatment?"

"Something like that."

Paul smiled.

Chapter 7

Paul felt emotionally handicapped when he visited New York City. Specifically, he became disoriented by the city's people—their number, their energy, and their variety. Paul looked in vain for a face that showed the complacent self-acceptance of the people in upstate New York.

Before starting on his usual itinerary, which took him to the reserved, pseudo-British atmosphere of Madison Avenue art galleries or the East-Fifty-seventh Street offices of Marnay Cognacs, Ltd., Paul always found himself headed for the nearest West Side IRT subway entrance, where he would board a local and make as many trips between Ninty-sixth and Fourteenth streets as his schedule or his nervous system would allow. Because eye contact with fellow passengers violated the unwritten rules of behavior—such as they are—Paul held a paperback book below eye level and engaged in an orgy of surreptitious glancing. He didn't speculate on what might be going on in the minds of the other passengers or on what some of the more spectacular racial mixtures might be; he simply revitalized his concept of the possible configurations and implications of the human face. Each time the train's doors opened to admit a new selection of subjects, Paul's pulse picked up.

Paul and Hillary had made the trip down to the city in his decrepit and unreliable car on Saturday morning. They traveled in silence, she studying her notes for the late-afternoon workshop, and he concentrating on the driving, a process he had never learned to take for granted. Even on the straightest three-lane stretches with light traffic, he expected other cars to appear magically and maliciously, bearing down on him from the opposite direction.

As they neared the city, Hillary put her work aside. She leaned her head back and closed her eyes. Paul was aware of the oddly attractive effect of her upper body. The dark strap of her safety harness pressed diagonally between her breasts, pressing them against her sweater. Hillary's pale hair lay in a glistening fringe across her shoulders. She raised her right hand and began twisting hair around her index finger, a habit that Paul thought inappropriate for a therapist. Her left hand rested palm down against the slight bulge of her belly. Paul thought of a small painting by Cranach—a leering, standing nude with the most erotically rendered tummy in the history of art. He hoped there would be time to take Hillary to the Metropolitan Museum, where the painting hung. As they looked at the canvas, he would brush his hand against the front of her skirt.

Paul was beginning to feel aroused. It was the wrong time and place. He asked, "Studying all done?"

"All done."

"Something interesting?"

"You tell me: 'Suggestion as a Therapy Technique Among Borderline Bipolars.'"

"It's about bears? Bisexual bears?"

"Bipolars are what used to be known as manic-depressives."

"What was wrong with manic-depressive? I sort of liked it."

"If the shoe fits."

"I don't think it does. I never feel very manic."

"And," Hillary said, "you're never very suggestible. I've suggested, for example, that we see each other more often."

Paul thought things were becoming too personal. "So—are bipolars suggestible?"

"I claim they are. I claim they respond to authority if they think they'll be allowed to share some of the authority."

Paul tried to work up some interest in Hillary's theory, but he was more interested in the fact that she had kicked off her shoes and was wriggling her remarkably long toes.

Hillary, noticing Paul's wandering attention, asked, "Are my toes really more interesting than my mind?"

"Depends on the eyes—and the brain capacity—of the beholder, I suppose. As you're already aware, my eyes are bigger than my mind."

"*Pas de problème,* sweetie," Hillary said. She unbuckled her safety belt and swung around to place her feet in Paul's lap. He was wondering, optimistically, if Hillary's fingerlike toes could deal with a zipper, when the name Freddy Stella appeared in his mind together with the image of a totaled sports car.

Paul decided he had better concentrate on his driving. He wondered whether he was developing a bipolar disorder that had an emphasis on the drearier pole.

While Hillary took care of her professional commitments, Paul took his subway ride. Then he reluctantly stopped in at Marnay Cognacs, Ltd., and—hoping the answer would be no—asked the receptionist if his brother, François, could see him. In the eyes of the Marnay family, François was the good brother—the one who was upholding an admirable tradition. Unlike Paul, who had been born in New York City and who was an American in fact and in temperament,

François had been born in Segonzac in the cognac region of France and was as devotedly French as the most snobbish Parisian.

François, one of the family's most accomplished "sea gulls," was, as usual, impeccably and boringly tailored, but he was featuring a slightly longer, straighter, and glossier hairstyle than usual. He greeted Paul with a smile that implied, I'm a busy man but I can spare a moment for my frivolous, helpless younger brother. François proceeded with a report— in French, of course—that Paul would have had trouble following even if his French had been fluent rather than utilitarian. It seemed that a sister was considering a marriage proposal made by a member of the Martell family. Sales were phenomenally good in China, where cognac was thought to be an aphrodisiac.

François then turned his attention to Paul. This attention always consisted of a request by François— who was as conservative maritally as in every other way—for a detailed description of Paul's most recent romantic involvements. Paul demanded a glass of the family's masterpiece, *Paradis: Age Inconnu,* on the assumption that Claude Rains had been right when he said in one (or was it several?) of his movies, "A good story always goes better with a cognac." The story didn't seem that interesting to Paul as he told it, but he resisted the temptation to exaggerate. François seemed satisfied with the fairly innocuous truth and was delighted to learn that his brother was sharing a hotel room with a social worker. *"Un travailleur social—formidable!"*

The social worker was indeed *formidable.* When Paul rejoined her in their room before dinner, Hillary was flushed with several kinds of excitement. She explained that her workshop presentation had been challenged by a lesbian cognitive therapist; hands had trembled, smiles had become fixed. After the workshop, Hillary had left the field of battle quickly and had gone to her room to wait for Paul and to relax in a bathtub full of too-hot water. The water hadn't relaxed her, but in an interesting kind of alchemy, had converted her combative passions into sexual passions. Paul found her lying nude, her body florid against the white bedspread. Her left hand was on her right breast; her right hand, its first two fingers glittering, was ruffling her pubic hair. Her eyes were closed, and she was humming an odd tune that might have been a cross between a medieval chant and delta blues. Paul stood watching and listening until Hillary's song turned into a pleasureful groan and she opened her eyes. She didn't seem surprised to see him.

"I'm having trouble relaxing," she said.

"I've got just the thing for that."

"I was sure you would."

Paul reached into his jacket and produced his flask.

Hillary's eyebrows moved closer together. "Is *that* the thing?"

"It's one of the things."

Paul opened the flask and handed it to her. Hillary sniffed it. Her eyebrows moved upward. She took a sip. She smiled. "What is it?"

"It's the Marnay triumph. It's older than both of us together. They call it paradise."

Later, Hillary said, "Your family produces all kinds of triumphs, all kinds of paradise."

Paul thought she sounded as if she might want to become part of the family—something that might have happened if they hadn't gone to the theater that night.

Chapter 8

Paul Marnay was usually embarrassed by what he saw when he went to the theater. Even when he was watching a play that interested him—which rarely happened—there was something about the experience that seemed ridiculous to him. The words *play* and *player,* he thought, were well chosen: grown-ups playing children's games. Paul couldn't accept the conventions of the theater—the falseness of the sets, the exaggerated lighting, the artificial speech. Stories, he believed, should be told and not seen. The last plays he had seen were revivals of Ionesco's *The Bald Soprano* and Beckett's *Happy Days,* which he agreed to give a chance because they were supposedly examples of the Theater of the Absurd. If anything could do justice to absurdity, he thought, it was the theater.

There were two reasons that Paul had accepted Hillary's suggestion that they see a play during their weekend in the city. First, there was simple gratitude for the pleasure she had given him. She had allowed herself to become unofficial for him, to put aside the earnestness of her social concerns and to suspend her analytical vision. They would sit in the darkness together and try to believe what was happening on the stage. The second reason Paul wanted to see the play—*The Companion*—was that it was about serial murder.

46

Hillary's reason for wanting to see the play was that a school friend of hers—Phyllis Arno—was in the cast. Paul hoped Hillary wouldn't want to go backstage after the performance. He saw himself standing by uncomfortably as the actress looked pleased while trying to remember which classmate Hillary had been.

The play turned out to be absorbing enough in a dark, puzzling way. A middle-aged woman and her blind father are traveling through the Midwest, stopping in small towns where the daughter finds jobs as a paid companion to old women, whom she kills. The daughter gets involved in a conflict with the son of one of the women. The son encourages the companion to kill his mother, and it's not clear which of the characters is the evil one.

For Paul, the strength of the play wasn't in its script but in the performance of Hillary's friend, Phyllis Arno, who played the companion. It was during the curtain calls that Paul realized what an accomplished actress Phyllis was. She gave the most startling demonstration of a phenomenon that had always intrigued him—the transformation that can take place when the actor steps out of character at the end of the play. Wearing the same costume and makeup that, in the play, had made her appear austere, poignant, and aging, she stepped to the apron of the small stage, and with a smile, made the audience realize that in reality she had nothing in common with the character she had played. Reality. Paul realized that that was the thing he had never understood about the theater: a play made the audience consider the nature of reality in a way that a painting did not. Likeness in a play was different from likeness in a painting. He also realized that if Hillary didn't suggest going backstage, he would suggest it himself.

Fortunately, Hillary led him quickly backstage without asking him if he was interested. She took his hand, but her thoughts were obviously not about him. There were tears in her eyes. Paul wondered what the tears signified.

When they got to the dressing area, Hillary was immediately and seriously embraced by a woman that Paul didn't recognize—a young woman with thick, auburn hair and a freckled bone-white skin. It wasn't until the unknown woman stepped back and he got a better look at her costume that Paul realized she was Phyllis Arno, who had removed a wig and wiped off her makeup.

Phyllis was the most impressive woman Paul had ever seen; not the most beautiful or exciting, but the most passionately tranquil and modestly self-assured. He didn't see Phyllis as a potential partner of any kind. She simply represented a different, and probably inaccessible, order of being . . . but one who could probably tell him something he needed to know. She probably knew the password.

Hillary made an introduction that Paul heard only vaguely. He said to Phyllis, "I didn't recognize you."

"That's the idea," she said, and held out her hand to him.

Paul thought: She's offering me something I've never been offered before. He said, "Shall we go somewhere?"

"Yes," Phyllis said, "someplace where we can forget about death."

Paul thought for a moment about the play and about the three people who had suffered fatal accidents in Dale Falls. He wasn't sure he wanted to forget about death . . . he just wanted to understand it. Maybe that's what Phyllis could help him do.

Hillary took Paul's arm, apparently realizing that

whether or not he had forgotten death, he *had* forgotten her. Paul looked into Hillary's eyes and saw a kind of passion he had never seen there before . . . a negative and maybe destructive passion. "Not nice," Hillary whispered to him. Then she said to Phyllis, "We'll wait for you in the lobby." Hillary led Paul out of the dressing cubicle, and he realized for the first time that Hillary had become interested enough in him to impose a code of behavior: She would accept his periods of congenial unmindfulness between evenings of niceness, but she would not tolerate indifference.

Paul knew that he would not have the emotional resources to bring the evening off. "Why don't I leave you two to talk," he said. "I'd just get in the way of your reminiscences. I'll meet you at the hotel."

Hillary smiled. She didn't argue. She's accepting my apology, Paul thought.

Waiting in the hotel room, Paul imagined the two women seated at a corner table in an old Chelsea bar. How would the other people in the bar see them? As lovers? As wives trading confidences about their unsatisfactory marriages? How would he paint them, Paul wondered. He had never had the ability to paint from memory. The more he tried to recall an image, the vaguer it became. The image of Hillary—the more familiar image—was fading, but he still had a strong recollection of Phyllis. Both women became Phyllis—the vital, inviting Phyllis who had been backstage, and the brooding, death-obsessed Phyllis who had appeared on the stage.

When Hillary returned to Paul, it was nearly dawn. She smelled of second-rate cognac and two kinds of perfume. The only thing she removed before she joined him in bed was her panties. As she lay beneath

Paul, she spoke of Phyllis. Paul closed his eyes and saw at first the imagined painting of two Phyllises at the shadowy table. Then he imagined a third, reclining Phyllis—one that he supposed Hillary might also be imagining.

Chapter 9

Randolph Bunche Johnson was known as Lamb to everyone except his father and the Internal Revenue Service. The names Randolph and Bunche were presented to Lamb by his father, who expected him to live a life of dignified public service in the tradition of A. Philip Randolph and Ralph Bunche. However, when Lamb was nine years old, his mother gave him a construction kit of a model Lamborghini P400 Miura sports car. (She then, in tragic irony, was killed in a traffic accident.) After his mother's death, the model car she had given her son permanently dominated his imagination. His friends began to call him Lamb, for Lamborghini, and then began to avoid him when they sensed that his obsession was carrying him outside the mainstream of their interests.

Except during the increasingly rare moments when a teacher or his father demanded his attention, the boy gave over his thoughts to the concept of the sports car—to an ideal design that he wanted to construct not as a model but as a working machine that would receive him into its single seat and fulfill the image he had of himself driving at exhilaratingly high speeds along a highway in the desert at dawn.

In his loyalty to this image, he sacrificed his formal education, his father's love and respect, and—most important to him—access to his father's growing fortune. When Lamb dropped out of his program of political science at an upstate New York college, he didn't return home but went instead to the nearby town of Dale Falls and began working as an auto mechanic. He spent his spare time reading about the principles of automobile engineering. He also began slowly to assemble his fantasy car and to resent his father's lack of understanding and lack of generosity.

Lamb and his father were caught in a classic genetic trap—the son had inherited the father's obsessiveness but not the object of his obsession. The father, although he owned a car, had never driven it, employing a succession of chauffeurs (all of them white, which Lamb thought was a little crude for a black man who was supposedly pursuing social justice).

When Lamb received the chain letter, he went into a state of moral paralysis. He sat down on an uncomfortable wood chair in a corner of his workshop and didn't get up for more than twelve hours. The chain had encountered a weak link.

Lamb found the idea of murder unacceptable. It wasn't that he objected to having his father murdered by an unknown person as the letter proposed; that would not require Lamb to act and would change his mood from misery to joy—assuming he was named the beneficiary of his father's will. But it was another thing to expect him personally to murder a stranger. Even if the stranger was despicable, as the letter implied, Lamb couldn't convince himself that he had the authority to end that person's life. But then he began to wonder if his hesitation might simply be a matter of cowardice.

He searched his memory for examples that might help him decide what to do. There was Hamlet. But that was a different situation—a matter of avenging (or not avenging) a father's murder. But wasn't the point of Shakespeare's play that Hamlet died because he was unwilling to kill—unwilling to dispense justice?

Lamb began to regret that his view of the world was so restricted. He couldn't think of any other example in fiction or in real life that could guide him. He realized that the only subject he knew well was a particular kind of automobile. The same realization had come to him once before—about a year ago—when a young woman had invited him to share her apartment, or at least her bed, and had demonstrated in the process that Lamb was—as he had suspected—impotent. That realization was enough to send him to a counselor for a few sessions. He was unsettled to find that the counselor was an attractive and fairly young woman, but he tolerated her prying and theorizing when he found that she was willing to let him spend much of his time talking about sports cars. However, when the counselor announced that his dislike of women (growing out of his love for his lost mother) was the reason his ideal car had only one seat, he lost the limited amount of confidence he had in the counselor. Any competent person, he thought, would have realized that nothing could have influenced the car's design except engineering and esthetic principles. A classic car, such as the Lamborghini P400 Miura, was more beautiful to Lamb than any woman could be. A car's beauty grew out of a graceful solution to problems in areas such as torque multiplication, compression ratio, or drag coefficient. After four sessions, Lamb gave up the counseling program and decided he was happy enough in his impotence—or would be happy if he found the money he needed to finish his car.

His decision on the choice offered by the chain letter gradually began to seem a simple matter of weighing the relative importance of two elements. On one side of the scales were two imperfect lives and on the other was one perfect machine. Did the creation outbalance the destruction? As he thought about the choice, he picked up the letter. What did it promise him?

If you follow these instructions, you will be able to release the beauty and power that lie frustrated within you. In exchange for two lives—one evil and worthless, the other well-meaning but futile and nearing its end—you will bring to the world a beautiful creation that will be preserved and respected as long as there are people who take pleasure in the grace of machines.

Lamb realized that whoever wrote the letter—the person who used the silly name "Chainmaster"—understood him as no one else had understood him. To ignore the letter's instructions would be to show contempt for the gods—to invite disaster, as the letter threatened. So, after a night of confused self-examination, Lamb decided to get to know Freddy Stella and the garishly painted Trans Am that the letter said he owned. And Lamb smiled when he noticed that he was experiencing an unfamiliar type of arousal—an arousal that was undeniably sexual.

It had turned out to be a simple and enjoyable matter for Lamb to develop a device that would uncouple the steering mechanism of Freddy Stella's car when its speed reached ninety miles per hour. It required patience and ingenuity to get the mechanism installed. But by offering to buy Stella's car at a temptingly high price and asking for a chance to give it a detailed inspection, Lamb accomplished his mission. He was surprisingly undisturbed when he heard of Stella's death.

The only thing that disturbed Lamb after that was the chance that his soon-to-be-late father might have disinherited him.

Chapter 10

After his weekend in New York City with Hillary, Paul returned gratefully to his studio. One of the things he liked about his life was that he wasn't forced to conform to an arbitrary routine.

Paul wandered through his studio, uneasily watching his image appear and disappear in the mirrors scattered through the room. It was a reflecting forest. Paul surrounded himself with mirrors not out of vanity; he had never liked the way he looked. It was the opposite—an attempt to keep his ego in check by reminding himself that his appearance, especially in profile, was not prepossessing. But Paul knew he was more honest about his appearance than most. When he began doing portraits he was startled to find that most people—no matter how plain or bizarre their appearance—thought of themselves as more than ordinarily attractive. It was particularly true of men. At first, he was afraid that a truthful portrait might offend an unattractive subject, but he soon realized that the same trick of interpretation that allowed a person to find himself or herself attractive—if not the fairest of them all—in a mirror, also applied when the person looked at his or her portrait. It was the eye-of-the-beholder principle at work, Paul supposed —the principle that apparently kept members of the Spanish royal family from being upset by Goya's obviously satirical portraits. It's hard for many of us to see physical flaws in ourselves.

But it's easy enough for us to see the ugliness in others, Paul thought—or to see evil in others. What about his own willingness to suspect that a probably random trio of deaths was not mere coincidence? Paul wasn't able to forget what he now thought of as the Dale Falls murders. The familiar image of the pigeon lady drifted into his mind several times each day and was beginning to be accompanied by impressions of Angela Bailey and Freddy Stella—half-formed images of the kind one might create for characters in a book.

Despite the persistent thoughts of these deaths, there were several reasons why Paul was not inclined to start an investigation of them. One reason was that when he thought of an investigation, he thought of Sherlock Holmesian exercises in logical connections —procedures that had never appealed to Paul as much as intuition had; logic was the specialty of his son, Luke. On the other hand, he also told himself that just because intuition wasn't an acceptable tool in crime fiction didn't mean it couldn't be effective in this situation. Didn't police occasionally call in psychics for advice when an important case was bogged down? What would probably be effective, Paul thought, would be for him and his son to investigate the deaths together. But his son no longer belonged to him, was no longer his to direct.

Paul walked over to the wreckage of the balsa wood

platform that lay where it had collapsed under Luke's weight. Gravity had defeated it—as it defeats us all, Paul thought. Something he had often noticed when painting portraits of middle-aged people was the tension of expression resulting from the simple attempt to resist gravity. The features are brought down; to relax is to sag. Gravity is the earth making its claim on us. Maybe that was part of the appeal of space travel—to escape earth's claim. But the space traveler then has to deal with the claim of the sun or a planet. There's always an irresistible force around.

Which reminded Paul of Phyllis Arno. Although Paul had decided it would be ridiculous for him to pursue a woman who lived in another city and who was involved in a demanding profession, he also knew that he was prepared to be ridiculous. Because his pursuit would involve commuting, he decided he'd better get some reliable transportation. Although he owned a car, he had never been much interested in it and wasn't even sure what make it was; he only knew that it was old, Japanese, and prone to breakdowns. Phase I of his campaign would have two parts: consulting someone at his local service station about what kind of car to buy and where to buy it; and then getting a new and substantial portrait commission to help pay for the car.

Paul also devised a way to open Phase II, the approach to Phyllis Arno, whom he thought of alternately as a citadel he would besiege or a goddess he would pay homage to. His campaign began with a phone call to Max Antell, a New York City agent who brought portrait painters together with people whose need to be portrayed was strong enough to make them willing to part with large sums of money for the privilege. Max had seen Paul's work at an exhibition a couple of years back and had invited him to call if he ever wanted to take on a commission in the New York City area.

Paul was pleased to find that Max not only remembered making the offer but currently had a client who was looking for a portraitist who worked in Paul's carefully finished but nonphotographic style. Paul agreed to get together a portfolio of his work and deliver it to the agent the following Saturday.

Next was a call to Phyllis Arno's answering machine to find out whether she was available for brunch on Saturday. Half an hour later, to Paul's delight and terror, Phyllis returned his call.

His mouth drying up rapidly, he said, "I'm the one who was with Hillary the other night."

"I know which one you are, Paul. You're the memorable one."

It took Paul a couple of beats to catch his breath. "Not everyone describes me that way."

"That's their problem. I make a career of trying to be memorable, so my opinion is expert testimony."

Paul was still uncomfortable. It had been too easy. Was Phyllis a girl who couldn't say no? He asked, "Is there any chance for us to get together on Saturday?"

"I've got about an hour around noon is all. Hardly worth the trip, I'd say."

"That's not what I'd say." A little dishonorably, Paul decided not to tell Phyllis that he had to go into the city anyway to see Max Antell.

"Then ring my doorbell at noon." She gave him an address on West Seventy-first Street and abruptly but alluringly said, "Good night, my sweet."

The connection was broken, and Paul replaced the receiver in confusion. Did he like women who said "my sweet" before the first date? He began to pace through the studio, trying to suppress some distinctly adolescent emotions—a blend of elation and fear.

Then, after a couple of minutes of pacing, he noticed again the remains of Luke's collapsed balsa wood construction. And he remembered in a rush of despair that the coming Saturday was his son's visiting day.

Should he cancel the commitments he had spent the morning making? Or could he take Luke along with him? During the day that wouldn't be a problem. He could deposit the boy at the Cooper-Hewitt National Museum of Design and let him revel in architectural drawings and models for a few hours.

But Paul had been making some other plans at the fantasy level: to get a ticket for the play Phyllis was in and to meet her after the performance; to stay in the city overnight. However, he didn't have overnight rights to his son (or to Phyllis, for that matter). Okay. Find the silver lining. Don't seem too eager. Have lunch. See the agent. Drive back with Luke. Behave yourself.

The next morning, Paul went to the service station where he usually bought his gas. He pulled up near the station's garage and looked for Lance, the attendant—a young black (but not very) man who would have qualified as handsome except for his constant expression of distraction and disconnection. Paul thought true attractiveness had to include some awareness of itself—some delight in its own effect. But this young man lived below the surface. Most of the people his age who did his type of job seemed to be featuring tattoos these days, but not Lance. His adornments, if he had any, were in his mind or emotions.

Paul looked into the dimly lit garage. "Lance?"

The attendant appeared from a back room. "It's not Lance," he said. "It's Lamb, as in leg of. Lamb Johnson."

It was, Paul thought, a set speech of the kind that all unfortunately named people had to develop. What had been in his parents' minds? Religion? Lamb of God? In any case, it didn't require comment. Paul proceeded with his business: "I need some advice."

Lamb glanced at Paul briefly and then looked at the floor as if he had noticed something unwelcome moving around.

Paul continued, "I want to get a better car—not a new one—and I don't know anything about them." Lamb glanced up again with an expression Paul couldn't interpret except that it probably meant he had Lamb's permission to do some more talking. "It should be able to hold four people and should have an automatic transmission. I don't care what it looks like, but I want it to be mechanically sound."

"Should it be fast?" Lamb asked. He seemed interested now.

"I'm not going to race it."

"When do you need it?"

"Before Saturday."

"Six thousand cash?"

Paul hesitated at the word *cash*. He supposed he could manage a certified check, but it would leave him without the reserves he needed to keep the poverty specter from tapping on his shoulder. Not understanding the dynamics of the marketplace, Paul (as well as the ex-wife he paid child support to) tended not to enjoy life when in debt or without savings. But maybe Max Antell could get him an advance on a new portrait. And he was curious to see what kind of car the odd Lamb Johnson would come up with. "Okay," he said.

"It'll be here Saturday morning at nine."

"Eight."

"Okay," Lamb said, and walked away. Before disappearing into the back room, he looked back and added, "You'll like it." Paul didn't find the attempt at reassurance too convincing, but for some reason, he didn't need convincing. He had the feeling that Lamb had too much respect for cars to misrepresent one.

At eight o'clock Saturday morning, Paul and Luke stood looking in amazement at the car Lamb had come up with. Luke's amazement was approving; Paul's was not. The car—definitely in the sports category—was white and didn't look as if it would hold more than one person comfortably. It also had a gearshift stick on the floor.

But half an hour later, Paul had handed over his certified check and was driving out of town with combined feelings of elation and apprehension. He had gone through with the deal for three reasons: first, because he hadn't wanted to be late for his date with Phyllis Arno, second, because Luke was infatuated with the car, and finally, because Lamb Johnson had insisted that Paul take a reassuring test run. It turned out that the stick shift wasn't needed in forward drive, and there was a rudimentary backseat that would hold two preferably legless people.

During the drive to New York City, Paul wanted to think about strategies for his meetings with Phyllis Arno and Max Antell. However, Luke wanted to talk—mostly about Lamb Johnson, whom he had gotten to know remarkably well in the few minutes Paul had left them together during his test drive. "Lamb is a really major guy," Luke said.

"He's got a minor name—unless it's short for Lamb of God."

"It's from Lamborghini, the Italian car designer—his idol."

"I guess no one has God for an idol these days. Or can God be an idol?"

Luke ignored the question. "You're lucky to have this car," he said. "It's a sort of sketch pad for the one Lamb is building in his workshop. The engine is mounted transversely in the rear, and it's got a three-element torque converter coupled to an automatic gearbox. Lamb thinks racing cars should have automatic transmissions. Too many races are lost by manual gear shifting. The drivers get tired and mess up the shift—strip the gears— and the car's out of the race. The auto-shift he's working on is electronically controlled. Up to two hundred miles per hour."

"Fifty-five's okay with me." Paul recalled the description of what was left of Freddy Stella after his sports car ran off the road. (Paul still didn't let himself use the term *accident* in thinking about it.)

As Luke chattered on about the car and about his latest engineering and architectural projects, Paul wondered whether life was more satisfying for people who were devoted to technology. The goals and principles were clear. A useful, comfortable building or a fast car had an objective reality that helped counterbalance the frailties of the people who designed and built them. Paul suspected that there was a lot more stability in the car he was driving than there was in the young man who produced it. There seemed to be an intensity in Lamb Johnson's personality that might become ruthless or destructive if it was focused on people rather than machines. Fortunately, Paul thought, his dealings with Lamb were finished—as long as the strange (now strangely attractive) car didn't break down.

"Dad," Luke said, "you're speeding."

So he was. It was easier than it used to be.

Chapter 11

Paul deposited Luke in the Cooper-Hewitt and left him standing in a state of mystical ecstasy in a room containing models of Buckminster Fuller's geodesic structures. Paul didn't share Luke's enthusiasm over the models. They seemed too much in the Tinkertoy mode; they were in the class of buildings that are intriguing as models but should never be built full-size.

Luke had cab fare to get him across town to the Hayden Planetarium, where Paul was to meet him later at one of Paul's favorite signs: TO SOLAR SYSTEM AND REST ROOMS.

Phyllis Arno lived in a fifth-floor walk-up apartment in the West Seventies—the overpriced co-op and condo capital of the world. The building was in a row of graceless brownstones that had been built originally in the late nineteenth century as family residences and had been converted first into assemblages of one- and two-bedroom apartments and then into full-floor cooperative apartments that were currently selling (according to Paul's ex-wife) in the half-million-dollar range. While waiting to be buzzed through the street door, Paul wondered how Phyllis scraped together the down payment (not to mention the monthly mortgage and maintenance payments). Off-Broadway productions such as the one Phyllis was currently appearing in didn't usually put their casts into the upper tax brackets. But maybe Phyllis had done some movie work.

Paul was trying desperately and unsuccessfully to breathe normally after climbing the five flights of stairs. But even if the climb hadn't winded him, he would have gasped when Phyllis opened the door. She was wearing a soft-cotton blood-red dress that contrasted with the paleness of her skin and clashed with the orange-red of her hair. She was either oblivious to her appearance or wasn't afraid to produce the bold effect.

Paul stood in a state of passion-induced confusion as Phyllis put her hands on his cheeks and placed her wet, partially opened mouth against his for a moment. She stood on tiptoe, leaned forward resting her breasts against his chest, then stepped back and smiled at his discomposure, turning her head away in a sidelong gaze.

Paul wondered whether the movement was spontaneous or whether Phyllis had worked it out through long rehearsal periods in front of a mirror. And then he noticed that there wasn't a mirror in the room—a room that seemed to be the combination living-room/sleeping-room usually called a studio apartment in the fantasyland of New York realtors. The room had probably been a servant's garret in the building's original form.

"You look as if you've misplaced something," Phyllis said.

"I was looking for a mirror."

"There's one in the bathroom if you need one urgently."

"Nothing urgent. I like mirrors; as things to look at, not into. I expected an actress would find them indispensable."

Phyllis shook her head—breaking up her sidelong

gaze. "I use people as mirrors. I ask the director—or whoever—whether an expression or movement is right. I don't ask a mirror; I don't even do my own makeup. What's important is how others see me, not how I see myself."

"But you have to be careful about which others you ask."

"I am careful about that. There aren't too many I trust." She turned her head away slightly. "I thought you might want to become one of them."

"I want to become something—a friend at least— but I don't know, and don't want to know, much about the theater arts."

"But Hillary tells me you know a lot about the graphic arts. And I believe her; I like the way you look." Phyllis moved her head and smiled at the floor. "That wasn't clear. I wasn't saying I like your appearance; I meant I like the way you look *at* things."

Paul tried not to show his irritation at the implication that Phyllis wasn't wild about his appearance. Not that he was wild about it himself, but he *had* been referred to with the questionably flattering term *interesting* on a few occasions.

Phyllis converted what might have become an awkward pause into a dramatic moment. She crossed her ankles and lowered herself with a continuous, dancerlike movement into a sitting position on the floor. Then she held an arm out toward Paul. He took her hand and wondered what was expected of him. There was too much moral difference between standing on the floor and sitting on the floor. He pulled Phyllis back to her feet. Although she didn't say anything about his maneuver, Paul got the idea he had done the right thing. He added a motto (a little belatedly) to his list of words to live by: When in doubt, show restraint.

They ate some overpriced pasta at a restaurant on

Columbus Avenue. During the meal, they were interrupted by people stopping at the table to congratulate Phyllis on her performance—not in *The Companion*—but in a soap opera that Paul had never heard of—a program she acted in most afternoons on her way to the theater. The confused pleasure that Paul was taking in Phyllis's company gradually turned to disappointment when he realized how intense the competition for her time would be.

Before either of them had finished the pasta, Phyllis sprang up and announced that she was overdue at the TV studio. Paul threw too much money on the table and followed her to the curb and helped her get a taxi. "I was hoping you would let me paint your portrait," he said. "But your schedule doesn't seem to allow for that kind—or any kind—of diversion."

"No. It's a while since I've been diverted. My portrait would have to be done by someone with a fast-shuttered camera, or by someone like those quick-brushed Impressionists who liked to paint women who were bathing or dressing."

Paul was going to announce that he could be quick-brushed when necessary, but he realized that he wanted to be able to spend more than an occasional few minutes, or even an occasional night, with Phyllis. He wanted to spend days with her—watching her do ordinary things. He didn't want to have an affair with Phyllis the actor; he wanted to live with Phyllis the person. But the person and the actor weren't separable.

As a taxi pulled up, Phyllis produced a sidelong smile and said, "Don't despair. Actually, bathing and dressing are two of the three things I like to do slowly."

Paul managed to hold his smile as the cab pulled away. But he wasn't amused. If he hadn't been in love he would have been offended. But because he was in love, he went back into the restaurant and ordered coffee and cognac and began imagining Phyllis standing with one foot raised to the edge of a bathtub and looking smilingly over her stark white shoulder.

Max Antell, although he had been born in the Bronx and although his travels had been limited to occasional forays into Connecticut and New Jersey, was the epitome of old-world charm. Curly white hair, floppy maroon bow tie, gourmand, gallant, connoisseur, certified bon vivant, he inspired thoughts of Vienna and the pre-Hitler Strausses. He convinced people through his mere presence that only the person whose image has been preserved in oil paints on canvas can be said to have lived to the fullest.

"What I most admire about you as a painter, my friend," Max said, as they worked out the details of the commission, "is that you do not tyrannize your subjects with a rigid, oppressive style."

"You mean I don't *have* a style."

"No, no. You realize that in portraiture, the style must derive from the sitter."

"Not according to Oscar Wilde. He said every portrait that is painted with feeling is a portrait of the artist, not the sitter."

Max, who had been pacing his office, leaned forward, laughed, and slapped his thighs. It was the first time Paul had ever seen anyone actually react that way to a joke. But he wasn't sure what the joke was. "Bizarre," Max said after allowing himself a theatrical chuckle. "A painter who reads. But you mustn't overdo it. You must remember that Oscar was Narcissus reincarnated. What your friend Max says is that most painters are so narcissistic—crazy van Gogh, for example—that they are only capable of doing self-portraits. Nobody knows or cares whether van Gogh's portraits of villagers at Arles were accurate in any sense—certainly not in the sense that Holbein's Thomas More is accurate."

"I'm not in either of those leagues, Max."

"Of course not. Those leagues have been disbanded. Down the street is a shop that does some sort of three-dimensional laser-scan portraits. All things are possible."

"We're antiquarians."

"Exactly. We're clockmakers."

And so they agreed on what kind of clock they would make. Paul's subject was to be a retired businessman, who would sit in his apartment at 10:00 A.M. for one hour each Tuesday and Thursday. He was paying a fee that indicated he must have been connected with a fairly lucrative business.

"He is spending a recent inheritance," Max explained. "He's virginal and humorless. Your portrait will be his offspring."

Paul shuddered and went to retrieve his own offspring.

On the drive back to Dale Falls, Luke was in an extraterrestrial mood. Wearing sunglasses that looked as if they had been made for eclipse-watching, the boy stared into the cloudless sky—or beyond it. "What's really scary about space," he said, "is its silence. When people go into space, they take noise along with them. I'd get crazed if I had to live in absolute quiet. I hate quiet."

"I've noticed that," Paul said. Then he purposely stopped talking. For a moment they listened to the sound of the car—a loud but satisfying deep buzzing.

Luke managed about twenty seconds of nontalking and then asked, "What would you hate about space travel, Dad?"

The "Dad" was something new with Luke after a few weeks of referring to his father as "Paul-O."

Paul had the answer ready: "What I would hate would be the lack of gravity." He remembered the thoughts he recently had about gravity as an enemy making its claim. But it was also a reassuring force. He couldn't imagine being without its comforting pull. It's like everything else that brings us comfort, he thought: Eventually it brings us death.

In Dale Falls, unknown to one another, three people who had recently been concerned with death were now enjoying the gains and release it had conferred on them.

Dwight Bailey, in his workshop, adjusted the escapement mechanism of a nineteenth-century long-case clock he had bought.

Lamb Johnson wrote a check for the Italian suspension system he would install in his car-in-progress.

Connie Nickens spoke with a bank officer about financing the restaurant she would soon open.

Someone had taught them not to fear death but to use it creatively.

Chapter 12

Paul had forgotten to turn off his answering machine before leaving for Manhattan. In the five years he had been using his machine, it had consistently supplied him with two unpleasant or insignificant messages for every pleasant one. And even the pleasant ones embarrassed him for some reason he couldn't understand. So he usually left the machine on only when he was expecting some good news. He hadn't been leaving it on much in recent months.

Paul didn't know which category the most recent message should be placed in, and he was sorry his son, Luke, was there to hear it. The voice was Hillary Brock's, and she wasn't being her usual articulate self: "Oh . . . you're out . . . as you tend to be lately . . . I just thought we might . . . oh, never mind . . . I know I have no claim . . . call me when you need your spirits—or your Fruit of the Looms—lowered . . . tah-tah."

The message, with its kaleidoscoping emotions, made Paul realize that he didn't want to see Hillary anymore. Although he had found pleasure with her, it was invariably labored. They both had to work hard for the pleasure, and it wasn't always worth the effort. Hillary, despite her humanitarian impulses and moneyed breeding, lacked essence; there seemed to be an emptiness at her core that forced her to struggle with her existence. Paul sensed that despite all her training and education, she still had no personal standards of right or wrong; she was capable of anything because nothing satisfied her.

Paul's sense of Phyllis Arno, on the other hand, was that despite her apparently more self-centered and unconventional life, there was a system of values at the center of her existence that gave focus and limits to her behavior. She was at ease with her life, and Paul wanted to be enfolded within that ease.

Wondering whether he might be guilty of cowardice, Paul decided he wouldn't return Hillary's call—or any of her future calls. His life was full enough without that complication. For example, he should be giving more attention to Luke. The boy was not demanding, and he had enough interests so that there would seem to be little time for him to brood about having a part-time father. But before long, he would be undergoing the terrors of adolescence, and Paul wanted him to know that his father was available and willing—even if not especially able—to help him through the experience.

Although Paul and his son had talked constantly on the drive back from New York City, they had talked, as usual, about safe, nonfamily subjects. Now, as Paul reset the answering machine, Luke wandered through the studio with what seemed to be a pensive expression. Hillary Brock's message could have upset him even more than it had upset his father. A kid had the right to expect his parents to get along with their lovers, if not with each other.

"Are you okay?" Paul asked.

"Sure." Luke was poking around in the wreckage of his construction.

"I thought something might be bothering you."

"Well, I think it's strange that no one seems to be sure where or when the mechanical clock was invented."

So much, thought Paul, for the problems of sensitive youth. He said, "I thought sports cars were your latest mechanical obsession."

"I'd like to build a clock."

The statement wasn't delivered with much conviction, Paul thought. It was just a random remark by a bored and tired boy. "I thought that was just a matter of hooking up a computer chip and liquid crystals or some such things these days."

"I mean a really complicated clock," Luke said. He was clearly beginning to work up some interest in the project. "Something with statues that parade around and hit bells with hammers . . . or maybe you could ring a bell with a laser beam. A Star Wars clock. A space clock."

"You'd need some sophisticated machine tools, I think, to cut gears. You might want to start with something simpler. I think you can get clock kits to assemble—to learn the principles with."

Paul was pleased that his son was interested in old technologies as well as new ones. Luke put a sketch pad on an easel and began to draw—quite skillfully, Paul was pleased to see—a clock tower populated by shadowy, menacing figures. In the Renaissance, such a clock would have put more emphasis on the forces of good—or God. Are my son and I living in an evil age? Paul wondered. He went to the classified section of the telephone directory and looked under the heading "Clocks"—where he found a listing for someone who offered "sales, repairs, new, old, kits." The someone was Dwight Bailey, and as Paul made a note of the number he wondered why the name sounded familiar.

That night, after returning Luke to his mother (who had a male visitor that Paul thought looked too young but not too bright), Paul decided to devote the evening to loosening his connections with Hillary Brock. His first impulse had been to use the approach he tended to use in all unpleasant situations: to do nothing and hope the unpleasantness would self-destruct. And actually, if Hillary hadn't been friendly with Phyllis Arno, there wouldn't have been any particular need for action. But Paul wanted to be sure Hillary understood the situation and that she wouldn't do anything —either inadvertently or consciously—to interfere with his attempt to become Phyllis's friend or lover.

Paul's day in Manhattan hadn't left him with much surplus energy, but he poured himself a large predinner California brandy and punched out the tones for Hillary's number. The tones played "Mary Had a Little Lamb," a fact that used to amuse him but now unsettled him slightly because "Lamb" made him think of his new car—an acquisition he still thought might have been a mistake.

Hillary picked up on the first ring and spoke her name in the approved business-administration style. Paul answered with his own name. Hillary's delivery became less businesslike: "I was just thinking of you."

"And obviously I was thinking of you."

"Actually, Paul, I was thinking of your body."

The voice was definitely unbusinesslike now, and Paul thought he detected the influence of vodka—a weakness of hers and a beverage he disapproved of—because it was practically undrinkable unless hiding behind something innocent and graceless like tomato juice, and because it led people to get into a falling-down condition because they could pretend they were teetotalers. Before Paul could change the subject, Hillary continued: "Things happen to *my* body when I think of your body."

Paul knew that unless he created a diversion, he was headed for dirty talk—something he had enjoyed in the past because it was so out of character for Hillary.

The subject had to be changed quickly. He didn't

try to think of a transition. "I bought a sports car today," he said.

The diversion wasn't successful. "Maybe we could initiate it tonight—let it experience Lover's Lane."

"It's definitely not built for lovers—except maybe car lovers. It demands the driver's complete attention."

"I think *I* could distract you, my sweet."

Paul tried another diversion. "I drove the car into the city today. I saw Phyllis Arno."

Success. There was a short but significant silence, followed by a menacing, "Oh?"

"I'm going to paint her portrait."

"You little—" Hillary's breeding caught up with her before she could finish the phrase.

But Paul was still offended. The word *little* was as disturbing to him as anything that might have followed it. Did she really think of him as a little man? His displeasure gave him the courage to say, "I'm in love with Phyllis."

The phone connection went dead. Paul finished his brandy and tried unsuccessfully to disconnect his mind. He told himself that Hillary had no reason to be upset and that there was no reason for him to feel guilty about the situation. But he knew he was breaking a bond, no matter how casual the bond was. He remembered Hillary lying in his arms, smiling securely, having given him her trust and her passion— maybe even her unspoken love.

The phone rang.

Hillary said, "I just wanted you to know that I'm not going to forget."

Paul wasn't sure how to respond and was grateful when she solved his problem by hanging up immediately. But his relief soon changed to uneasiness. Hillary's tone seemed to indicate not that she would always remember him fondly but that she was going to seek revenge for his disloyalty.

Why was there always a dark side to things? In Paul's experience, life wasn't a series of clouds with silver linings; there hadn't been that many clouds in his life. It was a matter of bright objects casting shadows. Maybe he simply paid too much attention to the dark areas. He promised himself he would ignore the shadows in his relationship with Phyllis—even in her portrait. He would paint her in a strong, diffused, shadowless light. He spent the next half hour imagining Phyllis both as a visual object—as a challenge in portraiture—and as a person. He was sure the portrait would be a success but wondered if the same qualities—the intensity and volatility—that made her an easy subject might make her a difficult companion. He was eager to get back to the city and find out—too eager. First, he had to take care of his local chores and commitments.

Paul went to his appointment book and found the note he had made earlier: "Clock kit, Dwight Bailey," with a phone number and address. And he realized why the name seemed familiar. Dwight Bailey was the man Luke had seen in the park the day the pigeon lady died and the man whose mother had died in the mysterious fall. Paul would try to see him the following week.

But first there was Sunday to get through—a day that had never been Paul's favorite. In his youth, there had been church services and formal, heavy afternoon meals with adults talking about how bad business and their friends' morals were. More recently, Sundays involved recovering from a Saturday night, combined with unsuccessful attempts to figure out his current financial status. The day's only pleasure—before the cocktail hour—was reading the *New York Times*. Not that the *Times* was exactly stimulating. In fact, Paul's theory was that the Sunday *Times* had been designed to meet the needs of someone who had (not too recently) been to college and had (recently) drunk too much.

One of the features Paul carefully avoided reading was the obituary section, which had been transformed from something depressing to something terrifying since the onset of AIDS. But occasionally the editors caught Paul off guard by placing an obituary in one of the regular news sections. The one that caught him this Sunday concerned the death (in New York City from a heart attack) of Franklin Johnson, a civil rights leader who was survived by a son, described as an automotive engineer who lived in Dale Falls.

Paul wondered if the automotive engineer was Lamb Johnson, who had just sold him an automobile.

Lamb Johnson, who would have preferred *not* to feel, became unfriendly when he was subjected to more than one emotion at a time. His father's death subjected him to at least three: joy at the prospect of inheriting his father's estate, grief that he hadn't expected or wanted to feel, and anger over the fact that he heard of the death at a time when he was composing his letter to Chainmaster explaining how someone might arrange for his father to have a fatal accident. Apparently Lamb's father had died naturally. Lamb had been cheated out of his reward for arranging Freddy Stella's death. Lamb didn't enjoy being cheated. He should be allowed to name someone to die in the chain, but who? Offhand, there was no one else he truly wished were dead. There were not many people in his life, and although there were people who had caused him problems—a parts supplier who had tried to cheat him, a woman who had deserted him after pretending to love him—he had nothing to gain from their death. He believed death should be sought only over matters of family honor, as in an ancient tragedy. But Chainmaster would be waiting to learn his choice for the next person in the deathchain. What should he do? He must write a letter explaining the problem.

Chainmaster would give him guidance.

The guidance arrived three days after he wrote asking for it:

Dear Mr. Johnson:

You must not break the chain, and you must not become anxious or confused. A name will come to you; a person will present himself or herself to you as being unworthy of life. That person need not be evil or totally reprehensible or be someone who has done you personal harm. A person who is merely frivolous can also be a danger to you or to society. Look around you, Lamb.

What is most important is to be true to your own nature and your obligations. You are a person who goes not the way of the crowd but the way that you have chosen and that has been chosen for you.

The name will come to you. For now, I will wait to hear.

Respectfully,
Chainmaster

Lamb was pleased that he would still be allowed to serve as a link. It restored his sense of order. However, it meant that his life would be unsettled until he completed his link by contributing a name. It was a disturbing situation, but it was also reassuring. With his inheritance and the chain, he would be able to concentrate on the pure world of automotive design. If anyone should offend or threaten him, he had a safe yet effective way to respond. He had purchased a reserve of protection and of vengeance. It was something anyone might find useful.

Chapter 13

During the next week, Paul did a lot of frowning—an expression that he knew not many people want to see. If he included even the hint of a frown in any of his portraits, he was certain to get disapproval from the subject. A frowning person is usually an unhappy person—a victim of circumstances or of the power of another person. People don't like to pay thousands of dollars to record the fact that they are easy to victimize or hard to please.

There were four inspirations for Paul's frowns. First, Phyllis Arno's busy schedule hadn't allowed her time to meet with Paul, although she had convinced him through a couple of brief but impassioned phone conversations that she wasn't losing interest in him.

The next problem was that the subject for the commission Max Antell had arranged was a retired sales manager whose physical distinctiveness, if any, had retired along with him.

Problem number three was that Paul had been unable to forget the chain of deaths. He had begun to deal with his obsession in a formal way and had constructed a chart summarizing what he knew about the deaths:

THE DALE FALLS MYSTERY

<u>Victim</u>: Edna Denning (pigeon lady)
<u>How Died</u>: Pushed (?) into river
<u>Suspect</u>: Dwight Bailey (clock repairer); seen by
   Luke at time and place of death
<u>Motive</u>: ?

<u>Victim</u>: Angela Bailey
<u>How Died</u>: Pushed from hospital window
<u>Suspect</u>: Connie Nickens was near scene of death
<u>Motive</u>: ?

<u>Victim</u>: Freddy Stella
<u>How Died</u>: Car crash
<u>Suspect</u>: Lamb Johnson had ability
<u>Motive</u>: ?

<u>Victim</u>: Franklin Johnson (Lamb's father)
<u>How Died</u>: Heart attack (how induced?)
<u>Suspect</u>: Lamb Johnson might have motive; did he
   have opportunity or means?
<u>Motive</u>: Inheritance

The new factor that emerged from the chart was that Lamb Johnson could have been involved in two of the deaths. But there were lots of question marks, and on the surface the deaths seemed to be a series of coincidences. He had to establish whether the people on the list knew one another. And in a town the size of Dale Falls, it was certainly possible.

Paul's first thought was to have Luke handle the investigation. The boy's inquiries would attract less attention than an adult's. And the first person Luke could talk to would be Lamb Johnson, with whom Luke had already established a rapport.

As Paul sat staring at his chart, someone began pounding on the door of his studio. The someone turned out to be Hillary Brock, and she was distraught enough to make Paul feel as if he were the social worker and she were the client. A taxi was waiting at the curb behind Hillary. The driver was watching Paul and Hillary carefully, apparently thinking he might see something dramatic. He got to see an impolite gesture from Paul, which was dramatic enough to encourage him to drive away.

Paul stepped back from the doorway and watched as Hillary closed the door behind her and leaned back on it in a movement he remembered having seen in movies from the 1930s. He couldn't remember how the dialogue should go, so he said, irrelevantly, "You took a taxi."

"I didn't trust myself to drive," Hillary said. She was wearing a rumpled green wool blazer over a striped front-buttoning nurse's dress—her hospital uniform.

Paul might have thought she was simply playing a role—fitting some vaguely remembered Hollywood mannerisms to her mood—except that she brought with her the scent of distress. Paul couldn't help distinguishing among subtleties of odors, and he had learned to distinguish easily between the straightforward perspiration resulting from physical activity and the variety that grew out of anxiety.

"Let me get you a cognac. Sit down. Relax." It was Paul's all-occasion suggestion. But before he started for the liquor cabinet, Hillary took his hand and pulled him toward her. She smiled as if apologizing for something. It was as if she had removed a mask that had been concealing her beauty. Paul was reminded that in conventional terms Hillary was more attractive than Phyllis Arno. But if the two women had stood side by side on a stage, no one would have looked first at Hillary; she would have attracted only the secondary kind of attention created by a handsome element of set decoration.

The comparison of Hillary to Phyllis was inevitable, and it helped Paul keep his perspective. He pulled his hand free and went to the liquor cabinet.

She didn't try to follow him, but said, "I'm the same person you found delightful a couple of weeks ago." Her tone was angry, not pensive.

Paul could understand why Hillary was upset. His loss of passion for her had been sudden and inexplicable. "You're the same; I'm not. I thought we once agreed that sex—like all delightful things—was mostly in the mind."

Hillary obviously wasn't going to be diverted by theoretical discussion. "You don't have to tell me how minds work. Just tell me if it was only Phyllis that changed your mind."

"Yes," Paul said. He wanted Hillary to go away, but he put two large glasses and a nearly full bottle of family cognac on the coffee table in front of the sofa, and motioned her to sit next to him as he poured.

As Hillary walked to the sofa, her anger seemed to lessen. "I can almost understand that. I'm fond of Phyllis, too." Hillary sat down, picked up her glass, and raised it in a toast. "To Phyllis." She clinked Paul's glass and then emptied her own in one swallow. Her eyes misted over. "What I want you to realize is that I'm losing *both* of you."

"I realize that."

Hillary continued, with what seemed like sincerity, "What I was thinking was that there's no reason why the three of us couldn't still be friends."

"Sure," Paul said. "I was hoping that, too."

"You two could be *in* love with each other . . . I wouldn't interfere with that . . . but you could *make* love to me . . . occasionally."

Paul decided that the best way to discourage this suggestion was to ignore it.

Hillary, who had taken off her blazer, quickly opened the front of her dress, exposing bare breasts and lifting them slightly by squaring her shoulders. Paul didn't know whether he should be excited, embarrassed, or pitying. Then he realized—as Hillary undoubtedly did—that it was impossible not to admire her breasts. As both a painter and a casual observer, Paul knew that the bosom was more likely to be flawed than most other parts of a woman's body.

But objective admiration wasn't what Hillary was seeking. She looked as offended by Paul's professional admiration as she would have been if he had laughed. In an angry gesture, she pulled her dress closed.

To give Hillary something else to do with her hands, Paul poured her some more brandy, which she drank without hesitation. He didn't join her because he knew he would have to drive her home—preferably soon. He rebuttoned her dress and put an arm around her shoulders. She had begun to weep, and she allowed Paul to lead her out to his car.

They drove in silence, and by the time they reached Hillary's house, she was almost asleep. Paul eased her out of the car and led her up the stairs. She leaned on his arm and became noticeably more in need of support once they were through the front door. Hillary had bought the house—a handsome but neglected brick building—under the illusion that she would have it renovated to serve as a combined home and office, but she hadn't progressed beyond paying a few high school students to spend a Saturday morning applying the wrong kind of paint to the easier-to-reach parts of the building's exterior trim.

Paul tried to disengage himself from Hillary once they were in the house, but she said, "I think I may need someone to accompany me to the john and hold my head for a minute, sweet. You can't refuse a request as unromantic as that."

Although Paul didn't trust either Hillary or himself to behave well in the emotional disarray of the evening, he couldn't deny that she was displaying a convincing pale, sweaty, presick expression. Hillary went into the bathroom adjoining the spare bedroom that served as her office. Paul waited, prepared to lend support if necessary.

Hillary's office contained—aside from an expensively mattressed, sheetless bed and a vanity table with an interesting (to Paul) three-paneled mirror—a desk, a computer, and a surprisingly large number of file cabinets. Hillary had apparently been working with the computer earlier. Its monitor glowed in what Paul saw as a threatening but irresistible invitation. Spelled out on the screen in garish colors and fuzzily defined letters was the case history of someone described as having a "histrionic personality disorder," which involved "a craving for attention, lack of genuine feeling, and a tendency to manipulate other people." The person had been abused and neglected as a child and was considered "sexually confused and incapable of forming stable relationships." The person worked in New York City as an actor. Her name was Phyllis Arno.

How convenient, Paul thought. It seemed unlikely that it was mere chance that brought him and this computer display together. He decided not to read more of the "case history," which he knew he would have trouble forgetting and which didn't necessarily have any truth to it.

Whatever Hillary was doing in the bathroom, she

was doing quietly and slowly enough to avoid distracting someone who might want to read a case history.

Paul went home, unplugged his phone, and fell asleep.

The next day, on his way down to New York City, Paul stopped to get gas at the service station where Lamb Johnson worked. He was relieved to find that Lamb wasn't on duty—which removed the temptation to ask questions about things that weren't Paul's business. However, Lamb's employer, a man who looked like a weight lifter, said, "So you're the one who bought Lamb's baby, are you?"

"Is that what he calls it?"

"That's what I call it."

"People don't usually sell their children."

"Lamb does."

Paul was going to end the conversation there, but his curiosity overruled him. "I suppose baby is safe enough for an uncoordinated person like me to drive."

"I'd think so."

"I've been nervous since that crash . . . Freddy Stella, wasn't it?"

"That car was sound. It was Freddy that wasn't."

"You knew him?"

"I knew his car. Lamb did some customizing on the engine. Probably shouldn't have. Making a car faster for Freddy was like putting an extra cartridge in the pistol of someone who was playing Russian roulette."

Paul tried to look uninterested, but he wasn't too successful. He smiled. He had added another connection in the murder chain. Lamb had the opportunity as well as the ability to sabotage Freddy Stella's car.

As he drove to Manhattan, Paul wondered why Lamb might have wanted to kill Freddy Stella. Or could it be that someone paid Lamb to bring about Freddy's death? Building sports cars is an expensive hobby, and Lamb might have been willing to engage in a little indirect assassination in exchange for enough money to complete the new car he was working on.

But there was also the chance that Freddy and Lamb had some hidden personal connection. In his reading of mystery novels, Paul had always thought that motive was the most interesting of the factors in the murderous equation. But it was also the most elusive and the least useful in proving a hypothesis. Motive was more useful in establishing whether something might have happened than in demonstrating that it had actually happened. Paul just wanted to know if some interrelated murders had taken place in Dale Falls lately, and to keep more from happening; he didn't want to uncover secret relationships, dark alliances, or hidden passions.

It was difficult enough these days for Paul to keep track of his own passions. His obsession with Phyllis Arno had reached a visceral stage. He understood for the first time that when the lover speaks of hungering for his or her beloved it is not necessarily a metaphor; there can be true physical pangs. Could it be that the stomach, rather than the heart is the true seat of amorous desire and that the heart was chosen as a symbol out of misguided gentility—out of a refusal to admit that romance wasn't much more noble than a desire for a bowl of stew and a glass of beer?

But wherever Paul's romantic desire was located, its strength and its novelty were undeniable. His previous romances each had the type of dynamics found in a baseball game: a series of low-tension encounters equivalent to pitcher-batter confrontations; then occasional scoring by one side or the other; then it was over. His marriage had been a high-scoring, extra-inning game, and he had, of course, lost it.

But Phyllis played a game that was new to him—one that so far seemed to be more like chess than baseball. He couldn't be sure, because he had never learned to play chess. In any case, the analogy was beginning to break down, because there wasn't any doubt that chess was not classified as a physical game—and his need for a physical relationship with Phyllis was beginning to be stronger than any he could remember feeling with anyone else. He craved physical contact with her, not so much out of lust as out of a mysterious sense of challenge. He needed to try out his touch on her the way a faith healer needed to practice on people with arthritic hips or asthmatic wheezes. Although he had never done any sculpture before, Paul thought that rather than paint Phyllis, he would like to model her in clay, feeling the moist slipperiness against his fingers as he built up her likeness. Perhaps his impulses had something to do with the quality in Phyllis that gave her such presence on the stage. Acting before an audience involved a tactile aspect that probably helped explain the lasting appeal of theater: more important than the words that were spoken or sung was the knowledge among the spectators that should they want to they could enter the action and ravish or maim. Maybe that was the basic tension of drama—not the playwright's creation but the restraint shown by the audience in honoring its unwritten agreement not to touch the performers.

As he drove, Paul let his right hand leave the wheel occasionally to run his fingertips over the surfaces of the sports car Lamb had built. There didn't seem to be any plastic. The seats had the feel of real leather; the instrument panel (which Paul only partially understood) was trimmed in wood. The car was probably worth more than Paul had paid for it. Underpricing was eccentric, but was Lamb more than just eccentric? Was he dangerous? Paul slowed down and put both his hands on the wheel.

Before he could see or touch Phyllis, Paul had to get through a session with Frank Whitby, who had commissioned a portrait through Max Antell. Whitby was a difficult subject, and Paul had not yet solved the problem of portraying him. The man's surface was bland and ineffectual. He had been the chief executive of an insurance company and had taken early retirement. His face was soft and round; he wore round steel-rimmed glasses and a dark blue three-piece suit. He posed seated in a large leather chair in the den of his Fifth Avenue apartment. Refusing to let Paul use the floodlit studio that Max had made available, he claimed he could only be himself at home.

It was while discussing the assignment with Whitby that Paul realized what the basic problem was: Whitby's strength and authority were in his voice—a resonant, ruthless instrument that belied his appearance. He could obviously be terrifying in a telephone conversation or in a boardroom, letting his intense, grating tones roll over the polished surface of a long table. But how could that power be represented visually? Paul was currently trying to depict Whitby as he appeared at the moment before speaking—at the instant when the power has been called up but has not yet been transformed to sound. The problem would be solved eventually, Paul was sure, but he wondered why Whitby didn't have his portrait done in sound—a gleaming laser-pure compact disc of a devastating boardroom announcement.

Close observation of his subject also led Paul to suspect that Whitby might become a devoted consumer of the Marnay cognac. The man apparently combined snobbery and false prudishness with a devotion (morning nips) to alcohol; a combination that would allow him to rationalize his addiction on the grounds of esthetics and cost. Not many devotees of Marnay cognac were willing to admit, as Paul was, that the product's alcohol content was as significant a factor as its taste and rarity.

After leaving Whitby's apartment, Paul phoned Phyllis and was pleased when she, rather than a machine, answered. He was more than pleased when she asked him to join her immediately.

The apartment was opulent with steam and scent. Phyllis, swathed in a damp white cotton robe, had obviously just stepped out of a bathtub that Paul could hear faintly draining with the brookish trickle of semiclogged pipes. Phyllis's face was feverishly pink, and her hair was highlighted with glistening, disintegrating tufts of tiny bubbles.

Paul took some of the bubbles into his hand and watched them turn to a fine liquid film on his fingers. The aroma was unsophisticated and unnatural but pleasing. He looked at Phyllis inquiringly.

"It's called Funny Foam. To entice kids who'd rather not bathe—and adults who remember childhood too fondly."

Phyllis's voice was huskier than Paul remembered. She would know about Frank Whitby's authority. But this was not the time for a professional chat.

"My play closed," Phyllis said. She sounded apologetic.

"Now what happens?"

"I never know what happens next. I don't want to know."

"Another play?"

87

"Nothing definite until July; Shakespeare outdoors near Saratoga. *The Winter's Tale*. I'm a statue that comes to life."

"Lifelessness would be hard to do, I suppose."

"Yes. People talk about lifeless performances, but that's not usually what they mean. The illusion of death is beyond us all. It's the opposite of projection. What saves us is that the audience is afraid to look closely."

"At a corpse, maybe. But at a statue?"

"I'd leave that to the director—which is what I always do in Shakespeare, anyway. I never understand."

"The language, you mean?"

"The language, the emotions. I don't think most audiences understand either. Shakespeare is for directors and critics. The actors and the audience are caught in between."

Phyllis's voice trailed off. She and Paul stood in the middle of the floor, close enough to touch. They smiled. Phyllis laughed gently—a whisper of breath through parted lips. Then there was one of those silent moments that appear unexpectedly in Manhattan; an instant when there is no passing traffic or distant siren; no neighbor's stereo or squabble; no passing plane.

Phyllis raised her arm and turned her head in a puzzling movement. Then she stopped as if caught in a vascular accident. Her eyes lost focus and she seemed to stop breathing.

Paul felt his own system moving confusedly in response. He remembered posters he had seen in restaurants. Someone's maneuver. You squeezed the victim from the back somehow.

Then he understood. Phyllis was rehearsing for *The Winter's Tale*—rehearsing effectively.

Paul's years of portrait work had given him a professional knowledge of what people look like when they try to remain motionless; they invariably looked grotesque. So Paul's instructions to a sitter always began, "Don't be afraid to move your body; just try not to let your thoughts move. Think of how you looked during your best moment."

Paul was having one of *his* best moments. Phyllis's attempt to imitate stone—or was it bronze or wood? —was disconcertingly effective for two or three minutes. She had disguised her breathing perfectly, and her body was motionless. But the flush in her cheeks was deepening. Her robe's translucent cotton, which had absorbed moisture from her body, was clinging and revealing, inviting the touch that Paul had needed and imagined in recent days.

Paul reached out and rested the fingers of his right hand lightly at the base of Phyllis's neck. She didn't move, but her breathing became perceptible in the slight rise and fall of her breasts. Paul trailed his fingers across her throat and down her chest and let them rest lightly in the deep dampness of her cleavage. Her breathing became erratic, and her breasts trembled slightly, the nipples transforming themselves invitingly. But Phyllis held her pose and her unseeing stare. She was making it plain that her reactions were involuntary. Although she was not discouraging Paul's touch overtly, he wondered if she might be doing so in subtle ways. She was beginning to make him feel guilty, as though he were taking advantage of someone who was unconscious. Also, he couldn't avoid thinking of Phyllis to some extent in the role she was playing—as a statue—and he couldn't imagine that anyone (Pygmalion not excepted) had ever been sexually aroused by a work of sculpture. There was something, despite the added dimension, that made sculpture more distancing than painting. It was the eyes that made the difference, Paul thought; the expressionless stare of the most erotic sculptured Venus was less engaging than the enigmatic gaze of the Mona Lisa.

Paul lifted his fingertips from the slope of Phyllis's breasts. He looked at her eyes, which seemed to have had their neurological connections severed. As he was about to step back and wait for the performance to end, Phyllis's eyes came back into focus. She looked at Paul, revealing the passion and invitation she had been concealing. She drew open her robe and placed his hands on her breasts, positioning his thumbs and forefingers at her nipples. For an instant, Paul thought of yesterday's encounter with Hillary, wondering how his reaction in the two situations could differ so distinctly from each other; how the sight of Phyllis's body could have so much more significance.

Then Phyllis's hands went to his clothing, quickly and surely disengaging buttons, buckle, and zipper. She said, "Let the artist be model . . . the actor be audience . . . I want to see you."

Paul's clothing was discarded so quickly that he had no time to experience his usual momentary regret over never finding time to keep his body in first-class condition. He was drawn into a confusing heightening of perception, with Phyllis's body as the focus— clearly defined in every detail and yet at the same time as featureless as the sun in its energy and intensity.

Paul had never before felt such urgency in a sexual encounter. His usual approach to lovemaking was leisurely and teasing, but now it seemed as if his existence might end at any moment if he were not joined to Phyllis.

Taking Phyllis's hands, Paul lowered her body backward to the floor. Despite the vehemence of the minutes that followed, Paul felt an innocence and newness that he had never known before. It was a new order of experience.

Lamb Johnson didn't like people who asked questions about him—especially if the questions concerned the work Lamb had done on Freddy Stella's car.

Paul Marnay had been asking questions; the man was like a fly that didn't leave you alone. No, he was more than annoying; he was dangerous—more like a wasp. Although Lamb wasn't able to tell himself why, he thought Paul Marnay was trying to cause trouble. Was it possible that Marnay had bought the sports car only because it gave him an excuse to snoop?

Lamb had just learned that his father's will specified his son could inherit a significant estate only on the condition that he earn a master's degree in political science and take and hold a job in government for one year. It was an impossible condition.

After asking some of his own questions, Lamb had begun to wonder why there should be people like Paul Marnay—people who didn't really work but lived as they pleased and who meddled in the lives of less fortunate people; sleeping with Miss Brock, the rich social worker. Lamb had seen her around the hospital, showing off her body in a way that wasn't right for an official person.

The more he thought about it, the more certain Lamb was that the world didn't need Paul Marnay. There was Marnay's son to consider, but the boy seemed sensible enough not to mourn the death of a part-time, selfish father. The fittest, the realists, the serious, would survive.

At 4:00 A.M., unable to sleep, Lamb went to his worktable and wrote a letter:

Dear Chainmaster:

I thought you would like to know that my employer told me that Paul Marnay, a resident of Dale Falls, has been asking questions about my connections with Freddy Stella.

That doesn't do either of us any good, does it? What *would* do us good would be to have him take my father's place in the chain.

He should be taken care of by a cautious, competent person. He visits New York City often, where deaths don't attract as much attention as they do in small towns.

Sincerely,
R. B. (Lamb) Johnson

As Lamb sealed the letter, he felt the way he did when he solved a design problem. He understood now that he didn't need his father's inheritance. He only needed a life free of interference.

Chapter 14

As Paul Marnay drove back to Dale Falls from Manhattan the next weekend with his son, he realized they were being followed. He probably wouldn't have noticed the car that followed them if it had been red or white, but its distinctive puttyish color caught his attention. It had the faded-liver hue that amateur painters often come up with to their distress after half an hour of mixing brilliant cadmium yellow, ultramarine blue, vermillion, and zinc white. The car represented a negation of color, which only a nonpainter would think of as unnoticeable.

Paul resisted his first panicky reaction to the situation, which was to try to force a confrontation with the person following him. He also resisted his second impulse, which was to notify the police. He recalled his unsatisfactory telephone conversation with Officer Ray when he tried to report his first suspicions.

Also, there was his son to consider. What was the point of bringing Luke into the situation?—particularly before it was clear what the situation was.

Paul decided just to keep his eyes on the rearview mirror for the time being and to postpone further decisions until he was back in Dale Falls and had dropped Luke off at Sherril's house. But Luke, as was too often true, knew more than Paul gave him credit for.

"You're spending more time looking at where we've been than where we're going, Dad."

Paul realized it was time to be forthcoming. "I think maybe someone is following us."

Luke didn't turn to look out the back window. "You mean that crapped-out '88 Dodge Shadow?"

"I suppose." Paul could tell a Van Eyck painting from a Memling, but he could make only the grossest of distinctions among car models: a Rabbit from a Rolls. Then he realized what Luke had said. "Shadow? Are you serious? We're being shadowed by a Shadow?"

"She's either following us or she's going where we're going."

"She?"

"I saw her when we stopped at the service area. She's old."

"How old? Older than me?"

"Granny-old. White hair."

Paul felt a little of his anxiety fade. Why would a senior citizen be following him? And even if that's what was going on, it was likely to be someone who was inquisitive rather than threatening.

Luke, who had been about to enter what he called "auto" hypnosis—the trance that can develop during highway driving—sat up and put his system into higher gear. "Why don't we lose her?" he said. "We've got twice the acceleration she has."

"And get stopped by the police?"

"We'd still lose her. She wouldn't pull over to watch us get a ticket."

"I don't want to get a ticket," Paul said. He had already earned himself more than enough tickets in the category known as "moving violations"—a term he admired but feared. Paul was a bad driver, not reckless but vague. He tended to forget what the rules were.

"There's not much traffic along here," Luke said. "Just push it up to a hundred or so for a couple of minutes. Then, is there a place to pull off along here?"

"There's a scenic stop, I think."

"So we'll pull off there and let her go by. Then we can follow *her*. Neat."

"Not so neat." Paul was having a bad day. He had driven to Manhattan through a no-visibility rainstorm; his portrait session with Frank Whitby had been unproductive; he hadn't been able to see Phyllis; and Luke had been fractious. If Paul hadn't had to get Luke back to Sherril, he would have stayed in the city. What he really wanted to do was to have a leisurely dinner with Phyllis in a country-style French restaurant his brother had been urging him to try; to go to a bar and have some cognac and hear someone like Marian McPartland play the piano for an hour; and then to share Phyllis's bed until it was time for Sunday brunch. Against such thoughts, the prospect of playing granny tag was doubly unappealing.

On the other hand, Paul wanted to find out if he was really being followed. So he boosted his speed up to seventy, then pulled off at the scenic stop, which would have given him a spectacular view of the Lord Howe Valley if he hadn't been more interested in watching the highway.

A minute later the suspected pursuer passed. The driver was a handsome, apparently sixtyish woman who was concentrating on the road and didn't seem to glance at the cars that had pulled off.

"Give her thirty seconds," Luke said. "That'll put her half a mile ahead. We can move up and just keep her in sight."

Paul didn't share Luke's enthusiasm, but he was pleased to see his son's energies engaged. One of the factors involved in Paul's reaction—and one he wasn't proud of—was parental competition. Occasionally Paul wondered if his efforts to please Luke weren't actually intended to make the boy think his mother boring or neglectful. In any case, Sherril wasn't likely to get involved in anything as exotic as tailing or being tailed.

Following Luke's instructions, Paul followed the Dodge as it proceeded sedately to Dale Falls and parked in the driveway of a newly renovated bungalow in an older part of town, a section that was being successfully gentrified.

Paul and Luke watched from their parking place half a block away as what Luke called their "subject" got out of her car, checked her mailbox, and went into the house. It was dusk now, and under the tall old trees that lined the block, it wasn't easy to see the woman they had been following. But Paul was certain it was no one he knew. Actually, he was beginning to

think she was someone he wouldn't mind knowing—
or wouldn't mind painting. As usual, he was having
trouble sorting out his reactions to a beautiful woman;
the pleasant blend of esthetic and erotic impulses
were at work.

Even from this distance it had been clear that the
woman, whatever her age, still had a full complement
of hormones. She showed none of the apologetic
bearing that sexually retired people usually develop.
Her hair, which was now a thick, whitish gray, had
most likely once been lank and mousy; the interesting
fullness of her figure had probably replaced a gaunt-
ness.

"So you probably want to paint her," Luke said.
"Right?"

"Something like that," Paul confessed. In a couple
of more years, Luke would know it wasn't that simple.

"Anyway, she wasn't following us after all," Luke
said. He was obviously disappointed.

"We can't be sure of that."

"Shall we make sure of it?"

"How?"

"First, we find out who she is."

"How again?"

"I'll go look at her mailbox."

"What if she sees you?"

"I'll make something up."

"That's not the point," Paul said. "If she *was*
following us, she'll recognize you. She'll know that we
spotted her." For the first time it occurred to Paul that
there might be some danger in the situation. "She
might not be alone in there. Let's just forget it. Your
mom's expecting you anyway."

"It'll just take a minute," Luke said, and got out of
the car. He jogged over to the woman's house and
went stealthily up to the mailbox next to the front
door. But then instead of returning to the car, Luke

walked over and pressed his face against a window, cupping his hands at the sides of his head. Lights had gone on in the house as the woman entered it, which would make it easier to see into the window. Luke stayed at the window much too long. Even if the woman didn't notice him from inside the house, someone might come along the street and see him. After an interminable five minutes, Paul saw Luke turn and jog quickly to the car. By the time Luke was in the passenger's seat, Paul had the car's ignition on, and they sped away to the squeal of tires.

Luke was smiling. "The subject's name is Ms. Sarah Hopkins, and she's got a circuit or two missing."

"Could you be more specific about the missing circuit?"

"She was talking on the phone. Standing up and not moving."

"There's something wrong with that?"

"Sure. You know how most people are when they talk on the phone . . . they gesture or twist the cord or doodle. They move around because they can't see who they're talking to. Ms. Hopkins just stood there with her free hand at her side."

"My son the psychiatrist," Paul said. He didn't want to admit that Luke's theory probably had some truth to it. But truthful or not, the theory didn't prove that Sarah Hopkins had been following them.

"And she's got lots of books," Luke added.

"A sure sign of derangement."

They rode in silence the rest of the way to Sherril's house. Luke was smiling when he got out of the car. "Is everybody crazy?" he asked.

"I think so, Luke. Everybody worthwhile, anyway."

"You're very worthwhile, Dad," Luke said as he got out of the car.

"No more snooping," Paul called out after his son, and immediately regretted it. The remark might be in the don't-put-beans-in-your-ears category. But Paul knew the beans had already been planted firmly not only in his son's ears but in his own.

Paul's evening was lonely in a way that hadn't been possible before he met Phyllis Arno. He ate some bread, a strong sheep cheese, and fresh figs he had brought back from the city. He also drank a bottle of the bad wine that his family usually distilled into good brandy; they bottled some of the wine for use at the family table, and no one had the courage to point out that it was virtually undrinkable. Paul called it The King's Clothes, or *Les Vêtements du Roi,* depending on how much of it he had consumed. And he eventually became fond of it, the way one might get to like a vulgar cousin.

After his meal, Paul added the name Sarah Hopkins to his mystery chart. He put her in the column headed "Suspect," although he didn't know what she was suspected of. He remembered how attractive she was, and he hoped she would not end up in the column headed "Victim."

During the next couple cf days, Paul spent a lot of his time looking over his shoulder. As he made his commuting trips into Manhattan, he spent more of his time looking at his rearview mirror than at the road in front of him. There was no sign of Sarah Hopkins or anyone else, and he decided he must have been mistaken about the whole matter. He was also encouraged because his failure to see a follower proved that he hadn't turned paranoid. He assumed that a true paranoiac would never accept the fact that he wasn't being followed.

As he glanced back and forth at the car's mirror, he was reminded that love and suspicion had distracted him from his looking-glass collecting. An antiques dealer on Third Avenue had been holding an elaborate Chippendale mirror for him, but it was similar to a rococo American piece he already had, with its phoenix finial, egg-and-dart molding, and florid pendants. Paul decided to see if the dealer still had it, but doubted whether its appeal would have increased. When a mirror's framing demanded a lot of attention it seemed to defeat the object's purpose. Was the frame meant to enhance the appearance of the viewer's image or to distract from unpleasant reality? More likely it was just the maker's attempt to draw attention to himself and to justify an exorbitant price—it was packaging. Paul was beginning to value the reflecting surface over its package. He hoped that was a sign of maturity and not of diminishing energies.

Chapter 15

After considering the problem carefully (as she did all problems), Sarah Hopkins had decided the cat has a better chance when the mouse knows it's there. The cat gives up the element of surprise but benefits from the mistakes the mouse is likely to make in its anxiety.

So Sarah had let Paul Marnay suspect she was following him. But she hadn't decided how she would kill him. The letter hadn't been clear about that and had only insisted that the death must look like an accident. Actually, the letter hadn't been clear about much. The instructions had been silly and a little desperate, basing their appeal on irrationalities and vague threats. Sarah wouldn't have paid any attention to the letter if it hadn't been for its opening sentence: *There is someone you wish were dead.* The simple truth of that statement was irresistible. And so Sarah Hopkins agreed to play Chainmaster's ridiculous but ingenious game.

The person Sarah wanted to die was Arthur Merrill, who had been her employer for ten years. Arthur was in charge of the reference book division of a large publishing house in New York City, and Sarah was a designer in the production department. When a Dutch publisher took over the operation and made Arthur the editor in chief with the assignment of reorganizing the staff, he fired Sarah without notice, although with a handsome severance payment. Sarah moved to Dale Falls to live in the small house her late mother had left her and that she had been trying unsuccessfully to rent out. As she settled into the house, Sarah also settled into a clinical depression that, after a year or so of mediocre psychotherapy, estimable medications, and born-again Christianity, receded enough so that she could take on some free-lance book-design assignments. She avoided friendships—particularly the free-lance sexual kind, which seemed more available now than they had in her younger years.

Sarah knew a little about Paul Marnay. She had seen some of his paintings and had been indifferent to them. Paul was obviously interested in likeness and not design. To Sarah, likeness was an easy concept; it resulted in Whistler's painting *Arrangement in Gray and Black* being known as *Whistler's Mother*. What obsessed Sarah was the concept of blankness and its absence. She believed that the less successful book designers were concerned with the elements that disturb the blankness. She knew that what was beautiful about a paragraph in Palatino italic was the space around it and that the beauty of a page lay in its margins and spaces.

But what bothered Sarah most about Paul wasn't the easiness of his art but the easiness of his life. Sarah thought the only lives that mattered were difficult lives. And if, while he was visiting Manhattan, Paul should be shot by a mugger while walking along Central Park West on a dark night, the world would be little the worse and might gain infinitesimally in its moral balance. It was unfortunate about Paul's son having to lose his father, but the boy had already lost him six days a week. Sarah would pray for the boy to escape his grief quickly, as she would pray for the frivolous soul of Paul Marnay and—eventually—for the putrid, selfish soul of Arthur Merrill.

Paul Marnay's life had reached one of those pleasureful peaks that develop gradually and are best appreciated in retrospect. As he was finding out, if you become too aware of a good situation, you can spoil it by wondering how long it can last.

The portrait of Frank Whitby was finished, and Frank, Paul, and Max Antell all liked it. Paul also realized that he had stopped carrying his silver flask and had completed the painting without a drop of liquid assistance. Frank Whitby liked the painting so much that he paid Paul a bonus and found him another client—a young woman who had distinctive features, an easy smile, and wanted a full-length life-size portrait in which she would wear a black plumed hat and a red satin gown. She wanted something in a style that was a cross between Romney and Whistler works she had seen in the Frick Collection.

Paul took the assignment eagerly, thinking it would be a pleasant stylistic challenge. He also wondered if giving priority to pleasure was the difference between being a painter and being an artist.

Not that Paul had to go out of his way to find pleasure. Phyllis Arno supplied him with more than enough varieties of that. Before meeting Phyllis, Paul had looked to a number of people for pleasures and gratifications. Now he was learning that Phyllis could be everything to him except an offspring, and fortunately, Luke was available to fill that role.

Luke seemed to have adjusted well to broken-home living—as had his parents. All three of them used basically the same technique of adjustment: self-reliance. They went their own ways. Another reason Paul was grateful to Phyllis was that she had kept his self-reliance from turning into selfishness.

A final note of pleasure was that the Marnay business was in one of its more prosperous periods, resulting in a bonus payment for family members, including those, such as Paul, whose contributions to the business weren't substantial.

Paul wondered whether his half-serious interest in the Dale Falls murders wasn't an attempt to supply some ballast to his life—to develop some of the shadows that add interest to a landscape. In any case, when Paul had any unoccupied time, he consulted his mystery chart and did a little discreet snooping. Most recently, he bought a nonworking antique clock in Manhattan and took it to Dwight Bailey for repair. The clock was an Empire pre-Victorian wall model with a mirror set into the lower of two doors. A combination clock and mirror seemed like a terrifying object to Paul. Not only did it remind you of passing time, it allowed you to watch as time worked its inevitable effects on your features. Paul recalled that the poet W. H. Auden had used the phrase "the Devil in the clock." A clock-mirror sheltered two devils.

Dwight Bailey was undoubtedly delighted to have the clock to work on. He looked like a tearfully grateful El Greco saint glancing at Heaven when Paul removed the wrapping from the case. As Dwight examined the clock's works, Paul examined Dwight. Could this man have pushed the pigeon lady to her death? Did he really fit into the "creepola" category Luke had consigned him to? Probably. Paul was beginning to believe that anybody was capable of any act if it made him or her feel happy or virtuous. And there was something unsettling about Dwight's appearance anyway, a slight hint of the idiot savant's reptilian stare.

But why would the pigeon lady's death make Dwight feel happy or virtuous? Obviously his happiness consisted of being allowed to regulate or construct little mechanical worlds. Had the pigeon lady's death made it easier for Dwight to do that? Apparently not. Could someone have, for some unimaginable reason, paid him to kill the woman? If so, the fee hadn't gone into clothing; Dwight was dressed like a recruit in some small nation's mercenary army.

So maybe it was a coincidence that Dwight had been wandering around in the rain at the time and place of the woman's death. And maybe it was a coincidence that Dwight's mother had died in a fall. Unless it was an example of trade-off murders as in Patricia Highsmith's *Strangers on a Train*. But who was the other party in the trade? Who wanted the pigeon lady to die?

Paul began to feel despondent. He understood now why the detectives in murder mysteries (Sherlock, Maigret) often lacked *joie de vivre*. But then there were Nick and Nora Charles. Maybe Paul needed a partner-in-crime-detection. Or maybe he should just mind his own business.

Dwight Bailey looked up from the clock's works. As his eyes met Paul's, his pleased expression changed to one of apprehension. Paul thought, Dwight doesn't hate people; he's afraid of people. He's the good soldier. He's not seeking happiness; he's seeking the virtue of obedience. "I'll have it going in no time," Dwight said, the pun apparently not intended. He looked relievedly back to the mass of gears and shafts. "I might have to cut a wheel for it, but the movement is nothing unusual. The maker was more interested in cabinetwork than clockworks."

Paul wondered if Dwight was being honest. There was a suppressed excitement in the repairman's manner, as if the clock had a rare type of movement that he was going to keep secret. Paul decided he was right to be suspicious of Dwight. A man who can't be honest about his profession shouldn't be trusted in anything.

Paul tried to test his theory: "The dealer I bought it from thought it might be unusual."

"What dealer is that?" Dwight gave Paul an annoyed glance.

"In New York City."

"A clock dealer?"

"An antiques dealer on Third Avenue."

"It's best to buy clocks from clock dealers."

"Actually, I'm more interested in the mirror in the cabinet that anything else. I collect mirrors."

Dwight nodded. He either couldn't think of anything to say or didn't think it would be good for business to say what he was thinking.

After a transitional pause, Paul said, "I like your place here." Dwight's office-workshop was in a newly renovated and modified room of his home. A separate entrance had been built into the room, which had probably been a bedroom; his mother's bedroom, Paul assumed. Without considering what he was going to say but realizing as he spoke that he was making a mistake, Paul said, "I understand your mother died recently."

Dwight slammed the two small doors shut on the clock, creating metallic resonances. He opened his mouth to speak but once again hesitated.

Paul thought, He's more sensible than I am, and said, "I'm sorry." He felt as clumsy as he had when he was trying to get information about Lamb Johnson; interrogation was not one of Paul's talents. He wondered why. Perhaps it required the ability to inspire trust—an ability Paul had never been able to develop. He hoped Phyllis and Luke trusted him, but he knew that everyone else—including his ex-wife and most of the people whose portraits he painted—seemed reluctant to put themselves, or their images, in his hands. It wasn't something he regretted, but it was something he didn't understand. Didn't people know that he neither practiced nor admired betrayal? Of course, Hillary Brock might argue about that, but exceptions always had to be made for love.

Dwight Bailey had turned his attention back to the clock, which obviously soothed him immediately. Paul looked around the workshop. There were dozens of clocks—standing, sitting, hanging, in a mad variety of styles. They were another demonstration that in design (as in most activities), people always go too far. In that respect, clocks were like chairs and soup tureens. Well enough was never left alone. Or maybe there wasn't any well enough—just tired or jaded tastes. As in painting, you could never go too far as long as you could demonstrate a mastery of technique.

Among the clocks displayed was a large, simple, caseless model labeled "Kit." Paul recalled that he had promised to get a kit for Luke.

Dwight had apparently finished examining the clock. "When do you want it?"

"As soon as possible." Paul realized he was becoming fond of the clock. The top door was decorated with a primitively painted landscape, obviously mass-produced but with some individual touches and probably done out of some pride in the quickness and facility with which it was produced.

Dwight said, "One of the weights is missing. I'd like to match it. That could take a while."

"A weight?"

"It's weight-driven. Didn't you know that?"

"I didn't ask about the insides."

"That's the most interesting part. You should have asked. Give me two weeks," Dwight said. "I'll call you."

"I'll take one of those kits, too," Paul said.

Dwight raised his eyebrows. "Do you think you can handle it?"

"It's for my son."

"Ask him to come in if he has any trouble with it. But it's simple enough."

"He wants to design a tower clock with life-size figures."

"I could show him how. But he'd have to work up to it."

"By way of a cuckoo clock?"

"Something like that."

Cuckoo, Paul thought. Only the expert knows if there's a cuckoo lurking in the cabinet, waiting for the right configuration of gears and levers to send it into its mad little performance.

The next visit was with Connie Nickens. Paul called her at the Postroad Restaurant and asked her to hold a table for him in a spot where it might be convenient for her to pull up a chair for herself between seatings and crises.

It was a dull night at the restaurant, and Connie spent a fair amount of time at Paul's table. He was flattered because she obviously was neglecting other customers to talk to him. She was also showing a new self-confidence in not being concerned with whether the owner might think she wasn't doing her job well.

But above all, Connie was looking good. She moved about the room as if she were dancing, weaving among tables and past waiters, her left arm around several oversize menus. Her thighs moved smoothly against the short, tight skirt of a challis dress that had a lot of burnt umber in its print. She made you understand that the phrase "radiantly happy" can occasionally be appropriate. It was as if there were a radiance-transmitter operating somewhere within her, and the radiance filled in the missing piece in the puzzle of her beauty.

As Paul eased his way through steamed clams, lemon-garlic chicken breast, and a spinach salad, Connie Nickens would settle across from him occasionally, handsome and alert. She would rest her fingertips on his hand as she talked to him, and when she had to get up and walk past his chair, her skirt would touch the sleeve of his jacket, a practiced, provocative grazing just short of bodily contact. There was another unattached male that Connie would visit briefly during the evening—a man who looked as if his silk shirt might be hiding a tattoo. Paul was glad not to be competing with the man for Connie's full-time attention.

Paul was sure directness was the best approach to take with Connie under all circumstances, so he said to her, "You know what everyone's up to around Dale Falls, Connie. You hear things."

"You mean things like a certain man-about-town painter is avoiding Hillary Brock in favor of a New York actress?"

"You hear more than I thought. And your sources seem to be accurate."

"In this case, my source is Hillary. You've hurt her, Paul."

"Yes. Well, that's not what I wanted. I don't like to hurt people."

"It's the hurt that matters; not whether it was intentional."

Paul doubted whether Connie believed what she had just said. He had other sources of information, and one of them contended that Connie was interested in formalized pain. "I'm sure the attitude of the inflicter makes a difference," Paul said.

"I guess," Connie said as if the thought were new to her. "But fortunately there aren't many people around who intentionally hurt people."

"I've been thinking there might be lots of them; even people who go beyond pain."

As Connie got up to greet an arriving couple, she said, "What's beyond pain?"

"Death." Paul wasn't sure if Connie had heard his reply. She had already turned away from him, so he couldn't tell whether her welcome-to-our-place smile was a little late in appearing or a little less convincing than usual. But there was no sign of hesitation in her movement away from the table.

Connie toured the room before returning to Paul's table, apparently not so much asking the customers if everything was okay as telling them it was. She joined in the off-key singing of "Happy Birthday" as a candle-studded cake was presented to a large family party.

"Thank God for birthdays," Connie said when she got back to Paul's table. "They can make the difference between profit and loss off-season." She clearly didn't want to return to their previous topic.

"We were talking about deathdays," Paul said and watched Connie's forehead crease slightly. "Haven't you noticed the deaths lately? You must have. The woman who fell from the window in the hospital . . . Freddy Stella."

Connie got up and left the table again. But this time there was no new arrival to greet. She walked into the kitchen and stayed there long enough to allow her to change emotions, whatever they might have been.

When she got back to the table, Connie had dropped some of her professional amiability. There was a hard edge of sarcasm in her voice. "My daily reminder to the chef that people have to eat his concoctions. He tends to think food is good if it looks good."

Connie was obviously still trying to avoid the topic of death. Paul, like everyone else in the world, was always ready with opinions about eating (which he liked to do) and cooking (which he let other people do for him), but he wasn't ready to be diverted yet. He put his hand on Connie's; he remembered that she tended to be more communicative when she was being touched.

"What's going on?" he asked.

"In the kitchen? It's always Marx Brothers time back there."

"Not in the kitchen, Connie. In the morgue."

She gave him a forbearing glance. "You tell me," she said. She didn't seem worried about what Paul might say in answer to that question. It was more as though she wanted him to demonstrate how little he actually knew.

"People are dying unnaturally for no apparent reason. I'd like to know the reason."

"Not everything has a reason, Paul. There's coincidence and accident. I know that's what the woman at the hospital was and what Freddy Stella was. And I'd guess that any other one was, too."

"What was between you and Freddy?"

"We had a relationship . . . not too simple."

"You don't seem too upset about his death."

"Did you want me to sit in a dark room for six months? Come on, Paul. You know I don't get too serious about any one man. If I did, you wouldn't like looking at me as much as you do."

Paul tried to suppress a little blush. It was true that he liked looking at Connie and that it wasn't because there was a great beauty or character in her features; it was because there was the implication that intimacy was a possibility. Paul had occasionally tried, without much success, to get that implication into a from-memory portrait. It had to do mostly with the eyes, but there was something else involved that he hadn't been able to capture. It was the same quality that explained the enormous and continuing appeal of Marilyn Monroe—the quality that persuaded any kind of camera (or viewer) that she was available for intimacy, but as a willing victim and not as a prostitute. The only portraits of Marilyn Paul had seen that had made her seem whorish were (significantly) some jumped-up graphics by Andy Warhol.

Paul had succeeded in sidetracking himself. Connie was looking around the room, but she apparently hadn't stopped thinking about their topic. "Look," she said, "why would a bunch of strangers go around killing each other? You should lighten up, Paul. I gather your life is sweet these days—about as sweet as most lives ever get. Right?"

"Right."

"Then why not enjoy it? Even I can do that, and I'm the one with Slavic blood."

"Touché," Paul said. "Or whatever the word is in Serbo-Croatian."

"So tell me about your new friend. Is she beautiful?"

"Not too."

"Is she intelligent?"

"I haven't asked her."

"Have I seen her?"

"Do you go to plays?"

"Movies . . . in my bedroom. Has she been in movies?"

"Not that kind."

"I don't *watch* that kind. I watch Martin Scorsese, Woody Allen, Blake Edwards. And I read cast lists."

"Phyllis Arno?"

Connie began to scan her memory. A usually suppressed intelligence showed through her concentration. "Phyllis Arno," she said after about five seconds. "She had a few lines in the last Woody Allen. At a cocktail party. She upstaged Mia Farrow. I'm surprised the scene got into the final cut."

"You amaze me. My respect continues to grow."

"I wanted to be an actress. But the reason I remember that scene isn't so respectable. I wondered if she had red pubic hair."

"I'll ask her that, too."

Connie smiled, slow-blinked a farewell, and went to do her rounds.

Paul chewed on some undressinged spinach leaves and thought about the odd arrangement of Connie's mind: her downplayed intelligence and her fondness for darkness both literal and figurative. And he also thought about one of her sentences: "Why would a bunch of strangers go around killing each other?" Paul hadn't said, or even implied that strangers were killing one another; he had just said people were getting killed. Had Connie inadvertently given him a lead? If so, it wasn't much of a lead. Why *would* strangers kill one another? Who would arrange that kind of lethal conspiracy in Dale Falls? Maybe that was the approach he should take: Look for a controlling person—a person who knew Connie, Dwight Bailey and his late mother, the late Edna Denning, Freddy Stella, Lamb Johnson and his late father, Sarah Hopkins, and possibly others, including Paul himself. What was it that all or most of these people had in common?

On the way out of the restaurant, Paul asked Connie if she'd ever heard of Sarah Hopkins.

"Another actress? Is this a trivia test?"

"Maybe, but I doubt it. She lives in Dale Falls."

"I've never met her, and she hasn't made a reservation here . . . at least since I've been here."

Paul was grateful that Connie didn't ask why he wanted to know.

When he got home, he called his brother and asked him to send Connie a case of *Très Vieux Spéciale.* François didn't ask why either.

And then Hillary Brock called and asked if she could stop over for a little harmless conversation.

Paul said, "I think not."

"Why?" Hillary asked.

Paul unplugged the phone.

Chapter 16

Paul usually felt a mixture of pleasure and fear when introducing a woman to his brother. The pleasure came from watching François react to the woman with a true connoisseur's appreciation; the fear came from wondering if the appreciation would develop into competition. Most women wrote François off as a member of the species Male Chauvinist Pig, but they were also aware that he was in the subspecies Refined, Discriminating European. Even though he treated women as objects, he was someone who had the deepest appreciation of and respect for those objects.

Phyllis Arno recognized François's capacity for being a devoted one-person audience, and she put on a subtle performance that was more pleasing to François than to Paul. But it wasn't extravagant enough to upset Paul.

The three were having dinner at Le Banquet, one of the midtown East Side restaurants that critics use as a conservative reference point when reviewing trendy dispensers of nouvelle cuisine. The restaurant's owner was distantly related to the Marnays, and he always gave François a good table and a lot of chat in French, but no break on the horrendously high prices that kept Paul away when on his own.

The meeting was the closest Paul could get to fulfilling the ritual of taking Phyllis home to meet his parents, and he had let François know in advance that

Phyllis might become the second Mrs. Paul Marnay. François made no comment. He was as conservative in his attitude toward marriage as in most of his other attitudes: Wives were meant to bear a child or two and to preside at formal dinners. François was fond of saying about his own wife, Simone: "Her emotional life is her own affair—or affairs." He never failed to follow the statement with an apparently genuine laugh. For this dinner with Paul and Phyllis, François had announced for some reason that Simone had a "prior commitment" that kept her away.

The early phases of the dinner consisted of François turning on the charm for Phyllis and explaining what to choose from the intricate menu. The chef seemed to follow three principles: make things look good; make them taste good; and don't make them taste the way they look as if they *should* taste. The meal was a series of pleasant surprises. The owner had a principle of his own: The cost of an item should be in inverse proportion to the size of the serving—the caviar principle.

Halfway through the second of three wines, the conversational topics began to darken up and to become more interesting to Paul. Phyllis had been describing the last play she had appeared in—which concerned serial murder—when she said, "According to Paul there are some kind of connected murders going on in Dale Falls."

"I'm delighted to hear it," François said. He had only visited Paul in Dale Falls once and hadn't been well pleased by what he found there.

"I can't share your delight about the murders, François," Paul said.

"Why is that? Moral outrage? Or fear?"

"Puzzlement, mostly. Why would an apparently unconnected group of people do away with one another in what looks like a series of unrelated accidents?"

François said, "Have you considered the possibility that maybe it *is* a series of unrelated accidents?"

"Yes, but what if it isn't? What's behind it?"

"Drugs," Phyllis said. "They attract a diverse crowd, and they start some major disagreements."

"No," Paul said. "Drug wars involve guns and lots of extroverted, apparently unemployed young men."

"Blackmail, perhaps," François said. "But I don't suppose anyone there does anything blackmailable."

Paul, annoyed at not being taken seriously, poked at a tiny assemblage of vegetable fragments that mimicked some kind of flower blossom. Even a dainty eater could have finished it off in one bite.

Possibly because he didn't want Phyllis to think he was insensitive, François changed his tone. "Just what is it that's happened, anyway?"

Paul went through the litany of deaths and in the process convinced himself, as always, that they were not random. Also as always, he couldn't be sure why he was convinced.

François listened to the litany politely but with an obvious lack of interest. His glance kept flickering over to Phyllis, particularly to the pale upper slope of her bosom, which was invitingly framed by the scooped neck of her black silk dress. Paul realized it was unreasonable to expect his brother to be more interested in an abstract discussion of dead bodies than in the presence of an attractive, intensely living body, but he carried his summary through to its sour conclusion.

"Our family has always been obsessive, Paul," François said. "What we've had to learn is to choose our obsessions well. I think maybe you're scattering your obsessions a bit."

Phyllis proved her loyalty to Paul by saying to him, although not enthusiastically, "If you were in an

Agatha Christie novel, sweetie, you'd find that your suspects—Dwight, Lamb, Connie—had hidden relationships; that they all had the same father or had been expelled from the same Sunday school."

François, who seemed always to be having root canal work done, added, "I'd find out who their dentist is. Dentists would not be above conspiracy—offering to reduce their outrageous fees for indigent patients who will eliminate others who refuse to pay."

"'The Deadbeat Murders,'" Phyllis said, before another course arrived and distracted everyone with its own mystery. It was one of the whims the chef occasionally saluted favored diners with—a palate-clearer between ordered courses. Paul, who was not the favored one anyway, had no idea what he was tasting: paper-thin slices of something meaty and pale under a pungent brown dribble of sauce.

"Sweetbreads?" Phyllis said.

"Blanched first in a white burgundy with thyme; then sautéed in butter and peppercorns . . . and . . ."

Some green flecks in the sauce gave Phyllis and François something to disagree about.

Paul didn't hear the disagreement because he had looked across the room at the restaurant's small, discreet window to see whether a predicted heavy rain had shown up yet; and in the window he saw the face of Sarah Hopkins. She was looking at him intently but with what seemed like a benign expression. Paul almost smiled at her as if she were an old friend. She was a striking woman, with the bearing and alertness of someone in early rather than late middle age. She resembled a thirty-year-old actor made up to play someone sixty-five. But across her forehead and upper lip were rows of vertical and diagonal lines that resembled a message faintly inscribed in runes. To most people, the message would have been: "I'm older than you think." But to Paul, it was: "I'm in pursuit."

While François and Phyllis worked their way enthusiastically through cheeses and dessert, Paul skipped ahead to coffee and brandy, with several refills. Phyllis and François were involved in a consumption competition that took on the qualities of a flirtation. There was nothing grossly sensual about their game, but they were obviously comparing perceptions and distinctions of appetite. It was a permissible intimacy, and Paul enjoyed watching them. They would be good in-laws to each other.

Everything began to seem good to Paul. When they left Le Banquet, he didn't even bother to look for Sarah Hopkins. She was there somewhere in the shadows among the bouquets of neon—as handsome and dignified a follower as a person could wish for. Paul was glad, for the woman's sake, that the rain had held off.

At Phyllis's apartment, she and Paul didn't speak, but undressed each other slowly, removing garments as if the process were their means of communicating with each other. Paul's duties in the game were simple. Once Phyllis had kicked her shoes off, she wore only three garments, each of them black and clinging. Her dress fell quickly and dramatically to the floor once Paul had lowered the zipper at its back. He released the clasp of her bra before she turned to face him. As she turned, Paul's index finger traced the line—white-edged and slightly concave, where a shoulder strap had been. His finger continued down the slope of a breast, across an aroused nipple, down to the curve of Phyllis's belly, hooking under the elastic of her panties, easing them to the floor as he sank to his knees. He rested his cheek against surprisingly luxuriant hair that had the intense color of new copper.

Phyllis raised Paul to his feet and led him to her

117

bed. Their bodies were dictating their actions, but it was a garbled dictation, Paul thought. His digestive system was in high gear after their meal and didn't want to deal with interference from rival networks—even from the reproductive network, which Paul's controls normally tended to give top priority. But he was finally learning, after three and a half decades of practice, to overrule the controls. He was secure enough to believe that Phyllis wouldn't think him unmanly or unloving if he used a little restraint. But he admitted to himself that his security was based somewhat on the fact that as Phyllis removed his shorts (red bikinis chosen for the occasion in adolescent bad taste) it was clear that immediate sexual activity was an option available to them. But the option Paul took was conversation and caresses.

"I'm becoming more mature, more moderate," Paul said. "Do you mind?"

"No longer the playboy of the western world, then?"

"Not unless you want me to be. I'll be what you want me to be, Phyllis."

"Attentive and admiring will do for the moment."

"I'm both of those."

Phyllis lay on her back with her right knee raised. Her hands were clasped at the top of her head, her arms bent and extended like wings. Her breasts were substantial enough so that even in this position they kept an assertive roundness. Her position seemed casual and unself-conscious, but Paul suspected it was carefully calculated. Phyllis needed admiration, and she tried to earn it. At the moment, Paul was sure, she wanted not just to have his admiration but to hear about it. He said, "Part of my love for you is that you seem to bring things to me—new attitudes and strengths." It was the first time Paul had said he loved Phyllis, and he wondered if she had noticed.

"I don't just give. I take. I might be taking more

118

than I'm giving. Sometimes I feel that way about my audiences."

"Is that what I am? One of your audiences?"

"No. You're my love." She had noticed.

Paul thought about what Phyllis had just said and realized that neither of them had been surprised by the word *love*. It was something they both had known was there. It was what they both had given and received. Paul said, "I'm not an expert on the subject of love. Does it add things and take things or just enhance what's already there?"

"I'm no expert either."

"I think I've either become more responsible, which I don't mind, or more solemn, which I *do* mind. I want to strike a balance between frivolity and pomposity."

"I don't see much danger of pomposity," Phyllis said. As if presenting evidence, she trailed a hand to the floor and came up with Paul's red bikinis.

Paul ignored the gesture. "Melancholy, maybe," he said. "This concern with murders. I'm not sure why they're important to me; it's not that I want to see justice done or that I care whodunit. It's the process."

"What *is* the process?"

"Some kind of evil, I suppose."

"An epidemic of evil?"

"Could be. But that would mean it was spontaneous. I think it's more like a chain reaction."

"Directed evil," Phyllis said. "I know something about that, or at least, about directorial evil." She turned toward Paul and ran her fingertips over the area below his navel, pausing at a patch of glistening stickiness. Then she rubbed her wet fingertips across her lips and kissed Paul's mouth. "Did you say you loved me?"

"I did. I do."

"Say some other things."

"Maybe it's time for doing instead of saying."

"Saying is important."

In their previous lovemaking, there had been sounds but no words. There had been an intensity that precluded words—a concentration that shut out not only words but images. There had been none of the fantasizing that Paul usually experienced—the thought of other encounters he had had or wanted to have. There was only Phyllis, engulfing, grasping, taking his body and all his senses. Paul wasn't sure that the experience permitted speech, or that words wouldn't diminish it. He was within her now, and the intensity was building. Maybe, he thought, this was where he would learn the words he had been waiting for—the passwords that would let him enter life's hidden room. It was certain that *some* kind of revelation was being presented. He tried his voice: "Won't words detract?"

"They'll augment. They're what makes it better for us than for our pets."

"What do I say?"

"You tell me what you're doing; what you're going to do; what you think about doing when you're not here; use the words you learned on street corners . . . the short words."

Saying the first few words, Paul felt shy; as if he were back on the street corners learning the words again on dark, humid nights, listening to the stories of those who had crossed the line of pubescence.

Phyllis prompted: "Tell me what you're doing . . . yes . . . and what is hard . . . yes . . . and what is tight and wet. . . ."

Mouth to ear, body to body, they began a dialogue that moved in arcs toward and away from muffled howlings, yelps, and gasps. It was dawn before they were totally silent.

* * *

Driving northward through the darkness, Sarah Hopkins sensed the landscape growing more elaborate around her. The earth's outlines, vague against the moon-brightened sky, became less regular. The sound of the car's engine became higher pitched and more threatening away from the city. The picturesque road was easier to veer off of. The simplest emotion, nurtured in solitude, took on irregular outlines. She recalled that the most accomplished mass murderers have been good country folk.

The big-city failings tended to be more on the farcical side. Sarah thought of what she had seen earlier through the window of Le Banquet. Paul Marnay and the woman (why did she seem familiar?) were in the shamelessly moonstruck phase of a romance—a phase that was either embarrassing or amusing to onlookers. Amusement had been the obvious choice of their companion, who Sarah assumed was Paul's brother. But Sarah was not amused. She had seen it all too often: The couple emerging from trysts wearing self-congratulatory smiles that featured the occasional pubic hair lodged between incisors, the total, gleeful surrender to the hormonal assault.

Sarah had never been one for total surrender. She had concluded after two marriages that her husbands' frequent sexual approaches were merely requests for assistance in an intricate and varied form of masturbation. The marriages had been appropriately childless and predictably brief.

Since leaving her second husband, Sarah had let her body seek its own pleasures, which turned out to be solitary but too subtle to qualify as masturbation. At the moment, for example, the cool spring air, moist and oxygen-rich from the increasingly dense stands of trees, moved across her face, between the buttons of her shirt, and up her thighs. She raised her skirt slightly—a small gesture but one that proved desire had not died. And with a shiver of pleasure, she turned her thoughts to the subject of death.

As was often true—a cause or effect of being a book designer—she saw the word that represented the direction of her thoughts. Uppercase, lowercase, in different typefaces and styles: *death.*

To kill Paul Marnay in his present circumstances would be to commit a murder and a half; his woman friend would suffer, too. But suffering is what most of the living do. Chainmaster was a natural force, a god, restoring the order of things. And who was the Chainmaster? Sarah wondered if she had passed him on the streets of Dale Falls, smiling a greeting in the broken shadows of the leafing oaks. Perhaps that had happened, but it was irrelevant. There's no need to have a personal relationship with the god. It's enough to respond when chosen—enough to know that Arthur Merrill, who had done away with Sarah's security and career with a few words murmured into a tiny tape recorder, would soon have his existence done away with.

But first there was Paul to dispose of. Who, Sarah wondered, wanted him disposed of? And why? But there was no need for such speculation. Perhaps one of the things that made a deathchain viable was that everyone's existence was offensive or threatening to someone. Sarah need not be concerned with judging Paul's habits. It was enough to observe his actions, as she had tonight, and to relate them to fatality. Watching him at the table, she decided she would have to learn more about death by accidental poisoning. How common is it, and what substances are involved?

Paul spent the next morning in his studio sorting through stacks of his paintings—exercises, sketches, mistakes, triumphs. It was, he thought, a record of moderate talent and remarkable persistence. There hadn't been much persistence lately, but maybe that wasn't a reason for regret. Maybe it was becoming less important for him to—in his ex-wife's phrase—to keep a piece of canvas stretched between him and reality. Maybe he should forget about painting. He could move to New York City and live with Phyllis. François would put him on the official full-time sales staff. He could put Dale Falls, with its mysteries and his own mistakes behind him. The big problem with that plan was Luke. Paul had promised himself that he would be available to Luke until the boy's eighteenth birthday—whether Luke needed him or not. But now Phyllis Arno was interfering with Paul's program of self-sacrifice.

About midmorning, Paul stood amid the tangled, disorienting images of mirrors and paint-daubed canvases, with depression settling like a stone somewhere near his liver. Maybe what he needed as an antidote was to get out of himself—to spend some time with a pragmatic, nerveless person. Ironically, the person who came closest to that description was Sherril, his ex-wife. He never precisely missed Sherril, but he recognized that there was the possibility of a singular kind of communication with her—the communication that, although not necessarily pleasant, has the magic of a well-learned private code that can infuse apparent banalities with depth and resonance.

Then it occurred to Paul that there was another antidote to depression. He searched out his old friend, the silver flask, and relieved it of some of its contents before refilling it. Then he dialed his ex-wife's number.

"Stone Realty."

"Hi."

Sherril's brisk, official tone became one of pseudoirritation: "Yes?"

"Does the demanding schedule allow for a drink with an ex?"

"An ex-what?"

She was saying yes; inviting a little folderol. "An ex post facto?"

There was a silence that was like a little curtsey. Sherril had been one of the few people of her generation to study Latin, and even though legal terms were about the only ones Paul could come up with, Sherril appreciated his effort. He wished he had known the Latin for "My place or yours?"—a phrase he was sure showed up in Sherril's translation of the play *Truculentus* by Plautus. Sherril's insistence on reading the translation aloud to Paul in the evenings had contributed to the foundering of their marriage. Paul had been driven to announce one night: "Either you, me, or Plautus doesn't have a sense of humor—and it's not me."

"It's not I," Sherril had said, and Paul was never sure whether she was defending her wit or just correcting his grammar. Either way, it was a rock through the matrimonial hull.

Paul wondered if Sherril was remembering the same bad moment. "Can you stop by this afternoon?" she asked. "Why don't you come over here? You know I can't deal with all those mirrors."

He was going to point out that he wasn't overjoyed with the odd combination of neatness and cats she lived with, but he just asked what time would be good.

Why, Paul wondered, don't cats come to see who's at the door, the way dogs do? He knew that scattered around Sherril's house—in the warm, comfortable places—were too many curled-up, lazily blinking, hair-shedding creatures that, despite being overfed, would demand to be let out later to stalk and kill a few migrating warblers that had the bad judgment to touch down in Sherril's backyard on their way from South America to Canada.

Sherril didn't like cats as much as she liked kittens, and she always seemed to have a litter or two she was tending while she was trying to palm off the parents. Her version of good-bye to her visitors was, "You don't know anyone who wants a cat, do you?"

Sherril was definitely off duty. She had some harpsichord music on the stereo—Rameau or Couperin— and she was drinking red wine on the rocks. The wine came from a spigoted five-liter cardboard box she kept next to her chair. The wine was "red table wine" from California; no specific year, vineyard, or type of grape indicated. It was an extreme example of inverted snobbery, but Paul preferred it to Sherril's usual uninverted kind. She began to talk passionately about the local real estate market, her eyes meeting his only occasionally. She claimed she didn't like to make eye contact with him because his gaze was indecent. Maybe she was right. She had made a change in her eyebrows, a reshaping to give them a Japanese thickness at the outer curves. It was the sort of change that would seem important to an estranged partner— someone who had become familiar with the detail of features and who was not present to be warned of impending changes or to see them gradually evolve. What other changes had there been?

Paul tried to remember the details of the body that was beneath her satiny rust pants suit. He could easily make a vivid visual recollection: the crevices and swellings of the body's landscape; the areola's hue; the hairs' paths and textures. But there was no emotional memory. He remembered her figure as he would recall the image of a favorite figure in a mythological scene by Rubens. It was a fond but dispassionate recollection.

Paul's revery was broken by the sound of a name.

125

Sherril was saying, "He calls himself Lamb, of all things. Luke says you know him."

"Hardly. Do you?"

"I know everyone, Pole." "Pole" was Sherril's not too accurate and unnecessary version of the French pronunciation of "Paul."

"So what *about* Lamb?"

"Not well socialized."

"Antisocial?"

"Oh, no. As harmless as his name."

Sherril sipped her wine and looked modestly smug. She probably did know something about almost everyone in Dale Falls. And if so, how could she fail to wonder about the recent deaths? "First thoughts," Paul said. It was a game they used to play when drinking together in the evening during the early years of their marriage, before they noticed that they didn't have a television set.

Paul paused as though searching for obscurities. "Dwight Bailey."

Without hesitation, Sherril said, "Beech Street . . . clocks . . . creepy."

"Luke calls him Creepola."

"Luke knows him?"

"He ran into him in the park one morning . . . before Dwight's mother died and about the same time another woman died."

Sherril ignored Paul's implication. She looked at him as if slightly annoyed and sipped her wine.

Paul tried another name: "Connie Nickens."

"Enjoy your meal . . . the hostess with the leastess." Sherril's reaction was edged with contempt, but Paul wasn't surprised. Women didn't like Connie.

"Freddy Stella," Paul said.

Sherril suppressed her first reaction, and after a moment said, "Must you be so morbid, Pole? You've been living alone too long. And speaking of that, let *me* try a name: Phyllis Arno."

"You *do* know everyone. Otherwise, no comment."

"I was just wondering if you're going to be dropping Luke back and forth to Manhattan every Saturday. You should be thinking of his needs before your own . . . at least one day a week."

Sherril was removing the cesspool lid, as usual. Paul closed it: "One more name," he said. "Sarah Hopkins."

Sherril didn't, as Paul feared she might, ignore his interruption and continue with her complaints about his treatment of Luke. For the first time since Paul had known her, Sherril looked vulnerable. Life was gaining on her.

Paul tried again: "Sarah Hopkins?"

Sherril shook her head negatively. The gesture was a lie or an evasion. She followed with a more definite evasion: a rambling, nasty, complicated story having to do with assembling property for a development. There were citations of obscure tax laws; tales of evictions and of life savings lost or fortunes made; the dropping of politically and socially prominent names. Paul had painted the portraits of two of the people mentioned and wasn't surprised to hear that the people involved weren't exactly selfless.

Sherril had stepped up her wine consumption during the story, and Paul had joined in with the drinking out of self-defense. Eventually, Sherril seemed to realize that she had either lost or had never gained her audience. They drank in silence for a few minutes, and she said, "You're still not interested in the real world, are you?" Her tone was more in the line of pity than of blame. Then, as if extending her pity to cover his lack of a live-in companion, she said, "You wouldn't like to adopt a cat? Isn't it time for that?"

They're taking over her life, Paul thought. They're becoming some kind of metaphor, the way cars are in Lamb's life and clocks are in Dwight's. (Should he call about the repaired clock?) Eventually the cats would triumph in their charming, indolent indifference. Paul took a glass-emptying swallow of the bodyless wine. Sherril rose a little too carefully and refilled Paul's glass and her own. As she moved, the room's scent changed slightly, becoming not perfumed but more intense. Sherril wasn't saying what her body wanted her to say.

Paul remembered Phyllis murmuring that words were what distinguished us from our pets. Maybe, he thought, we should keep pets around just to remind us of how not to behave. "Maybe it *is* time for a feline. What's available?"

Sherril's eyes narrowed in suspicion. "Really? Come along." She led Paul to what used to be their bedroom. She opened the door, releasing a zooish smell. Paul remembered Hillary Brock's violent allergy to cats, and thought she would probably expire if she walked into this room. Three restless tortoiseshell cats raced crazily down the hall and out of sight. These were the adventurers. The room was unfurnished, unless litter boxes and old blankets can be considered furniture. On one of the blankets was a large, light beige cat with several unfortunately placed black and brown scarlike markings. It had arranged itself in the classical alert-recumbent position: paws tucked under chest; tail pulled forward along the body-floor line.

It occurred to Paul that he had never made a painting of an animal. Their forms could be interesting but not expressive. In a sense, a still life, with its pure, dumb forms, could be more expressive than an animal portrait, with its implication of elementary emotions and limited consciousness.

"That's Grace," Sherril said.

"So it is."

"She might accept you."

"Easy, is she?" Paul went to the cat and squatted next to her. She raised her head slightly and blinked. Her gaze was more owl-like than catlike. Paul raised a hand slowly and ran a finger along the tips of the cat's white whiskers.

Sherril said, her voice swooping in surprise, "She *likes* you. She's smiling."

"Whatever you say." Paul picked up Grace and carried her to his car.

Sherril followed. "If she stays in the car, she's given herself to you."

There was a pause while Paul remembered an evening when Sherril had given herself to him—or as much as she ever gave—in a car. Then he said, "If she gets out, she's still yours." Grace went slowly through the car, sniffing, touching, looking. Then she settled into the passenger's seat, sprawling as if exhausted or seduced.

Paul got into the car. Sherril looked at him confusedly. She's jealous, Paul thought; she's recognizing that this man in the sports car is not the man she lived with.

"Thanks for the wine . . . and for Grace."

Sherril smiled. "Sure."

Paul tried his unanswered question once more: "Before we started in on cats, I mentioned Sarah Hopkins."

Sherril's smile faded. Her shoulders and new eyebrows lifted in a "beats me" begging of the issue.

Paul said, "She's the one who's parked down the street, pretending to read a newspaper."

Chapter 17

On this quiet spring night, Dwight Bailey, Connie Nickens, and Lamb Johnson found a certain sweetness in their lives. The sweetness had been gained at the expense of others' lives, but that seemed to be part of the natural order of things. Responsibility lay elsewhere, fatelike, with Chainmaster.

Dwight attached the driving weight to Paul Marnay's clock, feeling the transfer of gravity's power from his hands and forearms to the newly renovated movement. The cleansed, lubricated system engaged under the weight. A touch of the pendulum, and the wheels and levers began their slow, beautiful dance . . . a stately dance conceived during a better era . . . a time when each person knew his or her place and function in the movement. Most people didn't understand those things now. Paul Marnay, for example; he didn't care about the system that moved the hands. He cared about surfaces . . . mirrors . . . vanity. He would not have obeyed Chainmaster; would have let the chain be broken. If Dwight could choose another link in the deathchain, he would choose Paul Marnay.

Connie Nickens looked at the floor plan of the restaurant that would one day bear her name. There was a neatness in the diagram that pleased her in ways she was just beginning to understand. The pleasures she had once found in relationships with people had been random and feeble. There had been no sense of order, no design. As silly or horrible as the chain might seem to an outsider, it had authority and logic. Someone like Paul Marnay, despite his charm, was drifting from woman to woman, turning out his odd portraits, which seemed unfinished to Connie. The paintings were, like his life, undisciplined searching rather than orderly achievements. Why did Paul seem like an enemy? Connie wondered. Possibly because he had been corrupted by his advantages. Money and education had been given to him to no particular effect. He was more interested in consuming cognac than in learning the difficult methods of producing it. He was breaking the continuity; he was an enemy of an orderly society, drifting idly toward death. Connie felt a slight shiver of pleasure at the back of her neck, a sign she now recognized as pride. She was assessing and planning her life—things she had not done before receiving the letter from Chainmaster.

Lamb Johnson listened to the complex sound of the new engine as carefully as a piano tuner would listen while finishing a job for a concert pianist. But the piano tuner would not have the visual image that accompanied Lamb's work. Vibrating wire was incredibly simple compared to the hundreds of interesting valves, pistons, rods, pins, and cams that produced the surprisingly uniform sound of an automobile engine. Lamb wondered if Paul Marnay ever listened to the engine of his car; if he had ever looked at the engine to see even the grossest exterior forms of the mechanism Lamb knew in such detail. Maybe it had been a mistake to sell the car to a mechanical illiterate rather than to someone who would understand it. At the time, Lamb had acted out of a type of jealousy; he disliked the idea of selling the car to someone who, unlike Paul, would be likely to learn the personal intricacies of the car's mechanism. It had seemed in some inexplicable way like letting someone sleep with your wife. But Paul Marnay's ignorance meant he could be trusted. Now, however, that ignorance seemed offensive. Too many people live off the expertise of others, not serving as a link in the natural chain. Lamb realized now that he had sold his car to the enemy, even disregarding Marnay's unacceptable nosiness and meddling. Marnay would laugh at the idea of Chainmaster, Lamb thought, just as Freddy Stella would have laughed. And maybe that is why their fates were linked.

Paul spent the next Friday reacquainting himself with the building he lived in. If it had been the custom in Dale Falls to nail picturesque name tags to houses, in the English-cottage style, Paul's sign would have read: UTILITY. The building had formerly been a carpentry shop specializing in custom-made wood canoes that couldn't meet the price competition of aluminum and fiberglass. The shop's owner had obviously been in love with wood. The walls were paneled; the floors parqueted. Paul knew from experience that there were worse things to be in love with, and when he moved into the abandoned shop and added a bedroom, bathroom, kitchen, and skylights, he had everything trimmed in stained and varnished wood: oak, walnut, and beech. The effect was uniform and natural but not homelike. When Paul filled the main space with his collection of mirrors and with stacks of canvas stretchers, he created an area that visitors agreed was easier to work in than to relax in. The addition of some heavily upholstered chairs and a sofa in one corner didn't do much to soften the effect, but Paul wasn't too concerned about the matter anyway. Even though his work as a painter was considered frivolous by many people, it *was* work, and he needed space to do it in. Whether the space looked domestic wasn't important to him.

The reason Paul was house-tidying, (cleaning had been done the day before by a semiprofessional), was that Phyllis was going to come up from the city to spend the weekend with him. The prospect of having a houseguest, especially a lovable one, can rematerialize objects that have become invisible through familiarity or through dislike. (Where did that vase come from? Has it always been ugly and chipped?)

After a little unenthusiastic rearranging, Paul realized there are really only three important preparations to make for a guest: linen for the bed, extra towels for the bathroom, and cognac for refreshment. In the case of Phyllis, the extra bed wouldn't be a factor. Paul found a few towels and checked the cognac bottle.

The person who came in once a week to clean the studio—a dispirited young woman known as Ms. Williams—was given to furtive (and she apparently thought secret) nips at the bottle. The nips got heavy at times, but Ms. Williams always left at least an inch of the contents unconsumed. Feeling sympathy for anyone who had to clean his studio and respect for someone who found the Marnay brandy irresistible, Paul tried to be sure there was a virtually full bottle displayed on cleaning days. On the day after a cleaning, such as today, Paul put a fresh bottle next to the depleted one. But he had found the opened bottle was virtually full; mysteriously full, because Paul was certain there was more cognac in the bottle than there had been before Ms. Williams arrived. What was going on? Was she suddenly trying to cover her tracks by adding water to the bottle? Paul hoped not; theft was excusable, but adulteration wasn't. Before he could sample the cognac for purity, he was distracted by a yowl from Grace the Cat.

Grace seemed to like her new home, but Paul had panicked when faced with the astounding variety of cat foods available in the market he stopped at when bringing Grace home from Sherril's. He wondered if some local cult (former Egyptians?) was worshipping cats and was not so much feeding the creatures as making extravagant dietary offerings to them. He had arbitrarily picked out a few cans, bags, and boxes, but Grace had not shown enthusiasm for any of the contents. Now she was complaining. Paul thought a call to Sherril for advice was in order.

She was home and taking calls.

"Sher?"

"Yes, Ex."

"What does Grace like to eat?"

"It's not a matter of like. It's a matter of get."

"The market had more cat food than baby food."

"Cats are more particular than babies, and more manipulative. You must be strong. Pretend she's a wife."

Paul ignored the challenge. "Do they make generic brand cat food?"

"Yes, Paul. I remember your inclination toward the generic. Nameless peanuts with hundred-year-old brandy."

Paul allowed himself a moment of sullenness.

Sherril said, "Get kibble; dry food. Make it clear to Grace that it's kibble or nothing. If she wants meat, I assume you have a supply of small rodents around the house."

"*I* assume you're having a bad day, Sher. But why try to share unpleasantness?"

"Luke tells me you've been having pleasantness sessions in Manhattan."

Paul didn't know what Sherril was trying to say, but

he didn't like Luke being involved in it. "Thanks for the nutritional advice," he said, and hung up without asking, as he had planned, about Grace's preferred toilet facilities. He had also bought some litter at the market, but neither he nor Grace was much taken with it. He had been letting her out into the luxuriant crop of spring weeds that flourished in his tiny backyard, but that could get to be inconvenient.

Paul decided an immediate trip to the local pet emporium was called for. The only such store he knew about was in a nearby mall that terrified him with its vastness and the hair-dos of its clientele. But this was an emergency.

An hour later, Paul was back in his studio, on his knees at the kitchen door. He was surrounded by the components of an electronically activated "Pet Sesame" door and several new tools, including a lethal-looking saber saw. He wondered whether he should call his son, Luke, for help, but decided not to.

Two hours after that, his knees locked into a prayer position, his fingers smeared with blood, and his mood changing from irritation to pride, Paul was looking at a reasonably well installed cat door. Luke would be proud of him. Grace had lost interest in the project almost immediately and had wandered off to a sun-splashed chair. Now came the most important moment. To keep unauthorized creatures from using the new entrance, it could only be opened by the approach of a tiny transmitter that was mounted on a collar. The question was whether Grace would wear the collar willingly. After a suspenseful fifteen minutes, the collar and the door were accepted and proved workable. Paul felt the way he did when he completed a successful painting.

He was feeling the kind of elation that calls not for resting on one's laurels but for meeting another challenge while energy and luck are in a good alignment.

One cloud that had passed over his mind earlier took the form of Sarah Hopkins. As he had walked through the corridors of the mall, he twice thought he saw her in the distance. He wasn't positive; it could have been that he was simply beginning to imagine her presence. In any case, he knew that he would have to confront her sooner or later, and he doubted if there would be a better time than now. His success with the cat door made him feel capable of overcoming any kind of difficulty. He cleaned up the mess in the kitchen and put away his tools. If today were like most recent days, it would be easy enough to find Sarah Hopkins; he would simply have to look into nearby cars. But a walk around the neighborhood didn't turn her up, so he got into his car and drove to her house.

It was late afternoon, and the day was one of winter's leftovers. The cold wind didn't please Paul, but the flat gray light blending with the varied greens of early foliage created pleasing little vistas that offset his discomfort. By the time he reached Sarah Hopkins's house, he was in a peculiarly calm mood. He wasn't without tension, but it was distant, as if he had just awakened and was still enjoying the comforts of sleep while knowing the harsh, whiney buzz of his alarm clock would soon call him into the less comfortable world of full consciousness.

Sarah Hopkins looked as though she had been expecting a lover—one with poor taste. Her shiny eggplant purple pants suit was too formal, too young-wifey, and too flimsy to be appropriate for a home-alone evening in the autumn of life and the spring of the year.

"As I'm sure you know, I'm Paul Marnay."

"Yes. So you are. I'm Sarah Hopkins."

Sarah smiled warmly and looked into Paul's eyes in a way that made him feel welcome. But they said nothing more and she made no move to invite him in.

"I thought we should talk," Paul said. "Is this a good time?"

Sarah's smile softened into a look of pleased invitation. She stepped aside just enough to let Paul through the doorway but not enough to let him avoid brushing his arm against her breast and his hand against her hip. He was aware that their eyes were on exactly the same level, but she might have been slightly taller than he was. Her forehead was unusually high and straight.

"Sit down wherever you like. I'll get you a drink. I'm sure you need it."

Paul settled into a worn leather club chair facing the chair in which Sarah had apparently been sitting—a Scandinavian-looking rocking chair on which a large sketching pad rested. On the pad was drawn the design for the title page of a book: *Farewell, My Lovely* by Raymond Chandler. The words were penciled on the page with a delicacy that would not be matched when they were typeset and printed. There was a sureness in the sketch that could only have been gained through years of practice.

All the wall space in the room was lined with shelving, on which were casually, if not carelessly, placed a remarkable variety of books in no apparent order.

Sarah returned with two tulip-shaped glasses containing something in the spiritous beverage family. It had an admirable amber clarity, but it was too dark to be a good brandy. Paul sniffed. It was bourbon: his favorite drink next to brandy.

"It's not as fragrant as Marnay cognac, but it's more affordable. I have a friend in Kentucky."

Paul raised his glass. "To Raymond Chandler," he said. The bourbon was the best Paul had tasted. He reminded himself that this woman might not be admirable or might not wish him well. He also reminded himself that she was probably old enough to be his mother. He was not good at age guessing, but he placed her at a remarkably well preserved sixty.

"I thought you might be following me," Paul said.

Sarah produced a modest smile. "Yes. I think you're right," she said. She crossed her legs. Her height was centered in the area from the knee to the hip, not in her thickening waist.

Paul asked, *"Why* are you following me?"

Sarah took a large gulp of bourbon and kept the glass close to her mouth. "I'm attracted to you."

"You're lying."

"No. It's true."

Paul was about to tell Sarah to stop following him whatever her reason might be. But he had a sip of bourbon and said, "I'm only thirty-five years old."

"That's part of your attraction."

"I could be your son."

"Yes. But you could be other things, too."

A twinge of shame went up the back of Paul's neck. He was being drawn into a flirtation even though he knew this woman was not sincere. There was a remote glitter in her eyes that probably meant she was past needing anyone's affection; that she saw people as targets for emotions that were darker, though no less intense, than love.

"Please stop following me—whatever your reason for doing it." Sarah's smile vanished. The odd glitter he had noticed in her eyes became less remote. She's crazy, he thought. "And stay away from my house. I'll have you prosecuted if I find you trespassing."

Paul watched as Sarah decided what to say next. He wasn't sure what to expect. "You see," she said, "there was no point in your coming over here and trying to discuss it. You don't understand the situation."

"And you *do* understand it?"

"In a sense. I know what's being done, though not why or by whom. You don't know anything, Paul."

"How about Dwight Bailey, Lamb Johnson, and Connie Nickens?"

Sarah had watched Paul with an unblinking and, he concluded, an uncomprehending stare. He was sure the names meant nothing to her. If she had any connection to those people, it was not direct; it was through someone he hadn't named.

Paul stood up. He decided there was no need to say thanks for the bourbon (even though he would have liked to know how to get some). "I'll let myself out."

"I don't mean you any harm."

"It doesn't matter to me what you mean. Just stay away from me."

Paul found it difficult to be unpleasant to a woman —even a crazy, pursuing, possibly dangerous woman. He would have liked to stay to have another bourbon and learn a little about book design. As he closed the door, he felt the relief that goes with the completion of an unpleasant chore, but he also felt a little regret.

The last thing he saw in the house was the pad that lay on the floor next to Sarah Hopkins's chair: the elegantly inscribed words: *Farewell, My Lovely.*

Chapter 18

"In the end, everything comes down to mathematics and physics," Luke said. He was looking at his completed clock kit.

Paul saw no reason to remind his son of love and the grave—at least one of which the boy would eventually have an encounter with. Would he ever give himself over to the irrationality of love? It certainly hadn't happened so far in his dealings with his parents. On the other hand, Paul thought, Luke's parents hadn't been the best role models in that area. The boy might well have concluded that being polite and friendly was about as far as it was necessary to go in human relations. And he might be right, but in the meantime, Paul was still doing things in the traditional, messy, wrong way. And now it was time to explain the latest manifestation to his son.

Paul took the clock and pretended to be interested. It consisted of crudely machined aluminum and brass parts set in a transparent plastic frame. The parts ticked, meshed, swung, and nodded under the urging of a large, dangerous-looking spring.

"So this is your new friend?" Paul said. Then, with a little pride in what he thought was a clever transition, he continued, "I've got a new friend, too."

"I know." Luke didn't welcome the clever transition. He took the clock back and began to tinker with the slow/fast adjustment. "You can't regulate this very well. That's one of the great things in clock design history: the ways they worked out to compensate for the effects of even things like temperature and humidity."

"Her name is Phyllis," Paul said, hoping Luke wasn't going to end up with a Dwight-Bailey-type personality.

"I thought her name was Grace."

"Not the cat. My new woman friend. Phyllis Arno. She's an actress."

"I don't get that stuff," Luke said. He got up off the floor and began to walk around the studio, holding the clock up for reflection in the maze of mirrors.

"You don't get what? Friendship?"

"Plays and acting."

140

Paul wasn't going to admit that he had his own reservations in that area. "It's fun and games, basically."

"Are you going to marry your new friend?"

"Maybe. Live with her, definitely."

"Here?"

"I think so. For a while."

Luke had become a phantom figure, disappearing behind large, standing mirrors then reappearing either in reflection or in reality. "Do I still get to see you?"

"Sure. Don't you want to?"

"I don't know why there have to be women around."

"Are they that much different from men?"

"You know they are."

"They've spent a lot of energy in recent years showing that they're *not* different."

"Nobody believes that."

"So how are they different?"

"They talk a lot and they want to know a lot of people."

"Maybe you're judging by your mother."

"Maybe. And they're evil."

"Like your mother?"

"It's stepmothers who are evil . . . in the fairy tales."

Unfortunately, Luke was right about the fairy tales. Paul would have to leave it to Phyllis to prove Luke was wrong about real life. The conversation seemed to have ended. Men—real men—don't talk a lot. Paul added a coda: "Go look at the kitchen door, Luke."

While his son obediently but indirectly moved toward the kitchen, Paul wondered if Luke really believed that women were evil. Was Sherril evil, as she had seemed on his last visit to her? When he and Sherril first separated, Paul assumed that the fault lay with him and that Luke would be better off with his mother. But lately he had begun to wonder. There was something predatory about her reports of her dealings with her clients—not the greed and deception that was becoming more familiar among real estate developers, but a kind of delight in mass victimization. She seemed to enjoy knowing that others were being taken advantage of, whether or not she profited from their misfortunes. She was becoming a willing tool of developers in assembling their chains of victims.

"Fabulous," Luke called from the kitchen. Then he appeared, carrying the manufacturer's booklet for Grace's automatic door. "Does it work okay?"

"Of course. It was expertly installed."

"No, I mean does the cat use it?"

"She seems to. She's got a strong incentive—birds and mice. She brings them in and displays them."

Luke contorted his face in displeasure. This information didn't interest him the way it would have interested his mother. "Why don't they have this for people? Each family with a wristwatch tuned to their own frequency that would unlock and open their door?"

"They *have* got them for garage doors. Maybe it would be too easy to pick the lock on a house with some kind of frequency scanner."

"I guess. But I could use this in my tower clock. Use electronics instead of mechanical trippers with the figures."

"Speaking of clocks," Paul said a little hesitantly and guiltily, "Phyllis Arno is supposed to drop by at three o'clock."

Luke looked up at his father in alarm. "Oh, shit. Why didn't you tell me?"

"I just told you."

"What do I have to do?"

"Just say hello to her."

"And then what? Sit around and talk?"

"What's wrong with that?"

"Grown-ups talk too much. Kids like to *do* things."

It wasn't that simple, Paul thought. Part of the reason children devoted a lot of their time to games was that they wanted to avoid the tensions of formal conversation—to sidestep the difficulty of finding something interesting to say, especially to a stranger. "So you can listen to us until you get bored and then you can watch video. I brought some tapes back from the city."

"Like what?"

"Young Frankenstein and Blazing Saddles."

Luke didn't show the interest Paul knew he was feeling. The boy was devoted to the movies of Mel Brooks, especially to the sequences featuring bathroom jokes—which Luke would rewind and rerun until he had memorized every image and sound.

Paul gave his son a moment to savor the videotape prospect before saying, "But if you'd like, I can take you back to Sherril's."

Luke assumed the expression he used to get when his horses lost. He had developed a handicapping program as a computer project at school recently and had taken it as an affront every time he lost one of his theoretical bets. Although the program had broken even (which is better than most devotees do), Luke saw the program as one of his lifetime's few unqualified defeats.

The choice between meeting and not meeting Phyllis was apparently in the no-win category for Luke. Finally, he said, "I'll stay." Paul was grateful that the meeting was considered the lesser of the evils.

Phyllis arrived in a burst of energy that immediately obliterated the mild anxiety Paul and Luke had fallen into while waiting for her. She barely acknowledged her introduction to Luke, treating him as someone who knew her well enough not to require elaborate, reassuring greetings.

"I need some help," she said. "Out at the car."

She wore a military green combat outfit but still managed to look excitingly earth-motherly, at least to Paul. The trousers were tight around her hips, and the fatigue jacket was unbuttoned, revealing a white T-shirt that was tight enough and thin enough to allow a slightly too small khaki bra to show through. It was an outfit for someone who was intending to do some work but who didn't want her companion to forget about the pleasures of leisure.

Phyllis's car turned out to be a military-type light truck. "A weapons carrier," she said. "But weapons aren't what I'm carrying."

Paul, Luke, and Phyllis wrestled the cargo out of the truck and into the studio. The object they moved—about three-by-five feet across its base and three feet high—was the model of a stage set. As Paul felt himself lifting and sharing the model's weight with his son and his new friend, a sense of happiness settled over him, as if the three of them were involved in a religious ritual. When the model was placed securely on top of a workbench, Phyllis lifted off its top, revealing an assemblage of miniature, movable stage lights mounted on a network of tracks.

Up to this point, Paul thought Luke had not looked too interested in the set, which could easily be placed in the dollhouse category. But then Phyllis plugged the model into an electric outlet and produced a complicated hand-held control panel that put the lights through a sequence of changes in selection and intensity. Luke began to pay attention.

"I need someone to program this lighting sequence," Phyllis said. Still looking at the control panel, she said, "Could you do that for me, Luke?"

"Maybe," Luke said. *Program* was a magical word for him as long as it wasn't preceded by the word *television.*

Phyllis produced a sheet of paper. "I've got the sequence written down here. In the first column are the numbers of the lights. In the second are the colors—there's a little set of red, yellow, and blue tinting filters. And the third column shows the intensity, in percentages."

Luke moved hesitantly to stand next to Phyllis and to look at the paper, which she had put on the workbench. He didn't allow his body to touch hers. "What about the duration?" he asked.

"That's not automatic. You do that manually after the sequence is programmed."

"What about fades up and down?"

"That's part of the program—slow, medium, and fast." Luke studied the symbols on the paper, and Paul studied Luke. The boy had already shown a better understanding of the model's mechanics than Paul was ever likely to develop. But would Luke have any interest in how the lighting could help establish the tone and pacing of a play? Probably not. Phyllis had understood that and would ask him to help only with the mechanics and not the esthetics of the exercise.

Luke's hip was touching Phyllis's thigh now. He had either forgotten her presence or—which seemed more likely to Paul—had surrendered himself to her attractiveness. Despite her military costume, Phyllis looked more maternal to Paul than she had ever seemed before. She was playing a new role. She would set Luke at ease through the use of masculinities and then engulf him with earth-motherliness. Paul was sure that before the afternoon was over, Luke would go willingly into Phyllis's arms and let her clasp him against her breasts. A sour little wave of jealousy passed through Paul's chest; he realized that even though he would qualify for his own embraces, they would be somehow less pure and elemental than those Luke would receive.

The day was Phyllis's. She kept Luke absorbed in the miniature stage set; she produced some melted cheese and jalapeño pepper sandwiches with a choice of Dos Equus beer and lime slices or root beer and vanilla ice cream. She prowled the studio, looking at paintings and mirrors, saying just enough to make it clear that she was interested in what she saw, and stopping to confirm her interest occasionally by touching an object.

Luke finished programming the lighting a few minutes before it was time for him to go back to Sherril's. He surprised Paul by asking Phyllis, "So who decided what the sequence should be?"

"I did."

"How?"

"It's just for practice. I think an actor should know about all the things that go into a production."

"Then this sequence doesn't mean anything."

Paul didn't understand where Luke's questions were leading. The boy was facing Phyllis aggressively, almost belligerently. She said, "Lights don't mean anything in themselves. They only have meaning when they're part of a human situation. A dim light can be either romantic or scary depending on what's happening in the light or what an audience expects to happen."

Phyllis had sat down. Luke approached her. He leaned his groin against her knee and rested his hands on her thighs. Was this an innocent gesture, Paul wondered, or was Luke going to ask Phyllis to explain the facts of life? The boy was displaying an intimacy in his actions that Paul had never seen him use with his mother or with Paul himself.

146

Phyllis took Luke's hands and pulled him slightly closer to her, increasing the pressure of his body against her knee. "It's not that everything *has* to mean something; it's that everything *does* mean something. The problem is that everybody's got a different version of *what* things mean."

Luke was looking at Phyllis as if he understood what she meant. She got up and led him to the miniature set and pulled out of her fatigue-jacket pocket a tiny doll-like figure—an auburn-haired woman wearing a long green gown and holding her right arm out in an ambiguous gesture. Phyllis placed the figure in the center of the set and began to run through the lighting sequence. The expression on the doll's face seemed to change, and its gesture altered from threatening to beseeching as the lighting effects varied.

Paul was sure that Phyllis was teaching both him and Luke something. Luke's lesson seemed to be in how charming Phyllis could be, but that was something Paul already knew. His own lesson was more sinister: As he watched the tiny figure in the set, he realized how strong a need humans have to manipulate one another—not just to take advantage of another person occasionally, but to take a godlike control of and to manipulate another life as if it were a puppet.

Paul, Luke, and Phyllis stood in silence looking at the figure in the dramatically changing light. It was as if each of them were watching his or her own secret performance. To Paul, the figure resembled his ex-wife, Sherril. Her pose seemed imperious and commanding, as if she were issuing instructions; manipulating an unseen person rather than being manipulated herself. Why was this the scenario that Paul supplied? Sherril had not seemed unusually manipulative when he lived with her: She didn't try to change him. That had been the point of their separation: to avoid the destructive tensions of trying to change each other.

Paul's revery—and the model's performance—ended when Grace the Cat leaped onto the set, a monster that knocked the tiny figure to the floor. It was a satisfactory ending, although Paul couldn't tell what force Grace represented. The cat's curiosity was immediately satisfied, and she apparently found nothing of interest in the set. No reveries for her. Blinking in disdain at the set's array of lights, Grace jumped back to the floor and began brushing against Phyllis's ankles. Phyllis went to a chair and sat down. Grace immediately jumped onto her lap and curled up. Paul and Luke watched. Paul was envious and suspected that his son shared that envy.

Paul said to Phyllis, "I have to get Luke back to his other home." Phyllis looked up from Grace, whose ear she was rubbing and folding. Underplaying, as she had in her greeting, she said, "Bye, Luke. Thanks for helping me."

"Sure," Luke said, as if to a schoolmate. Then he added what Paul thought was—for Luke—an emotion-charged, "I'll see you." It sounded more like a request than an expectation.

On the drive to Sherril's, Paul said to Luke, "It's getting a little crowded in the studio these days."

"That's okay," Luke said. He was giving his approval to Phyllis and Grace. But Paul wondered whether the changes were actually for the better. If Luke became fond of Phyllis, it might set up new tensions between him and his mother. Paul always had the impression that the one-day-a-week visiting arrangement was just about right for all concerned. If Paul should marry or begin living with Phyllis, a new arrangement might have to be negotiated.

It was a misty, overcast day—the kind that heightens the green in the early foliage, making plants and bushes glow as if illuminated from within. As his car approached Sherril's house, rain began to fall, and Paul could see a disk of color moving from the house toward the curb. It was Sherril carrying a large scarlet umbrella and leading another person to a car at the curb. As Paul pulled up at the house, the other car drove away. The driver was Sarah Hopkins.

Sherril stood at the curb, her face an odd shade of red, apparently tinted both by the umbrella's reflection and by a slight, uncharacteristic blush. She said, "A new service for my extended family."

"Is Sarah Hopkins part of the family now?" Paul asked.

Sherril's blush returned. "Oh, that . . . just business. She wants an assessment on her house."

Paul let Luke out into the shelter of the umbrella.

Sherril said to Paul, "Coming in?"

"No. I've got to get back. A visitor . . . not business."

Sherril's sheepish expression began to change, but Paul didn't wait to find out what it would change to. He began to feel some sympathy for Luke, who would obviously have to answer some questions about Paul's nonbusiness visitor. Paul wondered how intense Sherril's questions would be and, especially, what kind of answers Luke would come up with. How would the boy describe Phyllis?

Paul set about concocting his own description of Phyllis as he drove back to the studio. He didn't try to verbalize the description but began to rough out a painting of her in his mind. His first decision was that he would do a full-size, full-length portrait. His next decision was not so easy. Would she be nude? He tried to keep his erotic requirements out of the decision as much as possible. Was Phyllis someone whose personality would survive in a nude portrait? Would her body dominate the way exceptionally good or bad bodies inevitably did? Probably not. She was trained to use her body expressively; its proportions were interesting but far from perfect. She had the kind of body whose total effect was more beautiful than any single feature. Perhaps what he would have to do, Paul thought, was to paint a pair of portraits, clothed and unclothed, in the manner of Goya's *Maja*.

When he reached the studio, Paul found his dilemma temporarily resolved. Phyllis's military costume was draped over the edge of a canvas, and her voice drifted in from the bathroom. Her voice was doing something he hadn't heard it do before: singing. She sounded like someone doing a creditable impression of the young Sarah Vaughan. The song was *My Kinda Love*, which has a gather-ye-rosebuds lyric. Paul was ready for a rosebud or two.

Paul called out a warning: "I'm back," and headed for the sound of Phyllis's voice. The bathroom door was open, and Phyllis stood next to the tub toweling the body Paul had been thinking of a few minutes earlier.

She said, "Is that a lecherous leer or a professional appraisal?"

"Strictly professional."

"I was afraid of that. I put on weight when I'm between jobs. Am I into the Rubens class yet?"

"You're barely—so to speak—into the paintable class. No one paints skinny nudes."

Phyllis put on a white terry cloth robe, one of Paul's, which left few hints of the form it was covering.

"You don't look pleased," Phyllis said.

"I'm pleased, but not *as* pleased."

"Was that really a professional assessment? Do you want me to pose for you now?"

"It's getting a bit late for that, I suppose. What other things do you have in mind? Food?"

"I can wait for that."

"Then why don't we set up the pose. I'll do a rough sketch."

"You know what bothers me?" Phyllis asked. She walked toward Paul and hooked her hands through the top of his belt.

"I'm afraid to ask."

"It bothers me that the painter has his clothes on and the model doesn't. It puts him at a psychological advantage."

"Isn't it the same as doing a nude scene in a play? Does the audience have a psychological advantage?"

"No. They're at a disadvantage. They're not doing anything but watching. The painter is using the model, but the actor is using the audience."

"So you want us both to be nude," Paul said.

"You guessed it," Phyllis said, and unbuckled Paul's belt. He pulled his Saturday sweatshirt over his head as Phyllis lowered his trousers and shorts in a single smooth motion. As Paul kicked off his loafers and stepped out of his garments, Phyllis knelt and pulled off his socks. Then she did some exploring with her lips and tongue.

"I'm liable to have an accident," Paul said.

"It wouldn't be an accident. It would be by design —to rid us both of a distraction."

"You make it sound like an unpleasant chore."

"Is that what it feels like?"

"Umm." Paul wasn't able to articulate any words.

Phyllis had stood up. She took the index finger of Paul's right hand. She said, "Do you want to have the accident here"—she placed his finger in her mouth for a moment—"or in here"—she lowered his finger to the dense, moist hair at the top of her thighs.

"You decide," Paul said. "But quickly."

Phyllis stepped back to the high-sided bathtub and raised her right leg and rested her foot on the tub's edge. She pulled Paul toward her, directing him awkwardly to an entry. Phyllis's contractions were immediate and grasping. Paul, in a semicrouch, responded with an instantaneous release. At the first spasms, he closed his eyes, losing his balance and falling backward, spattering his belly and the bathroom rug. When he opened his eyes, Phyllis was smiling. In a moment, they were both laughing and were on the floor in each other's arms.

"Things went awry," Phyllis said.

"As the best-planned lays often do."

They went back into the studio where Paul, reclothed, had Phyllis, still unclothed, pose on a velvet dressing stool with her back to him and her head turned to look at him over her shoulder in her characteristic sideways glance. The key light was on her back and on the shoulder away from her face. But her profile was stronger than he had expected in its contrast of deep shadows, and despite the sweeping curve of her back and the interesting flare and cleavage at the top of her hips, her face was the strong center of the composition. The pose was strenuous, and Paul worked quickly to complete a preliminary charcoal-on-canvas sketch.

Phyllis held herself motionless but without apparent tension until Paul said, "That's it for now. Do you want to see it?"

"No. I wouldn't want anyone to judge a performance of mine during rehearsal. I'll look at the painting when you think it's finished."

"And if you don't approve?"

"What's the usual procedure? What do you do when a client rejects a portrait?"

"It depends on the client and the objection. Certain kinds of changes I might make. But I usually have started with a signed agreement that says I make the final decision."

"No money back at the box office."

"No. That's what I tell a new client—that they wouldn't expect their money back if they didn't like a play or movie they saw."

"But they're not in the play or movie."

"That's what *they* usually tell *me.*"

Phyllis put on Paul's robe again. She was perched cross-legged on the dressing stool, obviously enjoying the intimacy of conversation, which Paul thought was the true cement of any love affair. It is talk, even though apparently casual, that fills in the spaces around the passion and that can eventually substitute for it if necessary. Phyllis wasn't eager to end the conversation. She said, "Has anyone ever destroyed one of your portraits?"

"Not that I know of. It's not likely to happen. It would be a little like committing suicide. Or at least tempting fate—like breaking a mirror or breaking a chain letter."

"Have you ever done that?"

"Broken a mirror?"

"Or a chain letter?"

"Several mirrors. But I've never gotten a chain letter; I've seen them—been shown them by people who wondered if they dared just throw them away."

Paul thought Phyllis looked a little unsympathetic. "I got one once," she said. "It said I might die if I ignored it. So I threw it away.

"I suppose there are two kinds of people in the world: those who throw away those letters and those who don't—the superstitious and the others."

"There are three kinds," Paul said. "Those two and the ones who start the chains—the ones who prey on the superstitious."

"And what kind of person does that? The same kind who sells amulets?"

"No. It's more sinister than that, I think. It's the

person who gets people to wear sheets with eyeholes in them."

Phyllis was either losing interest in the topic or she was feeling chilly. "Speaking of clothes, I think I'd better put some on for dinner . . . if we're having dinner."

"There are things I'd rather do—a clumsiness to make up for—but I also want you to believe I'm a civilized person. I thought I'd cook for you, unless you're losing courage and would like to eat out."

"I'm courageous."

Before Paul could outline the menu, Grace the Cat appeared. She went first to Paul and let herself be stroked. Her fur was cold and damp, exuding the smell of weeds and spring rain. Paul was surprised and grateful that the cat hadn't brought in any little corpses of mammals in the order *rodentia*. He was also surprised when Grace went unhesitatingly to Phyllis, bounded up into her lap, and curled up.

"That's Grace," Paul said.

"Hello again, Grace," Phyllis said. She raised the edges of her terry robe and toweled the cat's wet fur.

Phyllis's gesture revealed her thighs in an interesting way, and Paul decided it was time for him to get into the kitchen if they were ever to get around to dinner.

Chapter 19

The dinner was simple and successful. Paul had developed a repertoire of bachelor-type easy but elegant meals under the direction of his brother's wife, Simone, who had been raised near Lyon in a family that took food as seriously as the Marnays took cognac. Simone not only gave Paul helpful tips about kitchen behavior but offered to give him a little specialized information about bedroom behavior. Paul declined, however, thinking that he didn't want to put François's brotherly urbanity to the full test.

The central dish of Paul's meal with Phyllis was Simone's version of potatoes lyonnaise—a cheese, garlic, onion casserole with a soufflélike texture. The hors d'oeuvre was steamed clams; the entrée was sautéed veal scallops, and the vegetable was braised leeks; for dessert, fresh raspberries and cream.

In Paul's new semisobriety, he seldom bothered with predinner drinks, but of course he still served wine and a closing cognac.

Phyllis did most of the talking during dinner, going easily and articulately from one theatrical anecdote to another, confirming Paul's suspicion that the things that happened during the production of a play were often more interesting than the play itself.

Phyllis was affectionate and modest when she talked about her profession. "I don't think theater people are a special breed except in the sense that they're in a tradition that shows up everywhere and always. There haven't always been computer programmers, but there have always been theater people, the way there have been religious people."

"Or whores," Paul said.

"Or painters."

"Painters might have come first. Those cave paintings at places like Altamira and Lascaux seem miraculous to me. If there weren't so many of them, I'd think they're a deception. Apparently there were beautiful —by any standards—paintings before there was agriculture or a town. Why should that be?"

"Boredom," Phyllis said. She was apparently serious. "There wasn't all that complicated paraphernalia of civilization for distraction—commerce, writing."

"Television."

"The cave paintings—and the theater that must have gone along with them—were their TV."

"So you and I are primitive types," Paul said.

"I think we demonstrated that earlier."

"And we will again later, I hope."

"Sooner is all right with me," Phyllis said. Her face was flushed the warm red tint that she often featured in her clothes—a red that clashed with her auburn hair.

Grace the Cat, who was obviously as devoted to Phyllis as Paul was, had been flirting with her during dinner. Now Phyllis suddenly swept the cat into her arms and clasped it against her chest. Grace unsheathed her claws and dug them into Phyllis's T-shirt just above her breasts. The cat's action wasn't a display of anger, but of pleasure—the stretching, digging motion that shreds furniture and pierces skin. Phyllis closed her eyes and tightened her lips in what seemed to be pain rather than anger. A few traces of blood appeared on her shirt. She said, "You'll have to learn to control your passion, Grace." And she dropped the cat to the floor. Phyllis's color was chalky now.

"I think some restorative cognac is in order," Paul said. As he began to pour some into a glass, Grace bounded up onto the table, still excited from her little encounter with Phyllis. She collided with the almost-full cognac bottle, which slipped out of Paul's hand and spilled over the table.

Masking his irritation, Paul said to Grace, "You might as well get a little reward for improving our evening." He held the cat's head close to a bowl in which there was a half-and-half mixture of spilled cognac and cream left over from his raspberries. Grace didn't pull away, as Paul had expected, but tasted the mixture. Paul had once seen a puppy get eagerly and quickly drunk on cognac, but he somehow thought a cat would be more cautious. After the preliminary tasting, Grace began to lap the brandy up steadily.

"Is that wise?" Phyllis asked.

"It's always seemed wise to me," Paul said. "Grace has discriminating tastes."

But the cat's apparent pleasure didn't last long. She suddenly stiffened, and her coat bristled as though she were faced with a threatening dog. She turned awkwardly and jumped to the floor, her legs collapsing as she landed. For a moment, Paul tried to think of a drunk-cat joke, but it became apparent that Grace was more than drunk; she was having a seizure of some kind. "I think we'd better get her to a vet," Paul said, and went to get a blanket to pick her up with. But when he got back with the blanket, there was obviously no help for the situation. Phyllis was kneeling next to the cat and weeping. She whispered, "Grace is dead."

Paul poured some cognac from the overturned bottle into a glass and swirled it around. He put his nose close to the glass and inhaled. He had known the aroma of Marnay cognacs practically from infancy—from long before he ever tasted them. He had never encountered one with this aroma before. There was nothing obviously tainted about the smell, and most people would not have noticed anything unusual in it. But to Paul, it was like entering a house that had a new carpet in one of its smaller rooms; the house's defining scent had been altered.

"I think this bottle is for analyzing, not drinking," he said.

"Never mind that," Phyllis said. It was the first time Paul had heard her speak in anger. Her voice was grating and pitched lower than he would have thought possible. "What about Grace?" she asked.

"What *about* her? She's dead. But I do think I should have an autopsy done."

"You'd like to *what?*"

"Get an autopsy."

"How could you do that? *Why* would you do it?"

"We should find out what killed her. *We* might have been the ones to die."

Phyllis's expression was the one that a new lover who is less than totally secure dreads to see—the expression that indicates a veil has been lifted. It could mean either, "the person I love is not exactly the person I thought he was" or "I don't love this person after all." But Paul had no doubt about his love for Phyllis. She was sitting cross-legged on the floor now, stroking Grace's body, which lay in her lap as if sleeping. The blood stains from Grace's clawing had become more noticeable on Phyllis's shirt. Paul thought: She forgave Grace, she'll forgive me. He said, "We'll wrap her in the blanket and bury her in the backyard now. Then you should probably go back to the city."

"First, the burial, then make love to me. I want to stay here tonight."

Paul was pleased that Phyllis chose to stay with him, but he knew that in the morning he would resent her presence. There were several things he wanted to do that she would probably not approve of or would keep him from doing. Then he decided it would be better not to anticipate things but to take them one at a time.

The first thing was one of those practical considerations that complicate existence but keep it anchored in reality: Paul didn't have a spade or anything like one that he could dig a grave with. He said to Phyllis, "Does that weapons carrier of yours have any tools in it? A spade or shovel?"

"Nothing like that. It has some things to change tires and wheels with—wrenches and a jack."

"We can buy one. There's a never-closed, everything-imaginable store about a mile from here."

"Everything imaginable?"

"Just about."

"Pets?"

"No." It hadn't occurred to Paul that he would ever want to own another pet. His first attempt in the area hadn't been exactly successful.

"I think we should get another cat right away."

There was one logical source for a replacement: Sherril, the source that had supplied Grace. And Paul could also borrow a spade from Sherril, who did some occasional defensive gardening—not out of a fondness for flora but to keep the weeds from taking over.

"I'll be back in a few minutes," Paul said. He took the cat's body from Phyllis's lap. He raised Phyllis to her feet and kissed her reddened eyelids. "Will you be all right? Would you rather come with me?"

"No. I'll straighten things up here."

Paul went to the dinner table and took the cognac

bottle and the bowl that Grace had drunk from. He put them in a cupboard in the kitchen. "If you feel like a drink—of anything at all—don't get it from an unsealed container."

Paul drove Phyllis's weapons carrier to Sherril's. He thought there was less chance that anyone might have tinkered with it, and in any case, he felt more comfortable driving an army truck than a sports car. They were both pretentious, but people were more likely to respect the truck—to give it the right-of-way. Paul needed a little respect at the moment. As he drove, he tried to reach some preliminary conclusions and to work out a plan of action.

He would start by having some tests made to verify his assumption that someone had put a powerful poison in one (or more) of his bottles of cognac. He thought he remembered that there was a government office of toxicology that could probably tell him where to have the tests made.

Next, he would go to the police and insist that they at least listen to his suspicions. But what were his suspicions? One was more like a certainty: that Sarah Hopkins was responsible for the attempted poisoning. But could he convince the police of that certainty? Could he get them to look for her fingerprints on the bottle or in his studio? It would depend partly on his own persuasiveness in describing his suspicions about the poisoning and about the other recent deaths. And another important factor would be the personality and experience of the person he spoke to at the police department. He didn't feel confident about his chances in either respect.

When Paul got to his ex-wife's house, he was greeted by his son, who was holding an elaborately detailed diagram of what Paul assumed was the works of the tower clock Luke was planning.

"You couldn't wait to see my commendable clock,

could you?" Luke said. As always, he looked pleased to see his father.

"You guessed it. That and to check up on your mother. Is she here?"

"No . . . the sitter."

Sherril thought children should not be left alone in the house until they were fourteen. But Luke's independent spirit and precocity in the past year had been unacceptable to the string of "child-minders" Sherril had tried out. Most of the minders had been young women who were less competent and more frivolous than Luke in almost every respect, and the minders—after a single evening of a never-described minding experience—were either not asked back or refused if asked. Finally, Beverly Chapman was discovered. Beverly, at sixteen, wore starched dresses and looked as if she would spend most of her life resenting the process of menstruation. Before that process attacked her, Beverly's life had apparently been a lot like Luke's, and she seemed to see in him now—with great respect and envy—her own lost youth and innocence.

Paul took the time to look at and praise Luke's drawing. The clock, which was to be located on top of a tower, would be viewable either from the ground or from a circular platform above it. The theme of the clock was "Great Murders of History." Above the clock face was a life-size figure of Justice holding a balance scale in its left hand and a sword in its right. At each hour, figures would appear to reenact a famous murder of history. Each hour featured a different murder, and each was concluded by the smiting of the murderer by the sword of Justice (one smite for each hour). At noon, all twelve of the murders would be presented consecutively. Luke was still trying to decide which murders would be included. So far he had picked Cain and Abel, Oedipus, Julius Caesar, Lucrezia Borgia, Jack the Ripper,

Lizzie Borden, and Charles Manson. His ultimate choices, however, would depend on practical mechanical matters rather than a representative coverage of historical periods and methods. But there was no shortage of material to choose from. Murder had always been a popular activity and subject of literature and drama.

Beverly, her arms folded over her large bosom, said, "What's most impressive, Mr. Marnay, is that this isn't just a random plan. It's all related to an actual mechanical system . . . ratios and movements worked out on a computer at school."

Paul, doing his best to overcome his difficulty in keeping his mind on the plan, offered up some genuine praise before saying, "I have to borrow a spade and a cat."

Luke said, with amazing perceptiveness, "Grace died."

"Yes. I suppose it's elementary, Holmes."

"It is, but I don't think Holmes actually used those words to Watson." Luke had begun reading Conan Doyle.

Beverly said, "It's like 'Come up and see me sometime.' Mae West didn't exactly say that."

Luke obviously didn't know—and didn't want to know—who Mae West was. "Did she get run over?"

"Mae West?" Beverly said.

"No. Grace."

"Who's Grace?"

Paul said, "A cat." He started for the basement, sidestepping the question of how Grace had died. Paul found a rusty garden spade he had seldom used but had often admired for its strength and elegant design.

The next chore wasn't as simple. He cautiously opened the door to what Sherril referred to as the cat room (which Paul usually called—to no one's amusement—the cat house). He was greeted by an unpleasant aroma and by a few yowls. A night-light in a baseboard outlet gave the room an illumination that was the visual equivalent of its aroma. There were still several cats from the same litter as Grace, and Paul took the one that most closely resembled her. Paul assumed the new cat was a she but didn't take the time to look, because the new cat didn't seem too pleased to leave the room and was struggling violently to get free of Paul's grip.

A spade in one hand and a cat in the other, Paul said to Luke, "Tell Sherril I'll return the spade but not the cat—unless she wants me to."

"Shall I tell her Grace got run over?"

"Okay." Paul wondered whether Luke had noticed his evasiveness and was thinking his father had accidentally killed Grace but was ashamed to admit it. No one wants to admit to having taken a life. The percentage of murderers who plead guilty doesn't seem to be high.

Paul thought it would be best to leave the new cat in the truck until he and Phyllis finished burying Grace. Because the ground in the yard was stony, and because he wanted the grave to be of more than just minimal size, it took Paul half an hour to finish digging. He removed Grace's transmitter collar, wrapped her body in the blanket, and placed it carefully at the bottom of the grave as Phyllis watched. He asked her, "Do you want to say anything?"

"No. Not out loud. Let's just stand for a minute."

They stood, and Paul wondered what Phyllis was thinking. It was more like five minutes before she walked away and Paul began filling in the grave. As he worked, he thought of the other graves that had been filled recently—graves that might ultimately have been made necessary by the same chain of lethal actions that had made Grace's necessary.

After filling the grave, Paul brought the new cat in

from the truck. He put the collar on the cat, who upon examination turned out to require a masculine name. Phyllis thought "Tom" would do. Tom tried for a couple of minutes to pull his collar off and came close enough to being successful to make Paul tighten the collar another notch. Then he introduced Tom to the pet door and the outside world. Before Tom pushed his way through the door, he looked back at Paul with what might have been a good-bye-forever glance. If they did see Tom again, Paul thought, it wouldn't be until morning.

Back in the studio, Paul turned on the lights of the miniature set, together with a low-level random selection of the studio's lights, which were mounted on three tracks running the length of the room. Islands of light reflected confusingly in the thicket of mirrors.

Paul sat next to Phyllis on the sofa and took her hand. There was no longer any possibility of passion for him. Even the act of simple consciousness seemed beyond him. He raised Phyllis's hand and pressed his lips to it. She said, "Sleep now, my sweet." She moved to the end of the sofa. "Rest your head in my lap."

Paul pulled his shoes off and stretched out on his side, his head cradled against Phyllis's thigh and belly, where Grace had rested earlier in the evening. In the moments before he slept, he said to himself, as in a childhood prayer, "Bless you, Grace. Who will protect us now?"

When Paul awakened the next morning, Phyllis was gone and Tom had returned. Paul would have preferred to have it the other way around, but Phyllis's absence at least gave him more flexibility in arranging his agenda for the day.

As if to announce death as the day's theme, Tom had deposited the bodies of two pathetic mice next to the pet's door in the kitchen. Wondering how he might teach Tom to leave his presents on the other side of the door, Paul put some food and milk down for the cat and tried to suppress unpleasant associations. The suppression was good practice, Paul told himself; no one can get through life comfortably without the ability to eliminate quickly and efficiently the memory of unacceptable experiences. Paul suspected he would soon have a few more experiences in that category.

Sarah Hopkins was accustomed to doing things efficiently and accurately. She had been meticulously careful in placing the poison in Paul Marnay's apartment. No one could have seen her enter or leave, and he couldn't have known that she had tampered with his cognac. Chainmaster had supplied the poison and had assured Sarah that it would not be detected. The substance was supposed to produce a coronary thrombosis—not mock it, but produce it. An autopsy would reveal the heart failure, and the chemical could be detected only by elaborate spectrographic procedures that weren't available in Dale Falls and would be requested only when there was no obvious and commonly encountered cause of death.

Therefore, when she found the note from Paul in her mailbox, she felt an unaccustomed panic. There was a frightening congestion in her chest—the feeling that a small but powerful creature was trapped in her chest and was fighting to free itself. She put her fingers against her inner wrist and felt an unmistakable irregularity in her pulse. Was she, in a ludicrous irony, about to have a heart attack? She went to her bed and lay still until her pulse became regular. Then she tentatively read the note again:

Ms. Hopkins:
Your murderous attempt succeeded only in

taking the life of an inquisitive cat. There's no point in trying again to kill me. There would be more point in being concerned with the obviously loose hold you have on sanity.

I know what you've done, but not why. I don't need to know why, though, do I? You probably don't know that yourself.

Get help,
Paul Marnay

Sarah had failed Chainmaster. How could it have happened? There had been an aura of infallibility and certainty around the scheme. Chainmaster had sent a key that worked perfectly in the lock to Marnay's studio. Sarah entered on a day when she was sure he had gone to New York City. She knew of his devotion to cognac, and she knew that if she found an opened bottle in his studio, his early death was virtually certain. Her concern was with how she would arrange things if she didn't find an open bottle; she knew that expensive cognacs were usually bottled with elaborate seals. She was lucky, though. There was a newly opened bottle on a small oak cabinet that obviously served as a bar. Sarah removed the bottle's cork and broke the ampoule of liquid, marked "quinidine," into the brandy. She shook the bottle and sniffed the mouth of the bottle. She could detect nothing odd about the aroma—just the rich, complicated fumes that seemed to penetrate every cavity of her skull. It was an aroma she had always disliked because it seemed medicinal beneath its surface glamour.

The placing of the poison had not excited Sarah, but as she looked around Paul's studio, she had felt a pleasantly illicit emotion rise in her chest. She could understand how certain burglars might be motivated not so much by the hope of finding valuable objects as by the excitement of being alone in another person's home. Sarah had wandered through the studio, touching and caressing objects at random. She had worn disposable plastic gloves to avoid leaving fingerprints, but she soon decided that such precautions were unnecessary. She removed the gloves and let her fingertips run lightly—too quickly and lightly to leave prints—over surfaces. She touched rough, bare canvas and the fine bristles of brushes. In Paul's bedroom, she touched his clothes—the nylon of his odd, pantylike underwear. In the bathroom, her excitement reached a peak, and she felt a strong urge to urinate. She resisted the impulse. In just such a situation, she thought, would Paul be likely to return unexpectedly. But her need was uncontrollable. As she relieved her urge, she also relieved her odd general sense of tension.

Then she left immediately, wondering if Paul Marnay would sense that she had been there—if he would somehow sense the vague traces of her presence that were scattered through the apartment. But apparently that hadn't been the case. The note she received from Paul Marnay implied that it had simply been a cat's curiosity that had spoiled her plan—a random event; simple bad luck. Sarah wondered if it had been a black cat.

But it was silly to think about that. Her immediate concern was with this devilish Chainmaster. Sarah wished she could talk the situation over, but she had to satisfy herself with writing—slowly and uncomfortably—another letter. It took several drafts to complete the letter, which was an apology in its early versions but ended up being a simple statement of fact.

Chainmaster:
    My attempt to take the life of Paul Marnay has failed—apparently not through any fault of mine,

but as a result of the stupid curiosity of Marnay's cat. (The cat, at least, is dead.)

Marnay knows about the attempt, and I think you should find someone else for the assignment. I am going to forget I was ever involved in the mess. Of course, I won't reveal any of this to anyone else. Your secret is safe. No one can connect me with you or with an attempt on Marnay's life.

Sarah Hopkins

Sarah hoped the optimistic concluding sentence was accurate. But her greatest regret was not her failure or any danger to herself but that now Chainmaster would not assign anyone to kill Arthur Merrill. It was Sarah's desire for Arthur's death that had drawn her into this idiotic situation—that had made her abandon all rational standards and behave like a superstitious fool. She realized now that what she should have done was to use the poison not on Paul Marnay but on Arthur. The chain letter had seemed like a message from a higher power—something more than simple coincidence. It had seemed to offer immunity and absolution—invulnerability. But it was only a game of chance, and Sarah had never had the unseeing faith, the devotion to fantasy, that a gambler must have.

After mailing her letter to Chainmaster, Sarah sat in her kitchen for two days while a debilitating, irresistible depression enveloped her mind and body. Twice, she went into the bathroom to relieve a growing pressure on her bladder, but the attempt made her remember the visit to Paul Marnay's studio, and the memory was paralyzing. She returned to the kitchen, where the evening's growing darkness paralleled the darkness that was breeding in her mind.

* * *

Although Lamb Johnson was aware that some changes were taking place in his attitudes, he had not tried to characterize those changes. If someone had suggested that he was becoming less certain of the distinction between right and wrong and was less contemptuous of people who spoke seriously of love, he would have denied it. But the suggestion would have returned to his mind in those increasingly common moments when he was not thinking about the design of his new car. He had begun test-driving the car, and he found that instead of listening for signs of stress in the engine or suspension, he was recalling voices of customers. Instead of watching the instrument panel, he would stare at the horizon and bring to mind images like tiny clips from a film: the way a young woman's hair framed her cheek; the uncertain walk of a child.

But most often he thought of Paul Marnay, who was driving into the station more often than was necessary —carelessly driving the car to which Lamb had given months of his life in planning and construction. It was as if Marnay were taunting him; letting his big-city actress drive the car. Yet the woman looked good in it. The white skin of her body was like the white paint of the car's body. Her reddish brown hair was like the leather of the seats. And she drove with more appreciation of the car's response than Marnay did. It was plain that Marnay was more interested in her than in the car, and such a thing seemed wrong to Lamb. Then there was Marnay's son, Luke, who seemed to like and be liked by his father. But the virtues of the child should not be visited on the parent.

Things were not always what they seemed, but it was safest to assume the worst. Lamb assumed that Marnay was his enemy. Things did not always work efficiently, but it was necessary to keep working on them until they worked as they should. The fact was that Paul Marnay should be dead. Chainmaster had promised. Was Chainmaster just another incompetent person? It was time to write another letter:

Dear Chainmaster:
I did as you asked. I did it quick and I did it right. Now what about Marnay? He stops by to smile at me, and I can tell that he'd make me suffer if he could.
Have you ever seen a chain break? A real chain under pressure, pulling too much of a load? It whips around like a force of nature. It'll take off the head of anyone close.
Is the chain going to break?

R. B. Johnson

Lamb received his reply quickly:

Mr. Johnson:
The chain will not break. I will personally strengthen it by eliminating the weak link.

Chainmaster

Sarah Hopkins did not receive an answer to her letter. Instead, she received a visitor. Her final visitor.

Chapter 20

The margins of Paul Marnay's life were wider than those of most people. He stayed busy but seldom felt stress. There was time for a leisurely meal, a conversation, a drink, or an affectionate encounter. His portrait assignments seldom had firm deadlines, and each established its own pace. But Paul realized now that if he wanted to preserve his life, he must enjoy it less for a while. His first sacrifice began with a phone call to Phyllis Arno. He let the phone ring more than the usual six times. When Phyllis answered, her voice was sleep-dulled, as he had expected: "Yes?"

"Sorry to wake you."

"I'm sorry you couldn't have done it in person . . . without words."

Paul paused and allowed his imagination to produce the image of such an awakening. Phyllis was not making this easy. "How are you feeling?" she said. "Safe and sane?"

"Safe, anyway. Or I think I am. But if I were sane, I probably wouldn't tell you what I called to tell you, which is that I think I shouldn't see you for a while."

"How long is a while?"

"I'm not sure. I'm going to talk to the police and then, with or without their help, I'm going to try to clear up some of the recent odd events. It could take days or weeks."

"Not weeks, Paul. You have to see me—long enough for both love and talk—at least once a week. At least that."

"I suppose that's reasonable."

Phyllis responded in a Mae West voice: "Reason has nothing to do with it, Big Boy."

Paul tried unsuccessfully to be amused. "I just don't want to put you in harm's way."

"There are all kinds of harm—like the harm it would do if you would forget about me."

"That's not a possibility."

"And besides, you might need someone to do some acting for you. I'm not known in Dale Falls, and I like to improvise roles."

"I'll have my agent call your agent," Paul said. He meant to ignore the offer, but as he spoke, he realized that Phyllis might indeed be able to help him. He wouldn't rule the offer out entirely.

"I want you to call me, Paul. Frequently." Phyllis then proceeded to demonstrate some of the possibilities the telephone offered for closeness.

Later, before hanging up the phone, Paul said, "I'll try to call you every day." But he wasn't convinced that was the best idea. Phyllis had already diverted him enough to make him forget his plans for the morning. It took him five minutes to remember that he was going to visit either the police station or the house of his cleaning woman, Ms. Williams. And it was another ten minutes before he could convince himself that it was still necessary.

But eventually he found himself at police headquarters. "Is Ray here?" Paul asked a young woman he assumed was the desk sergeant. She had the required three stripes on the arm of her shirt, but not, as he would have expected, the look of a bored veteran. She looked like someone out of a television commercial, not out of a Hammett or Chandler novel.

"Lieutenant Ray? No, he isn't here. Maybe I can help you."

Two mysteries were solved: Ray was a lieutenant and a he.

"When will he be here?"

"What does it have to do with?"

"It's confidential. Something I spoke to him about recently."

The sergeant ran a forefinger across her long, delicately painted mouth and stared at Paul. "I'll get him for you."

"I thought you said he wasn't here."

"I lied."

"You lied?"

"The first thing we learn at police academy is that everybody lies. Including you, I suppose, Mr. . . . who?"

"Marnay."

The sergeant began typing on a computer keyboard. "Marnay comma Paul," she said.

"You already knew my name."

"Mmmm."

"Then why did you ask?"

"Just to see if you'd lie."

"Wasn't that dishonest?"

"Everyone's dishonest." The sergeant didn't look up. "I have to record the purpose of your visit."

"I think someone tried to kill me."

The sergeant glanced up quickly at Paul as if she were violating regulations. Then she looked back at her keyboard. "Do you have this kind of experience very often?"

"Doesn't everyone?"

The sergeant picked up a phone, pushed three buttons, and said, "Paul Marnay is here to see you." She hung up and said, without conviction, "He'll be out . . . in a while." Paul sat down in a green plastic chair that had been molded to fit a body considerably unlike his own. He got up and went to a bulletin board that was decorated with pictures and descriptions of criminals. The people definitely looked like criminals. Show anyone any of the photos, and the first word that would come to mind would be *criminal*. Mostly it was because the pictures were police mug shots or action shots from bank-robbery-in-progress films. But there were shots of missing children, who also looked like criminals. It was context, Paul supposed. If you put a photograph of Mother Teresa on that board, she'd look evil.

"See anyone you know?"

The voice behind Paul was familiar. It took Paul a moment to realize it belonged to Hillary Brock. "Not really," Paul said. "They all look like social workers to me." Then he turned. Hillary was standing close— almost touching him. He felt a wave of the peculiar embarrassment that ex-lovers often experience. He asked, "Here professionally?"

"Mmm. Consultation about a backsliding client."

Hillary wasn't trying to ease Paul's embarrassment by treating him as a casual acquaintance. She continued to move too close as he backed himself against the bulletin board. She wasn't using her social smile but looked frankly passionate. "I miss you, Paul," she whispered. "You miss me, too. I know you do."

Paul looked over at the desk sergeant, who was now giving him her full attention. He got his eyes back into close-distance focus for Hillary. He said, too loudly, "Fine. I'm fine. Things have been a little hectic. Doing a couple of portraits in Manhattan." He moved sideways, feeling cowardly, and putting about four feet of space between him and Hillary. She stopped her pursuit; the casual smile appeared.

"Just joking," she whispered. Then she said, at a normal level, "You're okay? I hear your cat died."

Where would she have heard that? Paul wondered. If she knew that, she probably knew how the cat died. Paul didn't think anyone but Phyllis could have known about the poisoning. But maybe Hillary had talked to Phyllis. Or maybe Phyllis had mentioned it to someone else. Maybe the police already knew about it. "I didn't think you even knew I had a cat," Paul said. Then he remembered that Hillary was intensely allergic to cats; another of those things ex-lovers know, and another thing that made him seem unaccountably embarrassed.

Hillary also looked as if she felt abashed, as if she had broken a confidence. "This is a small town," she said. "Small but busy. I'm afraid I'm late for an appointment at the hospital. Let's have a drink sometime. The three of us."

As she turned to walk away, her smile was replaced by an expression that would have been appropriate for a graveside. Paul's embarrassment changed to guilt. He watched Hillary until she was out of sight. He had never seen anyone move more beautifully; she had the elegance of a ballerina but without the sexless narcissism.

"Marnay?"

Paul turned to discover someone who had another, more unusual kind of elegance—a man who had exactly the gaunt, dissolute, film-noir face that Paul had hoped to see in an investigator but who was dressed immaculately.

"I'm Nick Ray."

Ray's voice, as Paul remembered now from their brief phone conversation, was all wrong. It was high-pitched and fluty enough to belong to someone who specialized in singing early Renaissance music. Paul was surprised that Nick Ray was a lieutenant. Was the public really willing to put its trust and safety in the hands of a countertenor?

Paul said, "I'd like to talk to you if you've got a few minutes."

"Okay."

"In private, if possible."

"Okay again. Follow me," the lieutenant said, and moved off in a peculiarly formal slouch that reinforced his air of elegance. He led Paul to a small, neat office and closed the door behind them. There were no file folders or loose papers on Ray's desk, and Paul wondered whether computerization or excessive neatness accounted for the bareness.

The two men sat down and looked at each other. Paul thought: We're wondering what kind of trouble we'll bring each other.

Lieutenant Ray spoke first: "Harry Dean Stanton."

"What's that?"

"If I look familiar, it's because you've seen a movie with Harry Dean Stanton in it. I remind people of him. I like to get that out of the way."

Paul was sure he hadn't seen Stanton. He would not have forgotten that kind of dark, emaciated, haunted expression. He was also sure Stanton didn't *sound* like Ray; audiences wouldn't accept him. It would be like watching *The Maltese Falcon* with Bogart's dialogue dubbed in by Truman Capote.

"So what can I do for you?" Ray asked.

"Someone tried to kill me."

Ray's expression of polite, skeptical attention didn't alter at Paul's statement. Did the police already know about the poisoning? Is that where Hillary found out? Paul said, "But maybe this isn't news to you."

"Why do you say that?"

"Hillary Brock knew. As she says, this is a small town."

Ray said, "I want to hear about it from you. Who, how, and when?"

"I'm not certain, but the who might have been a local resident named Sarah Hopkins; the how was definitely poison; the when was last night."

"Why would Sarah Hopkins try to kill you?"

"I don't know. But she's been following me."

"Are there other people who spy on you?"

"No. Never. I'm not paranoid, if that's what you're implying. And if you're wondering how I know Hillary Brock, I was a friend of hers—not a patient."

"You say you *were* friends. Past tense."

Paul resented the lieutenant's prying. Or could it be that Ray thought Hillary might have become Paul's mortal enemy. "We're acquaintances now, not enemies. I still like Hillary; I just found someone I like better."

"Someone less controlling, maybe?"

"That's not what I came to see you about."

The lieutenant said, with a look of vague amusement, "So what is it you want me to do?"

"Could you get me an analysis of this?" Paul produced a small bottle that contained some of the tainted cognac.

"You want me to do a urinalysis for you?" Ray asked. His expression changed to an unbelieving smile.

Paul blushed. "It's not urine; it's cognac. It's what poisoned my cat."

"You've got a cat with a drinking problem?"

Paul suppressed an urge to get up and walk out. But he reminded himself that the police had to be skeptical. And he obviously hadn't presented his information clearly. So he started again and gave Nick Ray a calm, logical summary of how he had been followed by Sarah Hopkins; how he thought there might have been some tampering with the cognac bottle, and how the cat had died.

Lieutenant Ray listened without comment, making

a few notes in a small notebook. When Paul was finished with his story, the lieutenant closed the notebook and put it in an inner jacket pocket. "What would you like me to do?"

"As I said before, you could find out what kind of poison was used. And that might lead you to whoever bought it and put it in the bottle. I've also got the bottle; you could check it for fingerprints. You could interview Sarah Hopkins."

"You're asking me to do a lot of work for what I would have to classify on my report as an animal poisoning."

Paul's patience ran out. He reached into his pocket and pulled out a sheet of paper he had brought along to show the police if they should seem interested in his report. Now, because of Ray's indifference, Paul thought the document might help create some interest. It was Paul's table summarizing his suspicions about the Dale Falls murders. He had added his own and Sarah Hopkins's names to the list, which now read:

THE DALE FALLS MYSTERY

<u>Victim</u>: Edna Denning (pigeon lady)
<u>How Died</u>: Pushed (?) into river
<u>Suspect</u>: Dwight Bailey (clock repairer); seen by
   Luke at time and place of death
<u>Motive</u>: ?

<u>Victim</u>: Angela Bailey
<u>How Died</u>: Pushed from hospital window
<u>Suspect</u>: Connie Nickens was near scene of death
<u>Motive</u>: ?

<u>Victim</u>: Freddy Stella
<u>How Died</u>: Car crash

<u>Suspect</u>: Lamb Johnson had ability
<u>Motive</u>: ?

<u>Victim</u>: Franklin Johnson (Lamb's father)
<u>How Died</u>: Heart attack (how induced?)
<u>Suspect</u>: Lamb Johnson might have motive; did he
   have opportunity or means?
<u>Motive</u>: Inheritance

<u>Victim</u>: Paul Marnay (intended)
<u>How Died</u>: Poison
<u>Suspect</u>: Sarah Hopkins
<u>Motive</u>: ?

As soon as Lieutenant Ray took the sheet of paper and began to read it, Paul realized he had made a major blunder. The summary would only convince Ray—who didn't seem to need much convincing—that Paul was some kind of lunatic.

As Ray studied the chart, Paul tried unsuccessfully to think of something to say about it. Then he simply waited for Ray to return it so that he could leave—if he would be allowed to leave. Maybe Ray would hold him for psychological evaluation.

Finally, the lieutenant looked up from the paper, but he didn't speak.

Paul said, "That's . . ."

"I know what it is," Ray said. "It's a lot like one I made. But it's a little better than mine." He stood up. "Let's go and see Sarah Hopkins."

Paul rode to the Hopkins house with Nick Ray in an undesignated police car. To Paul's relief, Ray didn't speak during the short trip. Paul supposed a person with an odd voice would tend to use it only when it was unavoidable.

There was no answer when Ray rang Sarah's doorbell and knocked noisily on the door.

"Her car's here," Paul said. "She must be around."

"Is she a jogger, do you know?"

"She might be. She's in good shape."

The lieutenant went to a window and peered in. It was the same window Luke had looked through recently. Ray went back to the door and turned the handle. The door opened, and he went in. Paul followed, asking, "Are we doing something illegal?"

Ray ignored him and produced a thin but piercing shout: "Anybody here? Ms. Hopkins?" There was still no answer. Nick looked around the room, and as he did so, put on a pair of thin plastic gloves he had carried in his pocket. "The electric clock isn't going," he said.

It indicated 9:30. According to Paul's watch, the current time was 10:15. The stopped clock wasn't the kind of visual detail Paul had trained himself to see. One detail he did notice was a peculiar odor that indicated something had burned. He couldn't tell what had burned; electrical insulation, perhaps.

Paul followed Nick Ray through the house and listened to the officer's occasional remarks, which were in the talking-to-yourself category. In the kitchen, Ray said, "Had breakfast; didn't wash dishes; two juice glasses." In the bedroom, he said, "Bed made."

There wasn't room for two people to stand comfortably in the bathroom, so when Ray went in, Paul waited outside. Nick was in the room longer than Paul expected him to be and didn't have any comments until he backed out into the hallway. "There's a dead woman in the bathtub. Electrocuted, I think. Go in there and don't touch anything. Just tell me if you recognize the woman."

Paul hesitated, then swallowed hard and looked

into the bathroom as the lieutenant stepped aside. Paul didn't have to enter the room. Despite the dim light—for which he was grateful—there was no doubt that the person who was slumped awkwardly in the tub was Sarah Hopkins. Her eyes, which were stretched open unnaturally, seemed to be focused on an electric cord that extended into the tub from an outlet near the washbasin. The knees of her long legs jutted stiffly out of the tub. Her expression was a hysterical grimace that might have been either terror or amusement.

With his training at collecting as much information as possible in a glance at a face, Paul had no need or desire to take a second glance. "That's Sarah Hopkins," he said, and walked out of the house and sat on the front steps. He thought of the scores of mystery novels he had read; the bodies seen as pieces in a puzzle; as incentives rather than impediments to thought and deduction.

Nick Ray followed Paul outside and went to the two-way radio in his patrol car and called to request that a homicide team and the coroner be sent.

"Homicide?" Paul asked.

"Oh, I think so, don't you?"

"I guess I haven't been thinking."

"No one ever uses a hair dryer while sitting in a tub full of water. Especially when she hasn't washed her hair."

"The dryer couldn't have just slipped in?"

"And turned itself on? Not likely. And she was a showerer anyway. Her collection of lotions weren't bath oils; they were the after-shower type. There's a shower cap on a hook. Somebody got here before we did and got her to take a bath."

"Couldn't it have been someone who spent the night with her?"

"No. There'd be some sign: night clothes, a tooth-brush."

Paul was beginning to think Nick Ray was not only a poorly organized investigator but a demented one. Was this silly theory based on anything but superficial observation and a hunch? It was ridiculous, and even though its silliness took some of the grisliness out of the situation by removing it from reality, the theory had to be challenged. Paul said vehemently, "How do you quick-talk someone into taking a bath—even someone who prefers to take baths?"

"You don't talk them into it. You make them do it when they're unconscious."

"What's this speculation based on?"

"The victim's clothes."

"I didn't see any clothes."

"You were distracted." The lieutenant began talking at a remarkably fast tempo—one that seemed appropriate for his voice. "The victim's clothes were in a pile on the bathroom floor. Underwear, panty hose, a pullover sweater, a skirt, and shoes." Ray had closed his eyes as he named the garments; he was obviously consulting some kind of photographic memory. He continued: "But there was no robe or slippers. Nobody does that. Nobody walks into the bathroom fully clothed and shod to take a bath without a robe or slippers or at least a change of underthings."

"People don't always do the logical or common-place thing, do they?"

"It depends on the thing. In this case, the range of variation is very narrow."

"So what happened?"

"A second party made the victim unconscious—probably with a quick-acting chemical, a capsule or injection—undressed her, put her in the tub, and threw the plugged-in hair dryer in with her. I'll have the coroner check carefully for disabling chemicals and a needle mark."

Paul was more skeptical than ever. There had been a certain logic in Ray's theory about bathing procedures, but the assumptions about injections and pills seemed completely unfounded. It seemed best not to argue, however, but to go on to a more difficult question: "So who did it and why?"

"Someone Hopkins knew and trusted. There's no indication of a struggle. Someone who could say, 'Here, take this.'"

"And who might that be?"

"We'll find out. Hopkins didn't know that many people here."

"She probably knew quite a few in New York City."

The lieutenant ignored the comment. He walked out of the bathroom and into a room he had only glanced into earlier. It was a home office and den containing a large desk and two file cabinets. Nick went to the desk and flipped quickly at random through a card file of phone numbers and addresses. "Business; names with firms and occupations," he said. He picked up a small, pocket-size address book. "Personal. Long-time friends; phone numbers and addresses updated over the years . . . personal services: dentists, doctors . . . a real estate agent named Stone—Sherril Stone. Isn't that someone you know, Paul?"

It was a rhetorical question, but one that couldn't go unanswered. "That's my ex-wife. She knows everyone who owns—or wants to own—property in Dale Falls."

"And everyone who dies an accidental death in Dale Falls."

It was a moment before Paul realized he was holding his breath. Was Nick Ray implying that Sherril had something to do with the murders? Or did he mean that Sherril might have been in collusion with Paul in some way? "What do you mean?" Paul asked.

"Nothing. No meaning. Just a random fact . . . one of many."

"I'd like to talk to you about this one."

But before the lieutenant could answer, some police officers arrived. Ray gave instructions to the new arrivals and then said to Paul, "Go home and wait for me."

One of the officers who had just entered the house came back out, holding, by the corners, several sheets of what appeared to be business correspondence. The officer said to Lieutenant Ray, "These were on the table next to the entrance."

The lieutenant read the top two sheets quickly. As he read, his somewhat complacent expression was replaced by a look that Paul interpreted as anger and humiliation. He looked up at Paul and said, "I thought I told you to go home." Ray looked at an officer—a young woman—who was standing nearby, watching the proceedings with interest and possibly with amusement. "Make yourself useful," he said, "and drive that person to his car."

The woman, who was probably not much older than twenty-one, motioned for Paul to get into one of the nearby patrol cars. She didn't seem happy with her assignment, or perhaps with life in general.

"Have I spoiled your first chance to see a nude murder victim?" Paul asked.

"Ray said it was murder?"

"That's what he told me."

The officer looked a little more pleased with life. "That letter was a suicide note," she said. "It was just inside the door. You couldn't miss it."

Paul smiled. "We missed it."

"Yes."

"Is the lieutenant good at his job?"

"He keeps getting promotions."

"Is he widely loved by his co-workers?"

"Loving isn't what his co-workers get paid for."

"Can he be trusted?"

"Nobody can."

End of conversation. Paul hoped his son, Luke, didn't decide to go into law enforcement—or lawbreaking.

Chapter 21

It took two hours for Nick Ray to show up at the studio. Paul spent the first hour thinking about the events at Sarah Hopkins's house. Ray had obviously been humiliated to have overlooked the suicide note, but at least the note confirmed his belief that the death had not been accidental. And suicide notes aren't always authentic. Paul wondered why the note was so long and hoped the lieutenant would be in a confiding mood when he arrived.

More likely, however, Ray would have a lot of questions to ask—questions about Sherril, or even about Paul himself. Could Sherril be involved in the chain of murders? Paul was certain that she had had some contact with Dwight Bailey, Lamb Johnson, Connie Nickens, and Sarah Hopkins. In fact, Paul had seen Sarah leaving Sherril's house. And it was possible that Sherril had at least spoken on the phone to everyone on the master list except Lamb Johnson's father, who had apparently never been to Dale Falls.

But why would Sherril kill or arrange to have killed any one of these people, never mind the whole group?

Paul couldn't let himself believe she could be knowingly involved—even indirectly—in murder. He had seen her in every significant kind of circumstance; he knew the limits of her capabilities. He and Sherril had separated not because she had a potential for being evil but because she had exhausted her potential for loving Paul.

But Paul also realized that only the rarest person would be willing to admit that he or she had had the poor judgment to marry a murderer. That was the fact behind the cliché of the loving mother who is convinced that her death-row son is a good boy.

Finally, Paul told himself that the burden of proof lay with Nick Ray. It was time to relax. The proof he was interested in at the moment was the eighty proof of Marnay cognac. He wanted to be able to walk across the studio and find Phyllis reading but ready to put her book down and hold out her arms to him. He went to the sketch he had made of her. It seemed successful to him as a likeness—as a reminder of a presence. He could sense all of her—even the parts that were not represented in the sketch. He understood the impulse that had led Picasso and other painters to represent all sides of a face or a figure simultaneously. His tension and confusion began to dissipate. His art had begun to perform one of the functions he valued it most for. It had taken him outside of himself; not exactly in the sense of escape but by offering him an alternative, more constructive, problem.

Paul set up his palette, found a couple of clean brushes, and began to build up the flesh tones of the sketch. After working for a few minutes, he realized he hadn't put out the glass of cognac he usually had within reach as he worked. He started for the half-basement that he used for storing his cognac and wine. He had planned to make an inspection tour anyway, to look for signs of tampering. The door was locked, as he always left it, and nothing looked out of the ordinary. Downstairs, the bottles were lined up in their usual comforting symmetry. Paul pulled out a few bottles at random from various racks and saw no indication that any seals or corks had been disturbed. He took an assortment of bottles upstairs, poured out an ounce or so from the one labeled *Réserve Familiale,* and sniffed it carefully before tasting it. Nothing unpleasant happened—*au contraire.* He worked steadily and contentedly until Lieutenant Ray arrived.

The lieutenant took an uninvited stroll through the studio, examining the rooms and their contents intently and professionally, but without touching anything. Paul was reminded of how Grace the Cat had looked during her first stalking tour of the studio.

As he trailed Ray, Paul began to describe the poisoning of Grace and the awkward tailing by Sarah Hopkins. Nick made no comments and asked no questions until they got to the description of the cat port in the kitchen door. Paul, who had to explain the working of the pet door in detail, asked, "Do you think this has anything to do with the break-in?"

"No. I just like to keep up with gadgetry."

They went into the kitchen to look at the gadget. Lying next to the port were three small corpses—two mice and a sparrow. The lieutenant moved the corpses with the toe of his shoe. "You've got a new cat?"

"Yes. Tom."

"I wish everyone had Tom's honesty and pride about the lives they take."

"Not everyone takes lives."

"Everyone wants to. That's what my job is about. To deter that universal impulse."

The lieutenant opened the door and went into the yard. The spade was still next to Grace's grave.

Ray said, "You're not good about putting your tools away." He picked up the spade and began to dig in the loose soil of the grave. "Exercise relaxes me," he said. "And we should have an autopsy done."

Paul wondered if Ray was simply suspicious of what was in the grave. The lieutenant was stronger than he looked, and the exhumation didn't take long. After he pulled out the grisly bundle, he glanced quickly into the blanket and then carried it out to his car and put it in the trunk.

Paul said, "Can you come in for a drink?"

"I thought you'd never ask," Ray said. His expression and bearing became more relaxed. He was an actor stepping out of his role. Back in the studio, he stopped in front of the painting Paul was working on. "Another friend of yours?" he asked.

"She was a friend the last time I saw her—at the deadly dinner. I hope she still is."

"I suppose this is the friend who got Hillary Brock relegated to the acquaintance category."

Paul didn't answer. He resented Ray's interest in Phyllis. Part of his resentment was the general distrust and discomfort he often felt around other men. Paul had always felt safer and more at ease with women than he had with men—a result, he assumed, of his having had a father whose major talent was philandering and who didn't try to conceal the lack of interest he felt for his wife and children.

Paul led the lieutenant to the studio's living area and poured two glasses of *Réserve Familiale*. He waited for his guest to start the conversation. The first topic was unexpected: "I gather you like to look at yourself." He glanced around at the mirror collection.

"Actually, I don't. I just like mirrors."

"I like to look at *my*self," Nick said. "I'm vain, as a matter of fact. But in a modest way." He took his first drink of Paul's cognac—a helping that was more in the category of a gulp than a sip. He smiled but didn't say whether he liked what he tasted. "Do you think you'd like to paint my portrait?"

"No. You're too sinister looking."

"Sinister but elegant."

"That's what I meant, actually: You're too elegant."

"It helps me in my interrogations—especially with women. They think I'm gay. They confide in me." Ray finished his cognac. "This is elegant, too; but not so sinister. What is it, about eighty proof?"

"Yes."

"The Hopkins woman had some bourbon that was a hundred and one proof."

"I know. She let me sample it. I meant to get the address of the maker."

"When was this sampling?"

"A couple of days ago. I went to see her to ask her to quit following me."

"She admitted following you?"

"Yes. She said she was simply attracted to me. I didn't believe her."

"You think she tried to poison you?"

"Yes."

"Why?"

"No idea."

"You didn't kill her?"

"I thought she committed suicide."

"What made you think that?"

"Wasn't there a note?"

"Anyone can write a note."

But not everyone can find them, Paul thought. He said, "Anyway, I didn't kill her—or anyone else. And I'm available for polygraphs if you think it would be helpful." Actually, Paul would have gone to considerable trouble to avoid polygraphs—on the assumption that his built-in guilt feelings would cause him to fail any such test. To make up for his reckless offer, he poured the lieutenant and himself another brandy.

Ray nodded his thanks. "I probably won't have to ask you a lot of questions—certainly not now. But I'd like to hear any theories you have about what's behind all these ostensible accidents."

"Like a good detective, I don't have any theories. I noticed a series of deaths that might or might not be unrelated accidents. The death of Sarah Hopkins might be another in the series."

"Had you planned to investigate the deaths?"

"I thought someone should. I've read a lot of mystery novels."

Ray sniffed his drink and then sipped it. "Well, *I'm* going to investigate this case, and I've only read three mystery novels. They overrate the importance of the detective. Intelligent detectives don't solve murders; stupid murderers do. The best thing you can do is forget about the matter. I'll let you know if I need your help, and I'll let you know how the case is resolved."

"You mentioned my ex-wife. Do you suspect her of being involved?"

"Yes."

"Why would she be involved in a series of murders?"

"I don't know. Why would anyone?"

"I suppose I'm a suspect, too?"

"Everyone is. You more than most."

"Why would I . . ."

"I said the best thing for you to do is to forget about it. Paint. Will you try to do that?"

"Yes. I can do that if no one follows me and I know you are investigating. Are you going to have me followed?"

"No. Are you going to paint my portrait?"

"No."

Ray finished his drink. "I like it here," he said, showing some mellowing effects from the cognac. "Wood and mirrors. I can't stand houses—especially houses that have had decorators turned loose on them."

The lieutenant got up and headed for the front door. His gait was steadier than it had been when he arrived—a sign of someone demonstrating that he could hold his liquor. As they passed a Queen Anne pier glass that produced a particularly soft, sepia reflection, Ray stopped to straighten his tie and adjust his carefully tailored jacket. But the practical act became something more frivolous as he noticed the counterreflection from other mirrors. He raised his hand to his thick, slightly greased black hair and made a couple of motions that might be described as primping.

"Do you sell these mirrors?" he asked.

"No. But I can give you the names of people who do."

"I assume you sell the cognac."

"My brother does. He also gives it away on occasion."

"Unfortunately, cops can't accept giveaways. But huge discounts are allowable." Ray smiled a just-kidding smile.

Paul hoped the lieutenant hadn't been soliciting a bribe but had been inviting some kind of businesslike cooperation that men of the world routinely make with law enforcers. It reminded Paul that despite his own playboy reputation, he was ignorant about the way everyday power was exercised.

At the door, Ray readopted his professional street persona. "Let me handle things. Go away, but not too far. Spend a few days in Manhattan. But leave a phone number with my office."

A couple of steps outside the door, Ray turned and asked, "Do you know anything about Arthur Merrill?"

The name didn't register with Paul. He shook his head.

"He was an ex-boss and lover of Sarah's. She was trying to figure out how he could have a fatal accident that would involve crushing his genitals."

"She didn't like him, then."

"I don't think so. She wasn't a good person to antagonize."

"But I didn't antagonize her. She must have been crazy."

"Someone is crazy," Ray said. "I guarantee you that. When we sort this out, we get a crazy person. Probably one who is loved and respected."

"So that lets me off the hook."

Ray smiled and walked briskly and apparently soberly to his car.

Paul assumed the lieutenant's smile meant the hook was very much in place.

He went to the kitchen and poured himself some cold coffee that he was sure was at least three days old. He sat uncomfortably wondering what to do with himself. The odd personality of Nick Ray had left him unsettled but at the same time reassured. Paul knew that he himself was incapable of putting together a rational assessment of the situation. He should follow Ray's advice and forget the whole messy business. And he would have been able to do that except for the death of Sarah Hopkins. He saw her terrified face and her large, awkwardly twisted body. What was he to her? It wasn't enough to tell himself she was crazy.

His thoughts were interrupted by Tom the Cat, who entered through the pet door and went to his food bowl, which was empty. Paul put out some unappetizing lumps of dried cat food and some fresh water. Tom ignored the lumps and drank a little water. Paul's heart went out to the cat. What kind of creature could eat something like that? What was in the refrigerator? Any kind of fish? Yes . . . sort of. There was some leftover caviar in a covered dish. Paul removed the cover and put the dish on the floor. Tom, who had been sitting in apparent annoyance in the center of the kitchen, went immediately to the bowl and, after some preliminary sniffing, ate the fish eggs—the large red variety—in two gulps. For a moment, Paul panicked. He remembered Grace's quick, graceless death. But Tom showed only signs of gratification. He walked over to Paul's legs and rubbed against an ankle. Paul could hear the beginnings of some extravagant purring. It was the first manifestation of pleasure he had encountered in hours.

But pleasure seemed out of place after the puzzling and gruesome events of the day. Overcoming his always-present urge to be with Phyllis, Paul decided to settle for a telephone conversation with her. But as it turned out, even that wasn't an option, and he had to be satisfied with hearing her voice on her answering machine. In an odd way, he did find satisfaction in hearing Phyllis announce that she wasn't able to come to the phone, and he called her number three times in succession before letting her know that he had called.

Partly to keep himself from wondering what Phyllis was doing and partly because the impulse was irresistible, Paul began to think about Sarah Hopkins. The studio was becoming dark now, although traces of a strange orange-blue sunset were still visible through the skylight. Sarah's house, with its small windows, would be completely dark inside now. Would a police officer be posted there to protect the scene of the crime? Probably not. The Dale Falls police department wasn't big enough to allow stakeouts at houses in which it wasn't even certain a murder had been committed.

Paul went into the kitchen and began to assemble a dinner of triple-crême cheese on sourdough rolls, raw carrot strips, strawberries, and a half bottle of Morey-Saint-Denis. When Paul carried the food to the kitchen table, he found a typewritten note:

Dear Paul:
Very important that you meet me at Sarah Hopkins's house after dark tonight. There is something there that I want you to see. You can decide whether the police should see it. I'm not sure what time I can get there. Wait for me.
A Friend

The note wasn't signed, and there was nothing about the plain bond paper to show where it might have come from. Paul's first impulse was to call Lieutenant Ray and tell him about the note, but he decided to wait until after his dinner to make any decisions. Who sent or delivered the note? That was what Paul most wanted to know. And he might never know if he didn't go to Sarah's house as requested. If he gave the note to the police and they investigated, they would probably frighten off the person who sent the invitation. It would probably be possible to arrange to have the police back up the rendezvous the way they did in kidnapping ransom drops, but that sort of thing seemed to go wrong too easily. It might be safer if the police were involved, but there couldn't be much danger. If someone wanted to kill him, why would they lure him to a house that might already be under surveillance?

As Paul considered the matter, Tom the Cat slipped stealthily out into the yard to begin a night of exploration. Paul was envious. He wanted to do his own exploring and make his own discoveries. Obviously, the police would have searched Sarah's house in a thorough, professional way, and they would have uncovered and followed up on any significant evidence. And Lieutenant Ray had made it clear that he didn't want Paul to attempt any investigating.

But what if someone wanted to show him something in Sarah's house that would be significant and revealing to Paul but not to the police? On the other hand, what if someone was playing on his tabloid-reader's desire to be involved in sordid and violent events—using his less admirable tendencies to . . . to what? To incriminate him? To distract him or the police from something more important? Whatever the situation, Paul's desire to visit Sarah's home was growing. But what if the police were watching the house and caught him entering? Should he show them the note? Would they believe he had not written it himself? Another possibility was to tell them lamely but not untruthfully that he wanted to get the name of the firms that made and distributed the bourbon Sarah had served him. Paul's brother, François, liked to talk to accomplished distillers about their methods of production. He particularly liked to talk to the people who put out the less widely known bourbons, which were often family businesses that had strong similarities to the Marnay operation.

Now Paul had a legitimate, if stupid, reason to visit Sarah's house. He wondered if he might not have done so even if he had not found the note inviting him there. Most of us, he thought, are prepared at all times to accept a legitimatizing reason, no matter how silly, that will allow us to take part in some illegitimate action.

So now that he had a legitimate reason to visit Sarah's house, what about the practical aspects of the visit? The fuses had probably been replaced in the house, but it would not be a good idea to turn the lights on in the house. Paul was sure there was a flashlight in the trunk of his car. What else did he need? Maybe some morale strengthening. He called Phyllis's number once more, listening to her recorded announcement, but not leaving a message. Then he got into his car and began driving slowly through the streets of Dale Falls.

He saw Dwight Bailey sitting at the counter of his shop, talking to a customer and peering knowledgeably into the mechanism of a handsome, wood-cased mantel clock.

At the restaurant where Connie Nickens worked, she was visible leading some early diners—probably retirees—slowly to a table. As Connie had once described this group to Paul, "they walk slow, eat fast, and tip small." But they were reliable, keeping the kitchen and staff occupied until the partyers, serious eaters, bon vivants, and lovers drifted in.

As Paul passed his ex-wife's house, he saw her standing in the dining room with her arm outstretched. She was probably reinforcing some order she had just given Luke. Paul thought of the small figure in Phyllis's model set—the ambiguous figure he had seen as godlike and manipulative. Had Sherril been that kind of person when he lived with her, or had she become that way since he left her? Had her urge to manage people's lives become lethal? He doubted it.

But regardless of whether it was Sherril, someone had been lethal. Paul was now driving past the municipal cemetery at the edge of town—an immaculately maintained, parklike area where, he assumed, the remains of Edna Denning, Angela Bailey, and Freddy Stella rested and where a plot was being prepared for Sarah Hopkins.

Sarah's house was dark, and there was no one sitting in any of the cars that were parked along the street. Faint sounds of kitchen activities and the aggressive sounds of television programs (the noisiest of the visual media) could be heard from nearby houses. Paul parked up the block within view of Sarah's house and watched. There was no sign of activity in the house, but a police patrol car passed along the block and slowed perceptibly in front of Sarah's home. Several more cars passed, and it occurred to Paul that the house would be under surveillance by another group: the inquisitive. Paul hadn't seen or heard any news reports since Sarah's body was discovered, but he supposed the word would have spread, either through the media or informally, that there had been an unnatural death in Sarah's house. And a certain portion of the population would not be able to resist the urge to drive slowly past that house and say, "There it is," or "That's the one, over there"—perhaps crossing themselves, and feeling a vague excitement or sympathy. They would return to their homes with a sense of satisfaction over having done obeisance to death. They would also have seen, and presumably reported on, any lights that might have been moving through the house.

Nevertheless, with a growing excitement of his own, Paul walked to the end of the block and entered the alley that ran behind the houses. He felt much more vulnerable than he had in the car. He knew that pedestrians in Dale Falls automatically attracted attention. Anyone who was not walking on a direct path between a vehicle and the entrance to a building was a subject for speculation. But there was one exception:

joggers. Paul began to jog. Why be furtive? He turned and jogged to the front of the house. He went to the front door and rang the bell. If a police officer answered, he would mention Nick Ray's name and say he wanted to look at the label of the bourbon bottle.

He could hear the doorbell ring clearly. It was the long-outmoded alarm-type bell, not chimes or a buzzer. As he rang, Paul peered through the small window in the door. No lights went on in the house, and no one came to the door. But he thought he might have seen a shadow move across a window in the dining area at the back of the house. He began to panic. If he stayed on the porch much longer, the officers in the patrol car might return and question him. If he went inside, he would encounter the person who was waiting for him—and now that the confrontation was about to be a reality and not just an abstract possibility, Paul recognized that the person waiting for him might not wish him well. The wise thing would be to turn and jog back to his car and drive home. But before doing the wise thing, he tried turning the doorknob. It turned easily and the door opened before him. He went inside and closed the door.

"Anybody here?" he called. It was a pointless act considering that no one had responded to the doorbell. But it made him feel less like an intruder.

Paul stood and waited for his eyes to adjust to the deeper darkness of the house. Then he realized he had not brought his flashlight with him. But perhaps it was just as well that way; he would be less likely to attract attention.

As he waited for his vision to improve, he concentrated on the house's sounds—the only identifiable one being the whine of an inefficient old refrigerator's motor. There were not many other sounds, but the few that Paul could hear were unsettling. One of them could easily have been floorboards creaking under a person's shifting weight; another could have been the distinctive sound of a yawn—the sensual intake and release of breath amplified slightly by the mouth's little cavern.

Paul was beginning to realize that his eyes were not going to allow him to do any significant searching unless he used at least a little supplementary light. As he considered the problem, the refrigerator's thermostat clicked off the motor, which died with a sigh-like moan. The sound reminded him that the refrigerator could serve as a low-level light source. He made his way awkwardly to the kitchen and opened the refrigerator's door. The light seemed dazzling. He turned away from it and left the kitchen.

Was there anyone else in the house? Probably not; he or she would have said something. Either the person hadn't arrived yet or would not arrive at all. Paul thought it better if he kept busy. The living room and dining room were now clearly enough illuminated so that he could see the outlines of the furniture and the other larger objects in the rooms. Again trying to banish his sense of fear and guilt, Paul found the bottle of bourbon and took it to the kitchen, where the light allowed him to read the bottle's label. He took out a pad and pen and made a note of the maker's name, which was, surprisingly, Slavic sounding, and the address, which was, not surprisingly, in Kentucky.

Paul suppressed an urge to sip some of the bourbon from the bottle to see—he told himself—if it was as distinctive as he had remembered. He replaced the bottle in the other room and stood in the near-darkness wondering how long he should wait for someone to show up at the house. He was beginning to feel relieved that no one had met him. There was an odd sense of pleasure in being here, in placing himself at the scene of Sarah's death. He felt the way a believer might feel when standing on the spot where a sacred vision had been reported. He was finding not evidence but inspiration.

As he stood listening primarily to his own deeper than usual breathing and looking at gradations of black and dark gray, Paul became convinced that the situation was not static but that a subtle event was taking place just out of the range of his perception. He began to feel like a victim. This was the point at which the heavy object would be brought down on the private eye's head.

But there was another possibility. Maybe the point of the note hadn't been to lure Paul into a trap but simply to get him out of his studio. He would have to be careful when he got back there.

Paul became a little less apprehensive. Of course there wasn't anyone in Sarah's house with him now. It was time for him to leave. Then he heard the squealing of quickly braked tires and the slamming of car doors. Next there were footsteps, the opening of a door, and the unmistakable voice of Nick Ray: "Whoever's in there, just stay where you are for now. There are people with guns surrounding the house. I'm going to turn a light on in the living room. Then you just walk slowly into the light with your hands on top of your head just like in the movies."

The lights went on, and Paul followed instructions, squinting in the strong light.

Lieutenant Ray said, "Marnay, are you an idiot or a villain—or all of the above?"

"How did you know I was here?" Paul asked.

"I ask the questions," the lieutenant said. "So, any explanations?"

"Would you believe anything I told you?"

"Probably not, but lies can be instructive."

Paul wondered if there was any point in telling about the note that had been left in his kitchen—a note that he realized he had forgotten to bring with him. He doubted whether it would sound convincing. Only half conscious of his words, he said, "I just came here to get the name of the company that made Sarah Hopkins's bourbon. I wrote it down." Paul reached into his pocket and took out the slip, thinking somehow that it would justify his presence in the house.

"That's your whole story?"

"Yes."

The lieutenant said, "You broke the law by coming in here. My job is to see that people obey the laws. And I gave you specific advice—I told you to stay out of my way."

Paul was staring at his feet in the penitential posture he had learned to assume early in his life when confronted with an angry, accusatory parent or teacher. He spoke the words that went along with the posture: "Yes sir. I'm sorry."

He looked up to find that Ray was smiling. "Now you be a good boy and go home. And don't let it happen again."

Paul found enough courage to ask, "How did you know I was here?"

"I'm smart, that's why. And someone called to say you were here. That's the person I want to have a long talk with."

"Was the person a woman?"

"That's not clear. The clerk who took the call thought it was me making a joke."

Paul wished he could take the situation as lightly as Nick Ray apparently did, instead of feeling stupid and slightly ill. He went quickly to his car and drove to his studio, in front of which he found a parked patrol car containing a young man and woman in uniform. He knew he would be seeing a lot of the couple until the Dale Falls murders were cleared up. Judging from their expressions, they weren't any happier about the prospect than Paul was. Why, he wondered, do so many people spend their time doing something that neither they nor the person they're doing it to is pleased about?

Chapter 22

When he got into the studio, Paul made a careful tour, looking for unannounced visitors or anything that seemed disturbed or disturbing. He assumed that the presence of the police outside would discourage potential breakers and enterers, but the visitor who left the chemical gift in the cognac might have left some other mementos.

His answering machine was flashing. He switched it on hesitantly and was rewarded first with the voice of Phyllis Arno saying, invitingly, "If a fella needs a friend, I'm available." Next was an offer of a new portrait commission from Max Antell. Paul wondered if he shouldn't move to New York City where there's enough money, power, and fame available to keep people from having to develop deathchains. The most bizarre events in the news always seemed to take place in picturesque or unexceptional surroundings. Dale Falls had once been depicted in a national magazine as one of the ten most beautiful U.S. towns. It had a sound commercial base that looked preindustrial but was simply inconspicuously industrial, the way its people were inconspicuous when they decided to engage in unpleasant or evil activities. But as Paul's ex-friend Hillary Brock and his new acquaintance Nick Ray knew, the charming facade concealed a lot of unpleasantness that was looking for a way to express itself.

Paul began to pace around the studio, and a pensive mood settled over him. Why did people find it necessary to kill and exploit one another? Paul realized his life was easier and pleasanter than most, but even if he were without advantages—if he were one of the poor and homeless, he would believe life was a privilege. If he had to characterize life, he would say that it is a privilege that most people abuse.

As he walked through the shadows of the studio, his attention was caught by a penetrating point of red light. Most people were surrounded by such lights these days—little reminders of the existence of machines and gadgets. A stereo system or VCR saying Play Me; a coffee maker saying Drink Me. The new wonderland.

This particular light indicated someone had turned on his computer—a device that Paul respected but used only occasionally as a word processor and filing system to keep track of his business records and expenses. Luke had hooked it up in a way that Paul didn't understand—by modem, whatever that was— with the computer that Luke and Sherril used in their home.

Paul was sure he or Luke hadn't used the computer in the last few days. Probably Ms. Williams had turned it on inadvertently while dusting. The thought of Ms. Williams reminded Paul that he had meant to ask her about the tampering with the cognac bottle. He had been hesitant to ask her about it, because of her supposedly secret tippling, which he didn't mind, and he was afraid if he confronted her about it she might quit, which would leave him with the depressing problem of replacing her. Now he could talk to her about the computer before leading into the topic of cognac. And he realized it was important to warn her that drinking from any opened bottle of cognac could be dangerous—although he assumed that the danger was diminished now that Sarah Hopkins was dead.

Paul went to look up Ms. Williams's phone number. She was a taciturn woman who could have claimed more or less convincingly to be either black or white. She had opted for black and understandably might have regretted the choice, given the biases of most people who lived in Dale Falls. When she answered Paul's call, there were the sounds of young children in the background.

The conversation was mostly a monologue by Ms. Williams during which Paul found out that (a) she was positive she had not turned on the computer, (b) she hadn't noticed any tampering with any of the bottles in Mr. Marnay's bar, and (c) was ready to quit if Mr. Marnay was hinting that she might have drunk any of his brandy. Paul assured her that he was sure she wouldn't do anything dishonest and that even if she had drunk his liquor he wouldn't have minded; he was only concerned with her safety. To demonstrate his faith in her, he arranged to keep all his alcoholic beverages in a locked cabinet, to which she would have a key. Ms. Williams seemed pleased with the arrangement.

Next, Paul called Max Antell, who offered him a choice of two new portrait commissions. Actually, there was no choice from Paul's point of view because one of the subjects was a child. Few portraitists enjoy working with children, primarily of course because young people have trouble sitting still for reasonable periods. But Paul's objection was to the unformed, characterless features of most children. A child's face might show interesting echoes of his or her heritage, but it is not a fully formed image. Painting a child is like painting a plant before it blooms; it can be attractive, but primarily as a study in green.

The second commission was the kind that Paul reveled in: a wealthy, middle-aged woman who had the reputation of trying to offset her physical plainness with carefully cultivated charm and intelligence rather than cosmetic surgery. She would ask only insight and honesty of Paul. He told Max to arrange a preliminary interview, and he decided while he was speaking to the agent to let Nick Ray take care of the deaths. After Paul hung up, he wondered how he could have wasted his time on the deaths in the first place. They were important in an elemental way, and they were interesting and absorbing in the sense that a mystery novel is, but they did not engage his most individual abilities.

The thought of engagement reminded Paul of Phyllis Arno, and he reached for the phone to dial her number. But before he could pick up the receiver, the phone rang. It was Luke, who sounded excited, as he often did, but in an unusual way. "Dad? It's Luke."

"I know it's Luke. You're the only person your age who calls me."

"Some people mistake me for a woman."

"Horrors."

"It's not funny."

"No. How's the clock design coming?"

"Commendably. I took it to Mr. Bailey."

Apparently *commendable* and its variants were still

in Luke's vocabulary-building program, Paul thought. Then he realized what else his son had said. "Did you say Mr. Bailey?"

"Sure. Dwight . . . the clock man."

"You call him Dwight?"

"We're friends. He respects my intelligence."

"Do you respect *his* intelligence?"

"He has more like genius than intelligence. And he says my design has promise. And Mom has found a tower that we might be able to install it in. It's in a town about twenty miles from here. The tower is old and made of stones and has a clock in it now that doesn't work. The town thinks that a clock with famous murderers in it would be a good tourist attraction. They might put up the money. Dwight could build it if he had enough money, he thinks. He's a more interesting guy than you think. Also, he's on the list."

"What list?"

"The Chainmaster list?"

"The *what?*"

"The new file on your computer . . . the file labeled 'Chainmaster.' What's that all about?"

"I think you'd better tell *me*. You've read it; I haven't."

"You haven't read the letters? Then why are they there?"

"What do they say?"

"They're disgusting. They're signed by Chainmaster, telling people to kill other people."

"Which people?"

"Dwight, Mr. Johnson, Ms. Nickens, Ms. Hopkins. There are people mentioned called Freddy Stella and Angela Bailey."

"Where could the file have come from?"

"We're the only two terminals on our hookup.

Somebody had to put them in there or here, and *I* didn't do it."

"How long have they been there?"

"They weren't there yesterday. I look for messages every day."

"Messages from who?"

"You."

"Have I *ever* sent you a message?"

"No."

"I wouldn't know *how* to send you one."

"Well, you never know."

Paul was touched and a little abashed that Luke was that hungry for contact with his father. Or could it be that Luke was simply snooping to see what his father and mother had been up to in their correspondence?

"Luke, you haven't told anyone else about this, I hope."

"No."

"Well, *don't* tell anyone. Don't mention it to your mother or anyone else until I get back to you—which will be soon."

"Okay."

Paul hung up and went to his computer terminal and called up the Chainmaster file. He read it through once, fascinated but incredulous. Then he went to his bedroom and lay down—an action that he took when emergency thinking was required. What should he do? Even though he assumed someone had planted the file, there was still the remote possibility that Sherril could have written the letters; therefore Paul didn't want to tell Lieutenant Ray about them. A man couldn't incriminate the mother of his child. Or could he? If Sherril was involved in murder, she might put Luke's life in danger. And then the ultimate suspicion occurred to Paul: What if Luke himself was involved in the chain? Was this the crazy, amoral kind of thing a kid might dream up as an exercise in manipulation, without connection to reality? Certainly the clock tower was a slightly sick—although apparently commercially appealing—idea.

But aside from the matter of who the instigator was, how could the scheme have worked? How could someone get people to kill just by asking? Only a certain kind of person could be suggestible enough to do such a thing. There must be something in the letters that Paul didn't understand. He would have to let Lieutenant Ray take them over. No, not when there was even a remote possibility that Sherril or Luke might have written them.

This kind of speculation had to stop. But how could he stop it? His telephone put an end to his indecision by ringing and giving him a clear, but possibly unrelated course of action. It was Phyllis, who said, "What are you up to, sweetie? Should I be jealous? I *am* jealous, whether I should be or not. So what I'm going to do is come and stay with you for a while. I have to see a producer in Saratoga tomorrow anyway, and I don't think either he or his roommate—not to mention me—would want me to stay with them. I'll leave now; I should be there in about three hours, okay?"

"I've got some problems."

"I'll solve them for you. See you soon—and you can see me, too. And now you can tell me you love me."

"I love you."

"I love you, too. And don't you forget it. *À bientôt,* as your brother would say."

Paul felt relieved. Help was on the way. In the meantime, there were things he could try to figure out. Who had put the Chainmaster files in his computer and why? It would be a dreary but temporary activity. Then Paul realized that he needn't bother. There *wasn't* any way to find out who had used the printer. He had been operating under the artificial rules of all the detective fiction he had read, in which everything is ultimately discoverable and explainable. But in most people's lives, most mysteries remain just that. You'll only find out who did whatever it is if the person who did it decides to tell you.

At that point, a visitor showed up. Tom the Cat stood in front of Paul and seemed to be nodding his head in the direction of the kitchen. Paul assumed there were either some rodent trophies to be seen or that Tom was ready for more caviar. Paul picked up the phone and dialed Phyllis. She hadn't left yet. "It's me," he said.

"It's too late to stop me."

"Could you stop at Zabar's or somewhere and get a large quantity of the cheapest red caviar?"

"Frankly, sweetie, I'm not devoted to that stuff. Wouldn't you rather have some country-style pâté?"

"It's not for us. It's for Tom."

"Tom who?"

"Tom the Cat."

"Oh. Yes. Of course. Who else? You take good care of your friends, don't you?"

"You'll find out."

"I'm on my way. I'll also bring something suitable for human consumption."

Paul went into the kitchen, found and disposed of three gift mice, and put some dry food into Tom's bowl just in case the cat was desperately hungry. Tom didn't even sniff the food but simply glanced up at Paul and then walked away.

"Don't despair," Paul said. "Help is on the way."

In the three hours before help arrived, Paul did his best to keep his mind free of any images except those he might use in a painting. The most difficult moments came when he decided that the various bouts of perspiration he had experienced during the day had definitely left him in need of a shower. How could he step into his bathtub without recalling the contorted features of Sarah Hopkins? The answer was that he *couldn't* avoid that memory and probably wouldn't ever forget it entirely. As Paul closed his eyes and let the water sluice over his body, the image that occurred to him was not precise but had the menacing, blurred quality found in some of the more horrifying paintings by Goya or Francis Bacon.

For the first time, Paul thought about the possibility of painting a dead person; a thought he had never had previously, even though painters had always depicted corpses. There were countless Biblical scenes, from Cain and Abel to the deposition of Christ, that included corpses; and during the Renaissance, the corpse itself became an object of interest to painters like Leonardo. But Paul's whole concept of painting was as a process that depicted life. He wondered what the result would be if he tried painting his memory of his last glimpse at Sarah Hopkins. Whatever the result, there was no doubt that it would be a serious painting in the sense that a living portrait of her could never have been. Maybe that's why professional portrait painters are seldom treated with respect by art critics; there is a built-in frivolity in a view that excludes death.

After dressing (and admitting to himself that Lieutenant Ray was right in his theory about the illogical collection of clothes in Sarah's bathroom), Paul went to the easel that held his unfinished painting of Phyllis. He put it aside and set up a new canvas, on which he began to rough-in a heavy oil sketch of his memory of Sarah's corpse. He thought of J. L. David's painting *The Death of Marat,* in which the figure in the bathtub has such grace and dignity. There would be none of that in Paul's painting of the death of Sarah Hopkins.

Paul was still absorbed in his work when Phyllis rushed in, bearing packages and saturated with the coolness and the fresh aroma of the evening's spring air. As she promised, she had the exaltation and energy of a rescuer. "You can't put your arms around my exciting, pulchritudinous body until you take some of this stuff," she said. "Food (the harmless kind unless your digestive system is prissy), flowers, *du vin*. Even some mail; don't you ever collect that stuff? You might be missing an important announcement about collectibles or a guilt-inducing chain letter . . ."

Paul didn't hear the rest of what Phyllis said. Was everyone becoming obsessed with this subject? He had heard that such letters will occasionally sweep across a country, engaging the fear or greed of hundreds of thousands of people.

"Are you all right?" Phyllis said. She had her hands on Paul's shoulders and was shaking him slightly. "Is this some more of your small-town morbidity?" Phyllis led Paul toward a chair and as she did, she passed the canvas he had been working on. "My God, Paul. What is that? Have you gone all the way around the bend? Is that supposed to be me?"

"Fear not," Paul said. He got out his sketch of Phyllis, which looked much more finished and delicate than he had remembered it.

"That's more like it. In fact, that's a lot like it. You admire my back, don't you?"

"No more than your front."

"But most men seem to be primarily interested in the front. Full frontal is what stimulates them."

"We can discuss that later. I need about ten minutes now to make a phone call. Maybe you can feed Tom the Cat. And then we'll think about ways to celebrate life."

"And ways to reproduce it?"

"One way, at least."

Paul wanted to talk to Lieutenant Ray but wasn't sure what he wanted to say. Would Ray find the chain letter business idiotic? Probably. And it was likely that the lieutenant would find any kind of suggestion irritating after he had made it clear that he wanted Paul to stay out of the investigation.

But Paul wanted to make some kind of contribution to the solution of the case, no matter how insignificant. It was as if the murders had the form of a large, malevolent god standing threateningly nearby, preventing Paul from concentrating on the pleasures of his new love. It was necessary at least to make an attempt to propitiate the god before attending to those pleasures.

Paul stood confusedly holding the phone, thinking of detectives in fiction. What would they do in his situation? Most of them wouldn't *be* in the position of having to divide their time between a love affair and an investigation. Detectives such as Sherlock Holmes and Nero Wolfe didn't allow for such diversions as love, realizing as Paul now did that a person can do justice to only one obsession at a time. "I am," he said to himself, "a lover, not a gumshoe." He put down the phone and went to the kitchen, where Phyllis sat sleepily and beautifully on a chair next to the table. A cat that reeked of fish eggs lay exchanging warmth with her lap.

Phyllis said, "That was commendably quick." Her vocabulary was showing Luke's influence.

"It's the last thing I want to do hastily tonight."

"And what are these unhasty things you want to do?"

Paul didn't speak but went to Phyllis and removed a resentful-looking Tom from her lap. He knelt next to

Phyllis and rested his cheek where Tom had lain. "Nice," he said, not adding the obvious feline pun but wondering if it had also occurred to Phyllis. Paul turned his face downward into the soft material of the skirt that covered her thighs. The aroma—womanly, fishy, catty—was rich with life. Phyllis raised her skirt, dragging it slowly from under Paul's head. He kissed the smooth warmth of her skin and the damp, white cotton of her bikini panties. Phyllis separated her knees, and Paul moved his face between her legs. He could hear the delicate, bristly sound of his whiskers rubbing against her thighs. Paul started to pull away so that he could remove the panties.

"No," Phyllis said. She held his mouth against her body. And then she reached down with her left hand to raise the side of her panties. In her right hand, she held a pair of kitchen shears. She cut away each side of the bikini, allowing it to fall away.

Later, Paul said, "I had a bad moment when I saw you wielding those scissors."

"I was having a good moment. I had thought you might want me to put my knees together and spoil the effect."

The good, leisurely effects—including breaks for snacks and beverages—lasted into the morning. When sleep finally arrived, it was interrupted after an hour or so by the irritating sound (like a hysterical gargle) of the telephone. The unanswered call became a message Paul was to hear later: "Nick Ray here. Your cognac had quinidine in it—something medical people use to stimulate the heart. Too much of it stimulates the heart into a thrombosis; which is what your cat died of. Technically, it wasn't poisoned and you wouldn't have been either if you'd gotten there first. I'll keep you informed."

Paul hoped the optimism he sensed in the lieutenant's voice was real and that the next message would be conclusive.

The rest of the morning wasn't as leisurely as the night before had been. Phyllis had to drive to Saratoga to confer with the director about the production of *The Winter's Tale,* which had been set forward in the schedule and would begin rehearsals soon.

Then Paul got the kind of call that made him want to get his telephone disconnected: "Mr. Marnay? This is Dwight Bailey."

Paul had no idea what to say.

Dwight continued in the cool, expressionless voice that matched the emotionless gaze Paul remembered from their meetings, "Did you hear about the clock tower?"

"Luke told me a little about it."

"Could you come and see it today?"

"Why would I want to see it? What have I got to do with it?"

"Luke is your son. The tower means a lot to him."

"But how could I help him by looking at it?"

"You could talk to the mayor there and help raise money. You know rich people."

There was sense in that. But Paul was uneasy about having any dealings with Dwight. He'd rather deal with the other people who were involved in the scheme. "Let me think about it," he said.

"I'm going to be out there this afternoon. They want to get started as soon as possible. I need someone who's used to talking to people and working things out."

Paul started to suggest a lawyer, but he realized that Dwight was not the kind of person to reason with. "Okay. I'll meet you," he said, and took down the directions. They were to meet at three o'clock.

Then Paul called Luke and asked him if he could get

away from school in the afternoon to see the tower. As he suspected, Luke had no problem with that.

When Paul left to pick his son up, there was no sign of the patrol car that had been parked outside his studio the night before. No one seemed to be following him after he picked Luke up, either.

As they drove, Luke explained the latest version of the mechanism for the tower clock, and then he explained the operation of the car's engine and transmission—information he got from Lamb Johnson. "How fast have you driven her?" Luke asked.

"Probably not more than sixty-five. But I'm not sure. I can't find the speedometer. And if I could, I'm sure it would be in kilometers per something or other."

Luke pointed to one of the many dials across the car's instrument panel. "This is the one. You could at least double sixty-five without even trying."

"Why would I want to do that?"

"Emergencies. Or maybe just for fun."

"That's not how I have fun."

"I know. And you're a terrible driver." Paul didn't deny it. "What they ought to do," Luke continued, "is make cars for kids my age. An adaptor kit for the foot controls is all you'd really need."

"You wouldn't even need that for this car," Paul said. "You could reach the pedals if we adjusted the seat a little bit."

"Could we try? You could give me a driving lesson. We could go off on one of the back roads."

Why not? Paul thought. He headed away from the heavy traffic.

Luke asked, "So, do you think you'll be able to get them to build the clock?"

"If I can convince them they will become rich and

famous by building it. But it may take someone more convincing than I am to do that."

"Mom," Luke said. "She could convince anybody to do anything, I bet . . . anything at all."

Say it isn't so, Paul thought.

When they reached the old north route, which virtually no one used now that the new, wider, faster Northway was available, Paul and Luke traded seats. As he had assumed, Paul didn't have to give Luke much instruction. It had taken a few minutes to get the seat and mirrors adjusted, and Luke was not in the most relaxed of positions, but he had enough control and field of vision for safety. The low placement of the seats made Luke more comfortable at the wheel than Paul, who always worried about sitting so close to the road, imagining he was about to suffer buttock abrasion.

By the time Paul had begun to relax, being sure that his son had adequate control of the car, Luke announced, "I think somebody's following us."

It must be the police, Paul thought. How could I have missed them, even if they had switched to an unmarked car? He turned and looked out the back window. There were two people in the car, a man and a woman. The woman looked like one of the officers Paul had seen at Sarah Hopkins's house after the murder.

"Why don't we lose them?" Luke said.

"Definitely not. They might be police, and we're already violating a law by letting you drive. What we should do is stop and trade seats."

"We should get ahead of them first and then trade fast before they catch up. Then they won't know I was driving."

Before Paul could respond, Luke put his weight on

the accelerator, and the car surged forward with enough power to make Paul think they might leave the ground. When he got his breath back, he shouted, "Stop."

But by then, stopping seemed out of the question. Paul looked first at Luke, who was obviously terrified and unbelieving about what was happening. Fortunately, the road ahead was straight, and it was clear of any other cars as far ahead as Paul could see. He turned and looked back. Apparently, Luke's maneuver had surprised their followers into paralysis. Either they had stopped moving or Luke was still accelerating fast enough to make it look that way. "Slow down," Paul said, putting his hands on the wheel and trying to hook his legs under Luke's to pull the boy's foot free of the gas pedal. There was still no traffic ahead of them, but the road was beginning to curve. Finally, Paul could feel the car beginning to slow.

"I'm going to turn off," Luke said.

"Just stop."

"I don't want the cops to get us."

"They're going to get us anyway. They know who we are."

"But I want to see the tower," Luke said. He had his foot lightly on the brake now and was beginning to turn.

Paul was glad the car had a low center of gravity. It was the fastest turn he had ever been involved in, but the car was holding to the road. "Slower," he shouted.

They had turned onto a two-lane road that might have been on private property. It was paved in potholed blacktop that bounced the car around but didn't raise dust that would have attracted attention to them from the main road. Their speed was slowing a little too fast for safety now, and Luke wasn't coming out of the turn too successfully. A tree appeared a couple of feet to Paul's right. They were off the road. But they had also stopped—putting their seat belts to the test in the process. Paul reached over and engaged the hand brake. He and Luke stared at each other. They were both smiling.

The letter had come the day before. It hadn't been mailed, but had been placed in his mailbox without a stamp. If it had arrived a week earlier, Dwight would have been flattered to receive it, but now he was disturbed. His life had changed in a fundamental way. For one thing, there was a woman in his life. He didn't think he was in love, for the woman wasn't beautiful, and he believed only a beautiful woman could be loved. But this woman looked at him not just with respect but invitingly. Although he hadn't yet found the courage to ask her, he was sure she would not say no if he asked her to go out to dinner with him; and she would not pull away from him if he put his arms around her and held her to his body. And there also was young Luke Marnay, who visited and telephoned him; who respected his knowledge. For the first time, Dwight felt an urge to become a parent.

And then the letter came. It was as if it were from another life, but it could not be ignored:

Dear Mr. Bailey:

Once more I need your help. You are the strongest link in our chain. Paul Marnay is endangering your life and mine and must be disposed of quickly. The chain is complete but must be reinforced.

You know of a certain clock tower, which will one day make you famous. Ask Paul Marnay to meet you there so that you may show him how his son's plan will be executed. Push Mr. Marnay from the tower. As his life ends, a new life will begin for you. The chain and your involvement with it will reach completion.

You will go on to new, equally memorable accomplishments.

With respect and gratitude,
Chainmaster

Chapter 23

Paul got back into the driver's seat, consulted a map, and made his way to the site of the clock tower, which was a town called, appropriately, Tower. It was not a pleasant drive for Paul. He assumed a police radio call had gone out and that all the patrol cars in the area would be looking for his car, which he fervently wished—not for the first time—had a less distinctive appearance. As Paul looked for lurking or pursuing police cars, Luke studied the map and worked out a route through back roads.

The little time Paul and Luke had for conversation was centered on the design for Luke's murder clock. He still hadn't made his final choice of the murders to depict. He had established three categories to choose from: famous murderers, famous murder victims, and—an additional group—fictional murders. He thought murders from the works of Conan Doyle should be included, but wasn't sure about others. "What others, do you think, Dad? You've got more time for that kind of reading than I have."

"What do you mean, that kind of reading?"

"Fiction. For pleasure. I have to read stuff for school. And for pleasure I read mostly scientific things. I like the scientific detectives like Sherlock Holmes. What about the others? The old ladies and the tough guys."

"Some people think Sherlock Holmes was a sort of old lady, and he thought of himself as a tough guy at times, getting into showdowns with villains."

"You always try to complicate things."

"Things always are complicated. But I don't think you can use detectives in your clock. You're showing murders, and with a couple of exceptions, the detectives don't commit the murders. You can't have Justice smiting the detective."

"I thought of that. You wouldn't show the murder, just the detective and the murderer."

"I suppose you could do that, but there wouldn't be any action. You could put in Miss Marple with an all-purpose small-town English murderer. And an all-purpose private eye in a trench coat for Sam Spade or Philip Marlowe. But maybe you could let your investors decide."

"They might want to change the whole thing."

"It's the eternal struggle between art and commerce, Luke."

"Whatever you say."

Although Paul thought it was a little early to give out congratulations, he felt a remarkable amount of pride in what his son was doing. This was definitely the era of the entrepreneur if a ten-year-old could conceive and sell an elaborate project like the clock tower without seeming to feel the doubts and intimidation that Paul himself felt.

The town of Tower consisted primarily of one four-block commercial street leading to a too-large village green surrounding a square brick tower that was apparently modeled on the Campanile in St. Mark's Square in Venice. It was what the British call a folly and Americans usually classify as an eyesore. The proportions of the tower were not good. It measured about thirty feet on each side and had obviously been planned to be higher than its present sixty or so feet. But as a platform for a mechanical tableau that could be seen reasonably well from the ground, it was promising. There was a surprisingly small, handless clock face on one side of the tower.

As Paul and Luke walked toward the tower, a figure stood at its top silhouetted against the bright sky and waving at them. Paul assumed it was Dwight Bailey. He also assumed that Dwight wasn't bothered by heights. The tower had no railing, and the parapet of the tower appeared to consist of a row of bricks only one or two feet high. Dwight seemed to be standing with his feet touching the parapet. Paul planned to stand well clear of the edge when he got to the top. Surprisingly, the tower contained a working elevator, and Paul and Luke were spared the trek up a formidable circular stairway.

It wasn't until they reached the top and he saw Dwight Bailey's gently sinister features that Paul remembered that Dwight had been the one whom Luke had called Creepola and who had been in the park when the pigeon lady had been pushed over the stone wall in Falls Park. How could he have forgotten that and agreed to meet Dwight at the edge of a sheer drop? Paul stopped in the center of the tower's flat roof and put his hand on Luke's shoulder to keep the boy away from the edge.

"I looked at the clock's works," Dwight said. He had to raise his voice almost to a shout to be heard over the strong spring wind that swept across the top of the tower. "It seems to be in working condition, and it's more elaborate than you'd think . . . probably a copy of some famous European turret clock. It'll take a while to check it over."

Dwight made no move away from the edge of the tower, and Paul continued to keep Luke from moving toward Dwight. Their conversation would continue to be a yelling match. "Could my murderers be hooked up to it?" Luke shouted.

"Sure. But we would probably want to convert it to an electrically driven system. It would be fun."

Luke said quietly to Paul, "Why are we standing here?"

"Why is Dwight standing there?" Paul answered. "It's safer here."

"You don't trust him? He's my friend."

"Maybe, but I'm not sure he's *my* friend."

Dwight called out, "Do you want to see the clock face up close?"

"No, thanks," Paul hollered before Luke could answer. "It's a little cool up here. Why don't we go inside before we all turn into brass monkeys?"

Dwight stared unsmilingly at Paul and Luke for a moment and then began walking slowly toward them. Paul turned and led Luke down the stairway that led to the elevator. "Can't we see the works?" Luke asked in obvious disappointment.

Paul reconsidered. Now that they were inside the tower, there was less danger of a fall. The top of the clock's massive works, which were encased in a steel framework like a cage for a giant bird, were near them. A metal stairway led down to a platform at the base of the mechanism and to an enormous handle, which Paul assumed was used to wind the clock. Quickly, Paul led Luke down the stairway to the platform. "We're down here," he called to Dwight. He said, quietly, to Luke, "Keep me between you and Dwight."

Dwight, moving agilely down the stairs, said, "Do you want to wind it and see it work?"

Paul definitely didn't want that to happen. The prospect of falling into the massive, moving gears of the clock was even more terrifying than the thought of falling to the ground from the top of the tower. He said, "Isn't that dangerous? Couldn't you damage the mechanism?"

"No. I've been told by the owners that the clock never stopped working—it just needs adjustment of the mechanism and repair of the face."

"We'll take your word for it," Paul said. "We don't have to see it work today."

"Aww, Dad," Luke whined. Paul was glad to get a standard, childish reaction from his son, who often behaved too much like a reasonable little adult for Paul's taste.

Dwight's excitement was obviously growing. He glanced back and forth between Luke and Paul, apparently not sure how to hold the boy's attention or to overcome Paul's resistance. "Luke," Dwight said, "you can learn a lot from seeing the movement in operation." He moved cautiously down the steps toward them.

Paul tried to move backward, but his legs didn't respond; they merely tingled and trembled slightly. He was clenching his teeth. He was terrified.

Luke pulled free of his father's hand and took a step toward Dwight. The boy and Dwight looked at each other with identically intense expressions that Paul could not identify. There was a bond between them that, though temporary, was stronger than the bonds of family. Dwight and Luke met at the handle of the clockworks' crank. Face-to-face and without speaking, they began to turn the crank. A piercing screech, like the death cries of a small animal, rose from the clock's massive, slowly turning wheels and gears.

Paul was still immobilized by his odd fear, and now he began to feel a sense of shame. Even if he was able to move, he wouldn't know what to do. He was cornered. The only escape route open behind him was a metal ladder that descended about eight feet alongside the works of the clock. But was there really a need for him to escape? Dwight seemed to be ignoring Paul and wasn't likely to harm Luke.

Paul's tension began to ease as he watched his son and Dwight working together and exchanging odd little smiles. Although he thought he could detect a sinister element in Dwight's smile, Paul realized he might be seeing something that wasn't there—that Dwight was merely looking for someone to share his knowledge and enthusiasms with.

After three or four minutes of cranking, Dwight straightened up and said, "That should be enough."

Paul looked over the short railing that separated the platform from the clock's works. Below him, the works had begun to operate. He saw no logic in the movement. Toothed wheels engaged one another. Levers moved up and down, back and forth, all with an inexorable steadiness that reflected a vast power. It was a vision of hell to Paul, who imagined a human body landing in the mechanism and being enveloped by it. If some part of a body—a hand or foot—should become caught in the works there would be no escape from a leisurely death. The clock would become a slow-motion grinder, rending flesh, snapping bones.

Feeling slightly nauseated, Paul looked up as Luke moved past him and began climbing down the ladder.

"I can see the weights," Luke said. "Are they iron?"

"Cast iron," Dwight answered. "Like the frame.

Not much tensile strength. That's why it has to be so massive."

Although Dwight was speaking to Luke, he was looking at—and moving slowly toward—Paul, who stood with his back to the clock mechanism and the guardrail.

Paul realized that in his present position just a gentle push would send him sprawling into the mechanism. Once again the image of the meat grinder occurred to him. He knew that his safety depended on his moving away from the railing, yet he couldn't move. Was he being brave by standing his ground, or was he simply paralyzed with fear? The line between courage and cowardice, he realized, could be hard to draw.

Dwight was within arm's length of Paul now. He won't push me, Paul thought. He wouldn't do it in front of Luke.

Paul vaguely heard Luke's voice: "Come on down, Dad. Watch the movement. It's getting ready to strike."

Is *Dwight* ready to strike? Paul asked himself.

Dwight raised his hand and slowly grasped Paul's upper arm.

Luke shouted, "Here it goes."

A deep-pitched bell, somewhere out of sight, rang once with a vibration that Paul felt throughout his body. This is it, he thought, and closed his eyes. He felt a movement of Dwight's hand—a movement so slight that Paul couldn't tell its direction.

Then, finally, Paul was able to take some action. He wrenched free of Dwight's grasp and backed himself against the wall. Dwight looked at him blankly for a moment and then swung himself quickly onto the ladder, descending out of Paul's sight.

The clock's bell sounded again, shaking the platform. Paul went to the railing and looked down at Dwight and his son. Luke had his hands clasped tightly over his ears, and his face was contorted with pleased excitement. Dwight was grasping Luke's arm as he had grasped Paul's a few moments earlier and was looking up with the same ambiguous expression he had worn then.

Movement was coming more easily to Paul now that the danger was not to himself but to Luke. He thought of climbing down the ladder to rescue his son, but there literally wasn't room for another person to stand down there.

Paul shouted, "Come back up here, Luke."

"Why?" Luke asked.

"It looks dangerous down there."

"Dwight's here with me."

Dwight smiled up at Paul.

Then, with a suddenness that astonished himself as much as it did Luke and Dwight, Paul took action. Stung by the combined insolence of Dwight's smile and his son's defiance, Paul stepped halfway down the ladder. Holding a rung with his left hand, he stretched his right arm down toward Luke.

"Take my hand," Paul said harshly. In his surprise, the boy didn't hesitate. He reached out and allowed his father to pull him up the ladder and onto the platform.

"Move," Paul said, and pushed Luke ahead of him toward the elevators.

Luke frowned but didn't resist beyond saying, "What a grouch."

Paul was elated. His rescue of his son was accompanied by a surge of adrenaline and an even bigger rush of self-satisfaction. He felt as if he had taken control of his life in a new sense—as if only good things were going to happen in the future.

Paul was about to start up the stairway with Luke,

when they heard the sound of the elevator doors opening on the floor above them. Then a voice called, "Is the owner of that white sports car up here?" A police officer appeared at the top of the stairs.

Paul's newfound elation vanished. "Yes," he said, "we'll be right up."

When he got upstairs with Luke, Paul freely admitted having committed the various offenses they accused him of. They apparently weren't aware that Luke had been driving while most of the laws were being broken. Paul willingly blew into a device that tested his sobriety, and he was grateful that he hadn't brought along his pocket flask, because he would almost certainly have made use of it when he arrived at the tower.

When the alcohol test proved negative, the officers seemed to relax a bit. They stopped threatening to confiscate Paul's license and were satisfied to write out a summons, which Paul was glad to see was answerable in a courthouse several miles from the town of Tower. He wouldn't have to appear before people who might be responsible for approving the clock-tower project.

Dwight Bailey apparently preferred not to get involved with the police. He didn't make his presence known, and Paul didn't see any reason to bring him into a situation that was already complicated enough.

Paul drove back to Dale Falls with exquisite care, dropping Luke at Sherril's house and warning him to limit his contact with Dwight Bailey to telephone calls.

At his own home, Paul found messages on his answering machine—a situation that seemed to be inevitable lately. The first was from Phyllis, who wasn't going to be able to get back to the studio until about eight o'clock. The second message was from Nick Ray, who said it was just about dénouement time and that he would be dropping in for a drink and a revealing chat later in the evening. "An unlikely story always goes better with a cognac," he said. He apparently also watched reruns of Claude Rains movies.

Chapter 24

Paul took Lieutenant Ray's message as a cue to begin unwinding from a strenuous day and went to the new, locked, liquor cabinet. After looking for—and not finding—signs of tampering with either the cabinet or the chosen bottle, Paul poured a substantial unwinder. He sniffed it carefully before stopping off in the kitchen for a helping of pâté, rice crackers, and dill gherkins. Then he slumped down on the sofa and began to enjoy his snack.

The weather, which had been clear and breezy earlier, had turned strangely cloudy and still, and the studio was in semidarkness. Paul opened his eyes only when it was necessary in locating food or drink and transporting it to his mouth. There was no need to think about murder now; Lieutenant Ray was taking care of that. Paul's eyes were tired, perhaps irritated by the wind while he was on top of the tower.

Maybe the time was coming when he would need to wear glasses. He gave his eyes a little test by directing them at the studio's mirrors, following the shifting focus points and the illogical images. He began to imagine Phyllis was walking among the mirrors—

nude and blatantly provocative. He reached down and rearranged his trousers to relieve a growing constriction.

Then the imagined figure began to alter. She was no longer nude but wore a familiar uniformlike dress. She was taller and more slender; she was a blonde.

She was not Phyllis Arno but Hillary Brock.

Paul said, "Hillary?"

There was no reply, and the image vanished. Paul drank the ounce or so of cognac that was left in his glass, tilting his head back and allowing the last drops to fall slowly onto his tongue. Then he closed his eyes, giving himself over to exhaustion and sleep. But as he leaned his head back against a cushion, he heard a faint sound, like the whimper of an unhappy child. Paul sat up and glanced quickly around the studio. He saw nothing unusual. But in a moment, the sound resumed, this time more clearly defined. It wasn't a whimper, but a song—a mournful, carelessly sung melody.

The skin on the back of Paul's neck began to crawl, as if someone had placed a cold hand against it. Where was the song coming from? Why did it seem familiar?

Then once again he saw a figure move among the mirrors for a moment. It was undoubtedly the figure of Hillary Brock.

"Hillary?"

The figure disappeared among the mirrors, but the plaintive singing continued. Paul was now certain that Hillary was in the studio, for even though he didn't recognize her voice, he remembered where he had heard the song before—it was a melody Hillary had sung to him once as they made love. The wordless song had seemed amusing then, but now it seemed both pathetic and threatening.

"Hillary?" Paul said. "Hillary, I've had a hard day.

I'm not up to games. Why don't you come and sit next to me? We can have a drink. And we can talk, if that's what you want to do."

The song stopped, but Hillary didn't speak. The studio seemed darker. A draft sprang up, cool and strong enough to penetrate his clothing. It was scented just perceptibly with an expensive perfume he recognized as Hillary's.

The humming began again. Paul wanted to get up and turn lights on—to flush his visitor out of her hiding place. But his body wouldn't cooperate. He told himself that he was exhausted. What he wasn't able to tell himself was that he was in the grip of a fear more profound than the type he had felt earlier when confronting Dwight. What he was feeling now was the terror a child feels when cowering in the darkness, convinced that a malevolent being is nearby—a being that would be even more terrifying if it were to be seen than if it remained invisible. This was the kind of fear that makes grown-ups wish they were children young enough to cry out for Mommy or Daddy.

The humming stopped. Paul sat rigidly forward and scanned the room for signs of movement. Minutes went by and he saw nothing. He heard only the sounds of traffic and an occasional plane in the distance. Yet he couldn't relax. Eventually he felt another draft—fainter this time and at his back. He would have to turn and look behind him.

He counted slowly to ten, allowing his courage to accumulate. Then he turned quickly.

No one was behind him.

He turned back and waited for his breathing and pulse to slow down. He closed his eyes. Lighten up, he told himself. He wondered if he had been hallucinating. It was possible. But why was he obsessing about Hillary rather than about, for example, Dwight Bailey? Was Hillary more important to him than he was willing to admit? He thought back to the night in the hotel room in New York when Hillary had hummed the odd melody. Why did he want to remember that night? Hillary had been tense—still excited from having presented her paper at the conference. He could even remember the subject of the paper . . . something about bipolars . . . suggestibility . . . about people who are exceptionally open to suggestion.

Paul's neck began to tingle again—this time not out of fear but a growing realization: What is the ultimate act of suggestion? Wouldn't it be to induce someone to kill someone else? A therapist's crowning accomplishment: selecting a number of patients who were theoretically suggestible and then proving their potential by persuading them to commit murder.

Could Hillary be the instigator of the chain—the deathchain? It was a possibility. She knew a lot of people in Dale Falls—a lot of disturbed and unstable people. Had anyone in the chain ever been one of her psychotherapy patients in private practice or at the hospital? She hadn't spoken of her patients often, but Paul thought he remembered she had once mentioned having treated Dwight Bailey. And Phyllis had once said that only a bunch of crazy people could be involved in such a chain. Maybe that's exactly what it was, and Hillary was the person who knew who could be manipulated and how to manipulate them. But why would she do such a thing? What would she get out of the process? Could it simply be some kind of exercise in psychological dominance? If so, that meant Hillary was more disturbed than any of her patients. But Paul had read that the incidence of psychological disturbance was exceptionally high among psychotherapists.

Paul was no longer telling himself to relax. Instead, he felt a new alertness based on the realization that a

Hillary who was the Chainmaster and was lurking in his studio at the moment would put him in true and immediate danger. He sat forward again and waited tensely for his senses to bring him a message.

When the message came, it was loud, clear, and terrifying.

"Hello, Paul."

The voice came from close behind him; it was Hillary's voice. Paul turned his head quickly and found Hillary standing only an arm's length away from him. She was smiling unpleasantly.

"Did I startle you, Paul?"

"Of course."

"You frighten easily, my sweet."

Paul couldn't gauge Hillary's mood. Her eyes were wide with excitement, but she held her body languidly. With her weight on one leg, her pelvis pushed forward, one hand on her hip, and the other holding a large handbag, she looked like one of the potential victims in a bad movie about Jack the Ripper. But as she walked around the sofa to stand in front of Paul, there was nothing of the victim in her expression. On the contrary.

"May I sit?" Hillary asked.

Paul tried to say yes, but his voice wouldn't respond. His mouth was dry and his palms were damp. Hillary dropped her bag to the floor; it landed with an ominous, vaguely metallic thump. She leaned forward and pushed Paul's knees together. She pressed her fingernails into his legs with surprising, malicious strength. "Here's where I'll sit," she said. Still facing him, Hillary raised her skirt, parted her legs, and settled over him, her thighs enclosing his. Grasping his hair with one hand, she pulled his head back and held her mouth against his, her teeth bruising his lips. It was an act of aggression and not of affection.

In the midst of his pain and surprise, Paul was

experiencing a strong and peculiar excitement, but he knew that to submit to the attack would be to invite not pleasure but defeat. He tried to bring his body forward and push Hillary onto the floor, but she increased the pressure on his hair, keeping his head back and preventing him from gaining the leverage he needed. Her tongue was in his mouth now, and she quickly grasped his hand and guided it between her legs. Before he could pull his hand free, Paul was made aware that Hillary wore nothing under her dress and that she was moistly aroused. However, Paul had suppressed his own arousal—as Hillary's free hand had discovered.

Her grasp on Paul's hair relaxed, and she pulled her face away from his. She looked puzzled, and her anger seemed to be turning to something resembling despair and confusion. "I was sure you'd be up to it," she said. "I was sure fear would excite you."

"What do I have to fear?"

"Death. Most people fear that."

"Death?"

"Oh, please. You're slow, Paul, but you're not stupid." Hillary's eyes, close to his, seemed enormous, like those of an alarmed nocturnal animal.

Taking advantage of Hillary's slight relaxation, Paul pushed himself suddenly forward, struggling to gain leverage. For a moment, they were at a desperate balance point, Paul's superior strength neutralized by his awkward position. Then his hand went to her hair. He hesitated as he remembered the times he had stroked and kissed that hair. Then, with a simple backward yank, he was sitting upright, and Hillary was on the floor, next to her bag. She reached into the bag and withdrew a large, short-barreled pistol, which she pointed at Paul as she got to her feet.

Paul said, "I'm afraid I still don't know what this is about."

"I told you. It's about death—your death, Mr. Impotent."

"You'd kill me for nonperformance?"

"You seem to perform well enough with our friend Phyllis."

Is this simple jealousy? Paul wondered. Had he been wrong in his speculation about Hillary and Chainmaster? The speculation was, after all, based on nothing more substantial than the subject of a scholarly paper. He said, "Is this just because of Phyllis?"

Hillary backed away to a nearby chair and rested her bag on the chair's arm. She reached into it again and pulled out a length of lightweight steel chain that had a padlock on one end. "Phyllis and this," she said.

"Then you *are* Chainmaster?"

"Of course. Do you want to hear about it?"

Paul wanted time and would have said yes to an offered reading of the over-the-counter stock listings. He nodded. Hillary kept the gun pointed at him, but she didn't bother to pull down her skirt. Paul realized modesty was an irrelevant concept in this kind of situation, but he still found the sight of Hillary's parted thighs and pubic hair almost as unsettling as the sight of the revolver. Whatever Hillary was about to describe, it wasn't unrelated to sex, Paul thought— if *anything* was.

Hillary looked less tired than she had a few minutes earlier. Both her gaze and her grip on the gun seemed firm and steady. "I'll keep it brief, my dear," she said. "And don't ask a lot of questions. I'll tell you what I want you to know. It's really quite simple, and what you should keep in mind is that before yesterday, I really hadn't done anything very horrendous. I had simply made a few suggestions . . . in the name of science, actually. In my practice, I had developed a set of characteristics to define the extremely suggestible personality. I worked up a program on my computer in which I identified all the variables and applied them to all the people in the files—the files from my private practice as well as the hospital's psychiatric files. I came up with a list of people who—according to my theory—could be persuaded to do almost anything. And what would be the ultimate test for such a theory? The ultimate taboo . . . the taking of another person's life. And to do the persuading not through a complicated series of personal conferences but with a simple vaguely threatening letter."

"I've seen them," Paul said. "Why did you put them in my computer?"

Hillary didn't answer the question, but she changed her position slightly and pulled her skirt down, probably, Paul thought, to support her contention that she had been acting as a dignified scientist. She continued, "There are some assumptions I made that are apparently valid. One is that almost everyone knows someone that he or she devoutly wishes was dead. Another is that if the chance of discovery and punishment is low enough and if the person gets some encouragement, the person will kill quite cold-bloodedly to eliminate his or her nemesis. And with a certain kind of personality—actually, with certain diverse and not at all deranged personalities—very little encouragement is needed. I proved that."

"Not the sort of experiment most scientific journals would want to describe, though, I'd think."

Hillary ignored Paul's remark. "But as you see, until the weak link—and plain shitty bad luck—developed, I really hadn't done anything but write a few letters. I hadn't done anything wrong. The wrongs were done by the others . . . until yesterday. It was Sarah Hopkins. I hadn't been certain of her, but I relied on her hatred of her ex-employer. I thought it would be appropriate to have her dispose of my ex-lover—you, my dear. You and your cat were my downfall. I wanted to punish you for leaving me. And I thought, why not use the chain to punish you. That was my mistake. The objective, scientific procedure became an instrument of revenge. It got out of control.

"When Sarah messed up her attempt on you—I had gotten her an excellent poison from the hospital —she panicked. And then I panicked. The great irony in all this is that I turned out to be the weakest link of all. I hadn't put myself into the equation.

"In any case, I went to see her and told her I was Chainmaster. I asked her to return the letters I had sent her. She realized they were her life insurance and refused to give them to me. Then it was my turn to panic. I offered her a sedative that I carry with me to calm distraught patients. I gave her enough to put her to sleep. I undressed her and put her into the bathtub and threw the hair dryer in. The perfect crime. I wasn't prepared for the burning smell . . . or for the lights to go out. I had planned to search for the Chainmaster letters she had received from me and to destroy them. The house has those small windows, and the light wasn't good. I looked in all the obvious hiding places without any luck. I didn't have time to look thoroughly, but the police would. I had to assume they would find the letters. But what if they didn't have to search for the letters? What if Sarah was Chainmaster? I typed a suicide note and a confession summarizing the chain and taking responsibility for it. It seemed to be a logical thing to do. I couldn't stand the burning smell. I had to get out of the house."

Paul was not trying too hard to follow Hillary's story. The gun was beginning to waver slightly in her hand, and she was looking around the room distractedly. She seemed to be about to stand up, but she merely raised up for a moment to pull her skirt farther down. "I had an appointment with Lieutenant Ray. When I saw him, I knew he wouldn't be deceived by the suicide note. Then things really began to fall apart. When I was leaving police headquarters, I met you. I knew you were the one who had spoiled everything. I went to your studio and left the note asking you to go to Sarah's. While you were at Sarah's, I put the Chainmaster correspondence in your computer to implicate you or your ex-wife, Sherril, and I called the police and told them you were at Sarah's. Later I regained some perspective and realized the police would eventually find out I was Chainmaster. There was no way around that. But I wanted you to suffer. I delivered a note to reliable Dwight Bailey asking him to kill you. That didn't work. So here I am."

"And what next?" Paul asked. He could see that Hillary's control of her body—not to mention her mind—was weakening. Hillary was either going to drop the gun or use it. She didn't answer his question —and probably hadn't heard it.

Paul turned his attention away from Hillary slightly for a moment. He thought he had heard a noise in the background. Then he realized what the sound was— the mechanism of the pet door opening in the kitchen. Next he heard an intense yowl that probably was announcing that a certain caviar addict needed a fix. For the first time in several minutes, Paul felt as if he were in the real world.

Hillary turned her head toward the kitchen. She had a look of distress. "Was that a damned cat?"

"I don't know if he's damned, but he's certainly a cat." For some reason, the vague, fear-inspired nausea Paul had been feeling vanished, and he began to feel silly and giddy. It probably had something to do with the body's primitive mechanics of fear—too much or too little oxygen or an overdose of adrenaline.

Hillary said, "I can't tolerate cats. Literally, I can't breathe when they're around. I thought it was dead."

"I got a replacement."

Tom the Cat appeared at the door to the kitchen and yowled again.

"Oh, Christ," Hillary said. Then she shouted at Tom: "Go away."

"He's hungry," Paul said. "He eats caviar."

Hillary was beginning to look hysterical. "Do you think I give a fuck what he eats?" she shouted. "Let him eat this." She turned and aimed the gun in Tom's direction. The gun, which Hillary held loosely in one hand, went off with an explosion that seemed more appropriate to an artillery piece than a pistol. Hillary's hand jumped backward, and the pistol fell to the floor in back of her.

Paul moved quickly behind Hillary and kicked the gun away. It slid out among the mirror stands.

For a moment, Paul and Hillary stood looking across the floor. From where he stood, Paul could see four widely scattered reflections of the pistol in downward-tilted mirrors but could not see the pistol itself on the floor. There was no way to tell where to begin looking for it.

The cat had vanished.

Hillary sighed, and her arms dropped limply to her sides. Paul caught her from behind, wrapping his arms tightly around her and grasping his left wrist with his right hand. But a wave of energy swept through Hillary, and she began to squirm with a strength that surprised Paul. He almost lost his grip, and he realized that if she continued to struggle this fiercely he wouldn't be able to hold her. Neither of them spoke as the struggle continued.

And then Hillary's body turned absolutely limp. She caught Paul off balance, and they both fell to the floor. They lay still. Paul was unable to keep from thinking of other times they had lain together on this floor.

"Kiss me, Paul," Hillary whispered.

He did; gently.

"Now let me go." The whisper had turned husky and heavily sentimental. Paul thought the sentiment might be self-pity rather than nostalgia. Hillary continued, in the same tone, "I won't interfere with your life again. Let me go. Do that much for me. We had some good times, Paul. You owe me that much."

"You tried to kill me. Twice."

"Twice?"

"Once with the poison."

"Oh, that. I was confused."

"And tonight."

"Tonight was different. I didn't want to die alone."

That was the element Paul hadn't been able to identify in Hillary's crazed mood: She was thinking of suicide. And suicides have nothing to lose. "Then don't die, Hillary. Don't give up."

"I have to . . . it's unbearable . . . hopeless."

She's right, Paul thought. There was no hope. The only possibilities were confession and punishment. It was absurd but touching.

Tom the Cat had bravely reappeared and was pacing inquisitively a few feet away, his tail erect and twitching. Hillary's allergy was taking hold dramatically. Her breathing was labored, her eyes puffy and watering, her face splotched. Paul eased his hold on Hillary, changing his restraining grasp into an affectionate embrace.

"You've got to let me go, Paul. I can't breathe. I'll suffocate."

Paul kissed Hillary's forehead and released his hold.

Hillary moved instantly to her hands and knees. Scuttling to the cat, she grasped his tail and swung him violently across the floor. Then she crawled toward the pistol, which was clearly visible from floor level, free of the mirrors' confusing reflections.

Paul was finally able to react, and he lunged toward the pistol. But in his desperation, he collided with one of the standing mirrors, which tilted dangerously. Paul thought he had a chance of getting to the pistol before Hillary, but when the mirror—a particularly valuable early John Elliott—began to fall, Paul's reflexes overwhelmed him, and he reached out to save it, forgetting that his own life might be at risk. He rose to his knees and kept the mirror from hitting the floor, but he was at an odd angle and couldn't push it upright immediately. As he stood up and tried to stabilize the mirror, he faced Hillary, who was on her knees, pointing the pistol at him with both hands. For a long moment, Paul stood straining against the mirror's weight and looking into Hillary's eyes. He realized it might be his last moment, but surprisingly he felt no fear or regret.

Hillary stared at Paul unblinkingly despite the tears that ran from her eyes. Then she looked away.

Paul knew he was safe. He didn't try to stop her as she got to her feet and walked slowly out of the studio. He felt no relief over his reprieve; instead, the sense of euphoria he had felt during his moment of danger was quickly turning to nausea.

He concentrated on rebalancing the mirror that he held. He was looking at his own reflection—into his own eyes—when he heard the gunshot from the street. The shot was muffled, as if it had been placed tightly against a body or in someone's mouth.

Paul went to a window and looked cautiously out to the street. Hillary lay motionless next to her car. Paul hoped he wouldn't be asked to identify the body. He wouldn't want to live with the memory of even a brief close look at what was left of Hillary's head. He knew he should call the police, but his nausea was increasing, and he walked quickly to the bathroom, where he found Tom the Cat lying in a corner. Tom looked unharmed physically, but he was obviously unhappy. "It's all right, Tom," he said. "She's gone—thanks to you. A thousand thanks to you." But Paul wasn't able to concentrate on his gratitude. He sat down on the edge of the bathtub and waited to be sick. He supposed he would soon resume his charmed, pleasureful life. But he knew that after tonight, his pleasures would always be somewhat tempered. Hillary had destroyed not only the lives of her victims but the innocence of the survivors.

He had few other thoughts until he heard Lieutenant Ray's voice calling, "Anyone here?"

"I'm in the bathroom," Paul shouted.

"Will you be out soon?"

"I'm waiting to be sick."

The lieutenant pushed the bathroom door open. "You can do that later," he said. "Now you have to tell me what happened tonight. Or do you want to talk in here?"

"A friend of mine just died horribly."

"Lots of people have died. And Hillary Brock wasn't anybody's friend. Hadn't you noticed that?"

Paul left the bathroom tentatively and went to the sofa and sat down.

"Would a drink help?" Ray asked.

Paul shook his head.

"You *must* feel bad. Maybe you should lie down. The psychoanalytic posture is appropriate to all of this, anyway."

Paul stretched out on the sofa. His nausea eased slightly. "Hillary confessed to the murders—or to Sarah's directly and the others indirectly."

"Yes. Formal assignment of guilt is going to keep a lot of lawyers busy. Basically, I know what happened. I need details and confirmation."

"There are letters in my computer that will help."

"I need your statement now, before you start forgetting what Hillary told you tonight. I've got a tape recorder here. I'm turning it on now. Just tell me as accurately as you can what she said."

Paul went through a stumbling reprise of Hillary's confession, assisted by Lieutenant Ray's astute questioning. The lieutenant, Paul soon realized, understood the statement better than Paul himself did and that the statement was in the category of confirmation, not revelation.

Finally, the lieutenant turned off the tape recorder, and said, "I'll just get a printout of those letters and I'll leave you alone. Why don't I stop in for breakfast just in case something surfaces overnight? I'll call."

Paul was asleep on the sofa before the police left the studio.

An hour later, when Phyllis arrived, Paul wasn't sure where he was—not just what building he was in, but what planet he was on.

"What's going on, baby?" Phyllis asked.

Baby. That's what Paul felt like. A young, helpless baby.

"There's a roped off area out there around a chalk outline. And there's a cop who asks questions but doesn't give answers. What's that about, baby?"

"It's an ending."

"The end of what?"

"We'll tell you in the morning."

"We?"

"Lieutenant Ray's coming for breakfast."

"Speaking of food, what about dinner? I brought things."

"Not for me. Sleep is for me. You can eat with Tom the Cat. Nothing's too good for Tom . . . or for you, sweetie."

Paul remembered two more things about that night: being undressed by Phyllis and awakening sometime later to find the smooth, ample warmth of her breast against his cheek; "Poor baby," Phyllis said.

Chapter 25

Paul made his way, squinting in the skylight-filtered, mirror-reflected sunlight, to the kitchen, from which issued the sound of two distinctive voices and the aroma of French-roast, Hawaii-grown coffee.

Phyllis was wearing a white terry robe that revealed more of her chest than Paul thought appropriate in the presence of a visitor. The visitor, Nick Ray, wore a gray glen-plaid suit, a pearl gray shirt, and a mostly red paisley tie.

Paul kissed Phyllis, closing the top of her robe more securely as he did so. On the kitchen table was a selection of pâtés, cheeses, and breads. Next to the coffeepot was a bottle of cognac. Phyllis and the lieutenant looked healthy and happy.

"We were talking about acting," Phyllis said.

"I see a lot of the amateur kind," Nick said. "People playing roles that are meant to deceive me. I'm an unresponsive audience."

Phyllis had poured some coffee and brandy—half-and-half—and spread some young goat cheese on a chunk of baguette for Paul, who said to Nick, "And I suppose you do your share of performing?"

"Of course. This morning, I do the dénouement— my favorite role. Omnipotence."

There was truth in what the lieutenant was saying, Paul thought. Nick's manner was less formal than usual. The prissiness in his voice had been replaced by a hoarseness that was more appropriate to a retired boxer who has been hit in the throat too many times.

Phyllis said, with a tone that didn't display much sympathy, "Nick told me about Hillary."

"You don't seem upset by the news . . . or surprised," Paul said.

"I'm upset by the suicide, of course. But somehow I'm not surprised . . . by that or by the chain letter. I always thought Hillary was capable of bizarre behavior. That's why she got involved in psychotherapy. She was interested in bizarre behavior."

"That happens," Nick said. "It's like a cop who gets tired of being inside the law . . . who wants to get some of the action instead of just observing it."

"So was I the last to know?" Paul asked.

"There was a lot to know," Nick said, "but it really wasn't too well hidden."

"So when should I have known?"

"Certainly the morning you came to see me and ran into Hillary—when she knew your cat had been poisoned. How could she have known that?"

"Phyllis could have told her," Paul said, and looked at Phyllis. She shook her head.

The lieutenant continued: "And we mentioned, that same morning, that Hillary liked to be in control."

"I guess the problem is my memory. I don't remember anyone saying that. I remember the way Hillary looked and smelled, but not what she said. But I do remember that you said at one point that the villain would turn out to be a highly respected crazy person."

"A safe enough guess."

"So how much guessing did you do?" Paul asked. "What did you know and when did you know it?" He settled back to eat, drink, and listen.

"On the morning I just mentioned, I knew that Hillary had done something—when she knew about the dead cat. She had at least tried to poison you. Hillary had access at the hospital to quinidine, the poison used, and I thought she probably had keys to your studio. I didn't know Sarah had planted the poison, since the trail led back to Hillary, who in a sense was the real murderer or attempted murderer throughout. The people in the chain were merely her tools."

Nick Ray paused, and Paul realized he was beginning to find the lieutenant's voice soothing and hypnotic, as if it were a musical instrument used in a tribal ceremony. Ray continued: "I found out about the chain letter after Sarah Hopkins died and we searched her house. We found the letter from Chainmaster—it was well hidden—asking Sarah to kill you. As Hillary told you last night, she correctly assumed we'd find that. We also found some papers indicating that Sarah had been treated by Hillary. I remembered from her work as an adviser to the police that Hillary had also treated Dwight Bailey. That was enough. The phony confession that Hillary planted to make it seem that Sarah Hopkins was the Chainmaster wasn't plausible enough to be convincing. We established that all of the suspects on your list of murders had been Hillary's patients. I was ready to pick her up last night, but she got here first. So I didn't really solve the case; the weak links in the chain—and luck in the form of a cat—solved it."

"How could it have worked as well as it did?" Phyllis asked.

"It was based on sound human principles. As I think I've said before, everyone wants at least one other person to be out of the way permanently—and the only thing that keeps many of us from removing the unwanted person is the fear of being caught and punished."

"Speaking of punishment," Paul said, "what's going to happen to the members of the chain?"

Nick Ray took a long, slow drink of his coffee royale, which he seemed to find more stimulating than the last question. "That's not my domain," he said. "I haven't been asked to arrest anyone yet. I wouldn't be surprised if no one is ever arrested. It would be difficult to come up with proof that any of the deaths in the chain weren't really accidents. And even if there was proof, sorting out the legal ramifications of responsibility would be sticky. The real villain is out of the picture. The links in the chain are basically your ordinary slightly-out-of-sync citizens."

"But they're dangerous," Paul said.

"We're all dangerous. The ones we have to lock up are the manipulators—the Chainmasters. Or if you want to be melodramatic about it, the Hitlers. The tellers, not the people who do as they're told. We've already got too many weak links in jail."

"So I assume Sarah Hopkins was the weak link in this chain," Paul said. "If she hadn't been so clumsy about trying to kill me, the chain might not have broken."

"It might have lasted a little longer. But there are also elements like simple chance to consider. Lamb Johnson's father, for example. From what I've been able to find out, he apparently just had a legitimate heart attack. That upset Lamb's sense of justice. His link was weakening." Nick Ray's interest in the topic

246

seemed to be definitely waning. "Good coffee," he said.

Paul half-filled the lieutenant's cup with coffee and passed him the cognac bottle, which Ray unhesitatingly used to finish filling the cup, adding in explanation, "I'm not going into the office today, and there's someone out there to do the driving." He sipped delicately from the cup. "These are European customs, aren't they? Coffee royale; cheese for breakfast? Maybe I'll go there on my honeymoon."

"You're getting married?"

"Not exactly. Just going on a honeymoon. I understand Harry Dean Stanton is popular there. Someone might ask me for my autograph."

"That's it," Phyllis said. "I knew you were someone's double. He doesn't usually play cops, though."

"No. But I usually do."

"But not always," Phyllis said. She had reached that important point in an acquaintanceship—breaking through the primary role; seeing the person behind the mask. It's what the good painter does, Paul thought. Breaks through the mask.

The doorbell rang and the front door opened. It was Luke, who came into the kitchen and stood so that his arm touched his father's. "I thought I'd stop by on my way to school and show you my latest drawings," he said. "But I forgot them." He's heard there was trouble, Paul thought. He wants to be sure I'm all right.

The sun intensified through the skylight, taking on the quality of early summer as opposed to late spring. The yeasty aromas of bread and ripe cheeses filled the kitchen. Tom the Cat walked in, concluding a night and morning of some sort of hunting; he went to the bowl of caviar that Paul would see was always there. Phyllis's robe had loosened again. She and Nick Ray were laughing. Luke put his hand on Paul's.

I might not have been here for this, Paul thought. We're links in another kind of chain; the kind without masters.

It was two months later.

"What we've been involved in is a comedy," Phyllis said.

There had been several moments during the day when Paul had failed to see the joke, and he was sure the same was true of Phyllis. At midafternoon, they had been married in a civil ceremony, and in the evening, Phyllis played in the season's final performance of *The Winter's Tale* at the Summer Dale Festival. Now she was proposing a toast at a midnight supper with cast members and friends, including Paul's brother, François, and his wife.

"I mean," Phyllis continued, "a comedy in the Shakespearean sense that regardless of whether there were any really funny jokes and regardless of how many gruesome murders might have taken place, people get married at the end."

"The assumption being," François said, "that marriage is inherently and overridingly laughable in itself." Paul looked at Simone, François's wife. She didn't seem to be amused.

Paul wasn't amused either. Ever since that morning after Hillary's suicide outside his studio, he had felt that the world was in a state of equilibrium. Even though there were always people available to make cynical remarks about marriage, they were usually—like François—people who were themselves married. They might be on their second or third marriage, but it was obviously the condition they preferred to live in. There was something healing about a marriage ceremony—even one as perfunctory and unimaginative as the one Phyllis and Paul had just taken part in. There was an optimism—a willingness to admit the possibility of continuity and the occasional willingness to admit that someone else's needs and desires might be as important as one's own.

Paul's marriage to Phyllis was one of a series that had taken place since the truth of the deathchain had been uncovered by Nick Ray. After elaborate consultations among public prosecutors and defense lawyers, it was decided—as Nick had predicted—that the unprecedented circumstances of the deathchain made it unlikely that coherent charges could be brought against those who had taken part in it or that convincing evidence could be found that the deaths had not been accidental. In a sense, the only true murderer in the situation had been Hillary Brock. And as if performing acts of contrition, Dwight Bailey, Lamb Johnson, and Connie Nickens had each married in a space of three weeks.

The financing for Luke's Great Murders Clock Tower had been approved, and he was working with Dwight to complete the plans. The clock would be constructed under the supervision of Luke's mother, Sherril, who was also developing a Great Murders Theme Park to be constructed in conjunction with the tower.

Lamb Johnson had rejected his inheritance and the terms of his father's will in favor of opening his own custom-made sports car company (with financial assistance from the family of his bride). Paul had resold his sports car to Lamb and had bought a station wagon.

Connie Nickens, with the help of her new husband and with advice from Paul's brother, was about to open a restaurant featuring specialties of the Cognac region.

Paul had completed his portrait of Lt. Nick Ray and had sold it to him for one dollar. The lieutenant had enjoyed his European honeymoon but had not married. "Cops shouldn't marry," he said. He was soon to receive a promotion, not so much for solving the deathchain murders as for keeping them from being publicized.

Phyllis had received excellent notices for her performance as Hermione in *The Winter's Tale,* but as she had been aware when she accepted the role, its principal requirement was the ability to become prominently lifeless for a few minutes, and that illusion could be helped considerably by careful lighting. But it had allowed her to play her first Shakespearean role and to prove that she could handle the extravagances of Elizabethan language and emotion. It was a beginning.

The wedding was another beginning, Paul thought. He and Phyllis would be moving to Manhattan, where they had taken out an enormous mortgage on a studio loft in the Chelsea section. Paul had accepted a portrait commission from the leader of a rock group, and Phyllis had signed for a major role in the Broadway production of the latest play by Britain's most respected enigmatic playwright.

Paul's one regret was that he would be farther from his son, Luke. But Luke had in the past weeks shown unmistakable signs of becoming a remarkably self-sufficient and mature person—one who would deal with the approaching stresses of adolescence more efficiently without the well-meaning interference of an oversolicitous father. But there would always be a bed and a welcome for Luke in the Chelsea loft when he needed relief from Dale Falls and its murder-obsessed vicinity.

And there would be a place of comfort and honor in the loft for Tom the Cat, who, together with his sibling Grace, had made Paul understand why the ancient Egyptians had venerated the domestic feline.

* * *

Phyllis was concluding her toast. She raised her glass of Marnay *Réserve Familiale* and looked around the table. "Go together, you precious winners all; your exaltation partake to every one."

Paul recognized it as a quotation from the conclusion of *The Winter's Tale*. Were these the winners? Paul wondered. Is to live to win? Perhaps. But as he touched his glass to his lips, he thought of Hillary and the others in the chain who had not won. It's not a good idea to forget the losers, he told himself. If a few links in the chain had been transposed, we could have lost—as eventually we all will. Winning is a privilege, he thought, and privileges should not be abused.